Lucky Break

LUCKY IN LOVE SERIES - BOOK 2

ANNE STONE

MANCHESTER ROAD PUBLISHING

Lucky Break

Copyright © 2024 by Anne Stone

Manchester Road Publishing

This is a work of fiction. While the story takes place in the fictional town of Lucky, Ohio, there is a town called Luckey in Ohio that inspired the author. Names, characters, places, and incidents are the product of the author's imagination and are fictitious. Any resemblance to actual events, locales, or persons, living or dead, is coincidental.

Print Book ISBN: 979-8-9880584-1-0

Book Cover Design: RCMatthewsArtist

Edited: Bryn Donovan

Dedication

To my parents, Gerhard and Anne Klouman
Thank you for choosing me and for giving me a loving home and
a wonderful life.

"Parenthood requires love, not DNA."
Author Unknown

A Special Author Note

As I was finishing Lucky Break, intending to publish in January
2024, I lost a dear lifelong friend in October 2023. Her tragic,
senseless death zapped every bit of my creativity and energy and
left a hole in my heart. Subsequently, it took me a while to get back
to my writing.

The world lost a beautiful soul. Heaven gained an angel.
We miss you, Sara.

"Remember that sometimes not getting what you want is a wonderful stroke of luck."

Dalai Lama XIV

Prologue

Four years earlier

Kell Howard, the vigilant Marine that he was, sat against the wall to watch the rowdy crowd as he chugged down the last of his cold beer. In the two hours he'd been in the dive bar, he'd done some serious damage to the Coors on tap. He was home on medical leave, and the alcohol helped mask the pain of the healing gunshot wound to his upper left thigh.

Well, that, and the pain from the loss of his buddy, Petty Officer Michael "Leaks" Fawcett. But there wasn't enough beer in the bar to wash away that fucked-up memory.

Tonight, he'd taken the back roads and stopped at the first bar he came to. He wanted to drink himself into a stupor away from the watchful eyes of the folks in his hometown of Lucky. Kell squinted at the sign above the bar that read Bernie's Tavern. A typical place with a pool table, darts, and a few arcade games on one end of the room. A jukebox next to the bar kept a steady stream of oldies blasting over the buzz of conversations.

The summer evening was hot and humid, pretty typical for Ohio in August. Even dressed in a T-shirt and shorts, Kell felt the oppressive heat. He doubted hell could be much hotter. The ceiling fans rotated, but they gave little relief. Still, it wasn't as sweltering as the summers he'd spent in Afghanistan. Now that was hell.

He hadn't had a decent night's sleep since the ambush. But even with his eyes wide open, he relived that fateful night over and over. The sharp, loud report of gunfire still resounded in his ears. The throbbing pain in his thigh was a constant reminder of what he wanted to forget. No, he wasn't drunk enough. Not yet.

At the loud crack of the cue ball, Kell ducked, then cringed when he realized there was no danger. His instant reaction to the loud noise took him back to Leaks with that damn coin.

"Let's flip for it," Leaks coaxed with one of his shit-eating grins. The team recognized the look. Leaks never missed an opportunity to pull a prank. He loved to flip that coin he carried around in his front pocket.

"I'm not flipping the damn coin — put it away," Kell said as he rolled his eyes at his buddy.

"O-Man, lighten up." The men had dubbed Kell 'O-Man' because he hailed from Ohio. Though it wasn't long before his aptitude with the ladies gave a whole other meaning to the name O-Man. "Tonight will be smooth sailing."

But it hadn't been.

He moved to an empty booth along the wall farthest from the pool table. Downing the rest of his beer, he flagged his server. "Another."

"You sure you don't want to take a break, Mister?"

He narrowed his eyes, and he gave her a don't fuck with me glare he reserved for the new Boots. The petite server scurried back to the bar.

Three women in their early twenties, by his guess, grabbed the table next to his booth. They wore low cut tops and short skirts.

What's not to like?

When was the last time he'd been with a woman? Too long. But he couldn't miss the eye-fucking he was getting from the one in pink. Straight brown hair, petite with a pretty face, but she wasn't his usual type. He liked blondes.

One woman threw money in the jukebox and their group shimmied on the pseudo dance floor between tables. Bumping and grinding, putting on a show.

As he watched, Kell's shorts grew tighter, and he shifted in his seat. The eye-fucker gestured for him to join them. Why not? He was just drunk enough, so he slid from the booth. She was on him faster than it took to say horny.

The woman wrapped her arms around his neck and wiggled up close.

He did little more than sway. She had plenty of moves for the both of them. He was too drunk to feel the lingering throb from his thigh wound.

After three songs, she leaned into him and put her mouth close to his ear and shouted over the loud noise and music. "Love your tattoo." Her index finger traced over the Celtic design, which encircled his biceps.

After the next song ended, the woman said, "I'm Jodi, with an i. J.O.D.I. You wanna find a private corner and get better acquaint-ed?"

Was that her way of asking if he wanted to hook up? Tonight, his middle name was "Reckless." Wasn't that why he'd spent the afternoon and evening drinking? If she wanted a quickie, who was he to stand in her way?

"Sure, why not?" Before he could give her his name, she pulled him into the back hallway. He checked behind them and no one was following. One knock revealed the women's bathroom was vacant, and she pulled him in and locked the door. He swung her around and pressed her against the door.

She groped him through his shorts. "Nice," she said.

He grimaced. What could he say to that comment? Thanks? God, he was rusty at this.

With the deftness any gymnast would envy, she climbed all over him and her mouth was everywhere at once.

He took control, pinning her arms above her head with one hand. Then he wedged her mini skirt above her hips and pushed her thong aside.

She gasped when he touched her.

His gaze traveled over her face and searched her eyes. Did she still intend to go through with it? If he thought he'd find doubt, he was mistaken. Her eyes were glassy, but there was no hesitation. If he saw the slightest bit of indecision from her, he would pull back. He might be drunk, but he would never push a woman into sex. Even if he had to take matters into his own hands later. He wanted to make damn sure that she hadn't changed her mind.

He had a younger sister, and he hoped she would never find herself in a bar bathroom with a stranger doing the nasty. The thought made his stomach heave and was the wrong thing to picture if he wanted to stay in the game.

Kell withdrew his hand, releasing her arms. She unfastened his shorts, reached in, and pumped his dick. In her inebriated state, what she lacked in finesse she made up for in enthusiasm. His head may have hesitated, but his dick was ready, willing, and able.

She dropped to her knees, nodding toward the bandage on his upper thigh. "What happened here?"

Should he tell her the truth? What difference did it make?

"Gunshot wound."

"No, shit? Sweet."

Kell's brow furrowed, and he frowned with annoyance. Sweet was not a word he'd use to describe getting shot, and not because his thigh still throbbed like a son of a bitch. The wound was a constant reminder of that fateful night and he lived with the consequences every day.

Kell came crashing back to the small, drab bathroom when she wrapped her lips around his dick. He gritted his teeth and twisted her hair through his fingers. Shit, it had been a long time for him. He didn't want the party to end before it even got started.

In one swift motion, he lifted her off the floor and balanced her ass on the edge of the sink. Alcohol-induced lust swept his usual caution away. Still, he gritted his teeth and said, "You sure about this?"

"Yeah."

Kell found the condom he kept in his wallet. Rolling it on, he shoved in and took her fast. The whole thing took less than five minutes. When he helped her down, she pushed away seconds before she threw up, almost missing the toilet.

He handed her a paper towel. "Are you okay?"

"Yeah. Fine. Must be the wine-beer combo."

Kell disposed of the condom, then pulled his shorts up over the bandage.

She pointed to his leg. "How'd you get shot?"

That was the last thing he wanted to talk about. But he'd be a Grade A shit if he walked out on her without some conversation.

"Afghanistan. I'm a Marine, home on medical leave. Going back in a few weeks."

"Wow, I hooked up with a real live Marine. Cool."

He had served his country and was proud of his service. But he'd be starting his fourth tour soon, and he was tired. Losing Leaks had screwed with his head.

He opened the bathroom door and stuck his head out to make sure she could make a clean getaway.

"See you around," she said.

Kell nodded. *Yeah, sure.* He knew he'd never see her again. He headed outside for some fresh air and found a rickety bench lining the front porch. As he came down from his buzz, he realized he shouldn't drive himself home. He pulled out his phone and called his best friend, Chase Devine.

After the fifth ring, Chase answered, "Do you know what time it is?"

"Nope."

"It's almost two in the morning. Are you drunk?"

"Yep."

"I'll come pick you up. Where are you?"

"Umm, dunno. Oh, wait, it's a place on Old County 52. Corner of fifty-two and River Road. Bernie's, I think."

"I know the place. Sit tight. I'll be there in less than thirty."

"Thanks." Kell disconnected, shoved the phone in his pocket, then he leaned back against the wall and waited. True to his word, at zero-two-thirty, Chase rolled into the parking lot in his F-150.

With Kell settled in the truck, Chase asked, "Want to talk about what's bothering you?"

He shook his head. "Nope. But thanks, man. I appreciate you coming out in the middle of the night for me."

"Anytime."

He knew he could talk to his best friend. But some demons were hard to talk about and impossible to shake.

Chapter 1

Lucky, Ohio
Present day

He clocked the blue MINI Cooper doing fifty-five in a thirty-five. "Damn that woman." Sheriff Kell Howard swore as he shook his head and shifted into drive, hitting the gas. He flipped on the siren and strobe light in pursuit.

Even without the flash of coppery red hair, Kell knew the identity of the person driving the vehicle. A MINI Cooper was a unique car, and he knew of only one in the small town of Lucky.

He didn't expect a dangerous or lengthy car chase, but he was glad the pavement was dry. Despite the forecast, the snow had held off, but there was a bitter, icy wind blowing. Nothing unusual for late January in northern Ohio.

The car pulled over to the shoulder, and Kell stopped a few yards behind. He yanked the zipper of his coat up and winced when the zipper-teeth scraped his chin. "Shit," he muttered.

He shoved his hat on and stepped out of his vehicle. The wind whistled through the tall pines to his right, past the culvert that ran along the side of the road.

It was times like this that he questioned his decision to return to his hometown and his acceptance when the mayor appointed him as the temporary town sheriff. After his four tours in the military, it had been time to leave. He'd been back in Lucky for a little over a month when he got a call from Mayor Hendricks with the offer after the longtime sheriff, Ted Andrews, had a heart attack and took an early retirement.

Stalking to the car, he signaled for the woman to lower her window.

"Good morning, Sheriff. Is there a problem?" asked the woman. Puffs of frigid air were visible with every breath she took.

"You know exactly why I pulled you over. It's the third consecutive week we've caught you speeding on this stretch of road."

"Sheriff, I'm sorry. I didn't realize I was going over the speed limit."

Bullshit.

"It wasn't until I heard the siren and saw the flashing lights in my rearview mirror."

Kell clenched his jaw. He didn't bother to ask where she was going in such a hurry so early in the morning. He didn't care. "I warned you last week what would happen if we pulled you over one more time."

He reached for the handcuffs on his belt. "Please get out of the car."

The woman's smile slipped a notch. The reality of her situation may have finally registered. Good.

She opened her car door and stepped out. Her red hair, which was graying at the roots, framed her face. "You are not arresting me. What'll people think?" She pulled her coat closed and bounced from foot to foot to keep warm.

"You should've thought about that before you pulled this stunt again."

"But–"

"We warned you."

"Kell Jamison Howard!"

"Mom!"

She was a master at guilt and manipulation. She'd spent twenty-three exhausting hours of labor to bring him into the world and she never missed a chance to remind him.

"If you'd come home to visit once in a while. I wouldn't have to resort to such measures to see my firstborn, my only son. I can't even recall the last Sunday you were home for a family supper."

No one could say Ruby Howard didn't have a flair for the dramatic. She'd missed her calling. There was a stage somewhere with her name in bright lights.

"Look, Mom, we've been over this. I've stopped coming over on Sundays because the conversation invariably ends up with questions like why I'm not dating, why haven't I found the one? Or, this popular one, when are you going to make me," — he shuddered — "a grandmother?"

"I can't help it if I want to see you in a happy relationship."

"Try harder. Please."

"Oh, Kell, you don't know what I go through. All my friends have grandchildren. If I have to listen to Molly Turner talk about her beautiful, gifted grandson one more time." She stomped her foot.

Her whine petered out. Maybe she realized she'd hit a nerve and pushed him too far.

It wasn't easy, but he would not let her get to him. How many times did they have to discuss this topic before she would back off?

"These stunts won't change my mind. You're wasting my time and the time of my deputies. Have you given any thought to how it looks to the town? With the new sheriff's own mother continually breaking the law?"

"No, of course not. But Mayor Hendricks won't fire you."

Hands on his hips, he glared at her. "He might if you continue to play your games."

Kell hoped it wouldn't come to that. He was already halfway through two of the online law enforcement classes he needed to take.

"Kell, if you'd listen to reason."

"No, Mom, you need to face reality."

Kell had listened to his mother rant about his single status since his mid-twenties. Escaping into the military helped some. But since coming back to Lucky, she'd been relentless. What she wanted superseded what he wanted.

"But Kell."

He was firm on this subject. He'd seen too many atrocities overseas, and too many causalities of the war. There was no way he would bring a child into the turbulent world. He also couldn't get involved with someone while he was still dealing with all his other shit. No woman would want a man with his issues. He didn't deserve to have a family.

"You don't have to boycott our Sunday suppers. Megan and Chase miss you so much when you aren't there."

He smiled for the first time that morning. "My sister visits because somehow, she got off your nag list. For some mysterious reason, I get all your attention in that department."

She grinned. "That's a perk because you're my favorite son."

He shook his head. "I'm your only son and I see Megan every day, so she's not missing me. And I see Chase almost as often."

His little sister, Megan, owned the best coffee place in town, Espresso Yourself. Kell made a pit stop there at least once, if not twice a day, for his caffeine fix. It helped that he was bunking in the studio apartment above the store. And her fiancé, Chase, had been his best friend since elementary school.

Ruby's face reddened, and she frowned. Her scrunched expression reminded him of what she used to say when they were kids.

"Remember, you used to warn Megan and me if we had a sour expression on our faces," he teased. "Be careful. Your face might freeze."

She gasped, then with a good bit of indignation she said, "That's a mean thing to say to your mother."

Kell smirked. "Mom. I'm simply reminding you of your own helpful advice."

"Whatever. I shouldn't have to beg my son to come to Sunday dinner with his family. Why are you so stubborn? You're just like your father."

He stiffened. "Mom, you need to be careful with your comparisons." Being compared to a father who walked out on them would not win her any warm and fuzzy feelings from him.

She sniffled. "Sunday supper is not as bad as you're making it out to be."

"Not as bad?" He shook his head. "By the time I get back to my apartment, I have to medicate myself with antacid and ibuprofen."

"Oh, dear, but you're the big, strong sheriff with a badge and a gun. Not to mention a former Marine. I think —"

He cut in. "Don't forget the handcuffs." He dangled them in front of her face.

"As I was saying, I think you can manage a few hours with your family."

"Please turn around, hold your hands out," he asked.

"Go ahead, cuff me, if you must, but hurry, it's colder than a polar bear's butt."

"No kidding," Kell said. On that, they agreed. He placed one cuff on and had every intention of cuffing her other wrist when a call on his shoulder mic interrupted him.

Another burglary, this time at a medical clinic. It was the second one, in a town with a history of minor crime, and had his staff working long hours to solve the case. He unlocked the cuff and hooked the handcuffs back on his belt.

"It's your lucky day." And mine, he thought. "I'm warning you to think twice before you pull this stunt again. Next time, one of my diligent deputies will pull you over, and he'll haul you in for a date with Judge Franklin."

"George Franklin is a big old teddy bear. We went to school together."

Kell sighed in exasperation. "Stay out of trouble."

Her smug expression did nothing to reassure him. "Before you go, give your mother a kiss, young man," she said as she presented her cheek and he complied with a quick peck, then jogged to his cruiser.

Before the door shut, he heard her yell, "I've invited Megan's friend, a pretty doctor, for dinner on Sunday. Two 'o'clock."

"Mother!"

Chapter 2

Dr. Becca James was not in a good mood. She had to wake up even earlier this morning so she could get into the clinic to review her case files before her day got busy with patients. Thankfully, today was her dad's day to take the morning off to be home with Emma, her three-year-old, so she could get out of the house earlier than usual.

She had to adjust her schedule because she was going to court this afternoon. It would've been simpler to pay for the damn ticket. But it was the principle of the situation. The cop was in the wrong. She didn't care that he was her friend Megan's brother. He'd been a jerk, and she was going to fight the ticket.

Becca entered through the staff door on the side of the building, then went directly to her office, where she hung her coat on the hook behind the door. She dropped her purse and keys on the credenza and caught sight of the ticket sticking out of the side pocket of her purse. Seeing it ignited her irritation all over again. Sighing, she pushed her frustration aside. She had work to do.

As she reached for her white medical jacket, she noticed there was dirt on the carpet. She stepped into the hallway and saw dirt there, too.

Something wasn't right.

The custodial staff vacuumed nightly. Unless they hadn't come last night? Becca's gaze swung to the trash bin next to her desk. The bin was empty, so they'd been there.

She looked down at her shoes. They were clean. That meant someone else tracked the dirt into the building.

The fine hairs on the back of her neck and arms tingled as she took steady steps down the hallway, following the trail of dirt. Her eyes widened when she saw the supply room door ajar because it was always kept locked.

Had the office manager come in earlier? Although she had seen no other car in the lot, she called out, "Betty?" Betty Greene had been with the James Family Medical Clinic since they'd opened the doors five years ago. She was a diligent employee.

When Becca didn't get a reply, she stepped closer and peeked into the room. The medicine cabinet's glass doors had been smashed. Glass littered the floor. Cold and cough products were the predominant medication stored in the cabinet. Her uneasiness morphed into flat-out anger and fear.

She squinted to see in the darkened room and reached for the light switch, but her hand froze when the thought occurred to her that there could be fingerprints. She heard faint noises coming from down the hall. Was it coming from the break room? She heard whispering and thought there was some movement.

She wasn't alone.

Whoever trashed the room was still in the building.

She pulled her phone from her pocket to call 911, but it dropped from her shaky hands and fell to the floor, knocking against the wall with a loud thud.

She threw a hand over her mouth to swallow her gasp and ducked behind the door. She held her breath and listened. Praying they, whoever they were, hadn't heard her.

More whispers. Glass shattering.

Her heart thundered in her chest, and her pulse raced.

She held her breath as she quickly bent and grabbed her phone from the floor. Her brain told her to get out of the building, but her feet refused to cooperate. She stood frozen behind the door.

She waited and listened. When she heard nothing for what seemed like forever, she dialed 911.

"Nine-one-one operator. What is your emergency?"

Becca took a deep breath before she spoke. "Someone broke into the clinic."

"Where are you, ma'am?"

"James Family Medical Clinic on Pine Street," Becca said. Though she tried to keep her voice calm, she wasn't surprised when it came out in a much higher pitch.

"What's your name?" asked the operator.

"Rebecca James," Becca said.

"Are you hurt, Ms. James?"

"No, I'm not hurt. But they're still in the building. I heard glass breaking a minute ago." Becca trembled.

"Help is on the way."

"If I think I can do it safely, I'm going to wait in my car," Becca said. "I just want to get out of here."

"What's the make and color or your car?"

"It's blue. It's a Nissan Rogue."

"Can you remain on the line until help arrives?"

"All right, yes, thank you," Becca said.

Becca used the flashlight on her phone to survey the floor for a makeshift weapon and finally saw a bigger pile of broken glass. She darted from her hiding place behind the door and grabbed a serrated shard, then returned to her hiding spot. The slippery piece of glass was difficult to hold on to because of her shaky grasp.

She listened for more sounds. Were they still in the clinic? Where were they? How many were there? The silence was freaking her out, perhaps more than the unusual noises.

Her nerves were shot, and she couldn't bear to stand there another minute. Becca gripped the slippery piece of jagged glass and bolted for the exit. It wasn't until she was halfway to her car that she realized she'd left her coat, purse, and keys in her office.

In the relative safety of her locked car, Becca trembled, muttering, "Idiot. You should have grabbed the car keys."

"Beg your pardon?" The garbled voice of the 911 operator startled her.

"Oh, sorry. Just talking to myself." One habit she'd picked up during college and medical school to minimize stress and anxiety. "Right about now I'd recite Netter's *Atlas of Human Anatomy* if it would help settle my nerves," she mumbled under her breath.

"Did you make it to your car safely, ma'am?" The 911 operator asked.

"Yes, I did. Thank you for staying on the line with me."

"The police will be there in a moment, ma'am."

"Good. Thanks."

The sun had risen maybe twenty minutes earlier, but the dreary gray winter clouds blocked any warmth it might have provided. The cold, dark car did little to assuage her fear.

She was thrust back to another time when she'd waited in a dark, cold vehicle for rescue.

Absently, she massaged her stomach, now flat, and minus the small precious bump. A tiny whimper escaped her lips. She'd never forget that accident, though the intervening years had provided the needed time to heal physically. She half-expected to see her ex, Josh, slumped against the passenger door.

The doctors had assured her that the accident hadn't caused her miscarriage. The timing had been a fateful coincidence. But she still believed she could have avoided the car accident if she hadn't been fighting with Josh.

Two official vehicles sped into the parking lot with the sirens blaring and strobe lights flashing. She put her arm up to shield her eyes from the glare.

Two men dressed in uniforms approached her car. One rapped on her window and relief washed over her. The man opened the car door, and Becca attempted to step out, but collapsed right into his firm arms.

"Easy now. I've gotcha. I'm the —"

"I know who you are," she said. She remembered that voice. Her day was just getting better and better.

He drew back, and she felt his penetrating gaze. Was he surprised by her comment? To be fair, she had an advantage, since he was her friend's brother. But today she didn't feel like being *fair*.

"All right, good. Well, this is Deputy Gibson. What's your name, Miss?"

Ah, so he didn't recognize her. That figured. He probably handed out so many bogus tickets he couldn't keep all his *victims* straight.

"Miss?" he asked again, with more authority in his voice.

"I'm *Doctor* Rebecca James."

He turned to his deputy and said, "Go ahead in. I'll be there once the doctor is ready."

She couldn't see the deputy well. She just had a sense that the man was tall and lean.

Her attention refocused on the man beside her. "Sit back down." He eased her back into the car seat. "I need you to take a couple of deep breaths. It'll help," he said as he patted her shoulder.

She nodded. "Yes, I'm perfectly aware of that. I'm a doctor." She cringed at her sarcastic tone. But damn it, this day had ticked her off. She took a moment to study her friend's brother. His hair was more of a light brown, not Megan's beautiful auburn shade. Though his beard was darker and reflected some of the red, and his eyes were a lighter green than his sister's.

"Dr. James, where are you injured?"

"I'm not."

His brows knitted as he scanned her face and body.

He stared at her waist, then quickly said into the radio on his shoulder. "I need an ambulance at this address, Sally."

"Becca shook her head and leaned forward. "Don't be ridiculous. I don't need an ambulance. I just need a minute."

He studied her for a moment, and the skepticism was plain on his face. She assumed he was considering whether to believe her. Finally, he spoke into his shoulder. "Sally, disregard the request for the ambulance."

"10-4, Sheriff," came the garbled response.

"I don't know why my legs are so shaky. I should be over the initial shock."

"It might be the blood loss," he said.

"Blood loss? What blood?"

He pointed to her lap. "There."

"Oh." Blood covered her hands, and she'd smeared it on her blouse. That explained why the shard had felt so slippery.

"Damn it, I must have cut myself when I grabbed a piece of the broken glass. The medicine cabinet's doors had been smashed."

The censure she saw in his eyes was confirmed when he said, "You shouldn't have touched anything."

"I thought I could use it as a weapon."

"Here." He unfolded a bandana and wrapped her injured hand. While he was tending to her hand, she stole another glance at his face. Why did this man have to be the arrogant cop who ticketed her? Why did he have to be so handsome? Whoa, why was he turning pale?

She pulled her hand away. "Are you okay?"

"I'm fine," he snapped. She couldn't read his expression, but his words were abrupt.

"You don't look fine."

He shook his head, straightened, and took a few paces away from her, then returned to her side. He was back, kneeling beside her in the open door. "Never mind me. Let's worry about you." Then, in one smooth move, he reclined her seat and pushed her back. "Steady. Take a minute."

His tone was firm, and as much as she hated to admit it, comforting. She couldn't help but feel safe and warm with the heat radiating from the man's body. As he leaned in, he blocked more of the wintry air. She allowed herself to relax and melt into the seat. Closing her eyes, she took a deep breath, counted to ten, and exhaled.

Opening her eyes, she mumbled, "Usually, I'm much calmer in a crisis." She hadn't gotten through medical school and her residency without learning to deal with emergencies. The intrusion and violation of her property and the possibility of danger must have rattled her more than she realized.

He said, "As soon as my men give me go-ahead, we can go inside and get your hand cleaned and bandaged properly and get you warmed up."

"Thank you." Becca closed her eyes.

Even without knowing he was the sheriff or seeing his badge on his belt, she'd have guessed he was in charge. His no-bullshit, know-it-all attitude was a dead giveaway. The surgeons at the hospital had much the same air about them.

For a nanosecond, her hormones overrode her brain cells, and she imagined the feel of his arms engulfing her in a warm hug. But his next words interrupted her incongruous thoughts.

"It's freezing in here. Why didn't you turn on the heater?"

Sighing again, she said, "I left my purse and keys inside when I ran out of the building."

She didn't like the look on the sheriff's face. He was frowning at her as if she'd been the one who committed the crime here. She could live without his superior attitude and critical look of disapproval, thank you very much.

"Listen, Sheriff..." She tried to sit up again. "What's your problem?" To hell with him being her friend's brother. He was being a royal pain in her ass.

"You should lock your car."

"Yes, I know, but it's Lucky."

His brows arched again.

"There's no crime in..." she began, but his mouth quirked into a sardonic grin. Her statement was ridiculous under the circumstances. "Fine. I do lock my car ... usually. I forgot this morning."

His attitude didn't help her mood, and she blew out an exasperated breath.

There was static from his shoulder thing, and he replied, "Roger that."

Clearing his throat, he said, "My deputy just gave the go-ahead. When you're ready, I need you to come inside with me and walk me through what happened."

"I'm ready."

He helped her out of the car and kept his hand on her arm as he escorted her across the parking lot.

When they entered the building, he removed his hat and helped her over to one of the waiting room chairs. "Take a seat and don't touch anything."

She resisted rolling her eyes. Instead, she studied his features without the hat shadowing his face. He wore his hair trimmed neat, a little longer than the military cut he must have had for several years.

The man was over six feet tall, and an educated guess put his weight at a solid two-thirty. The word sturdy came to mind. She felt a flush creep up her neck.

"Sit tight. I'll be right back. I've got a first aid kit in my cruiser."

This time, she rolled her eyes. "We do have supplies, you know."

Apparently oblivious to her sarcasm, he replied, "We're not touching anything until we dust for fingerprints."

Kell gave her a smile before heading out. He should smile more often. He had a great smile. Becca leaned forward in the chair to watch as he walked to the door. The break-in should be the only thing on her mind. Yet here she was, blatantly ogling this man's butt. Good thing there wasn't a law against looking, or jail cells would overflow everywhere.

When he returned with a bottle of water and the first aid kit tucked under his arm, he took the seat next to her and said matter-of-factly. "Give me your hand." She nodded, extending the wrong hand.

He chuckled. "The injured hand."

"Oh, of course. Sorry."

Oh, my gosh. She knew her face was becoming flushed, but he didn't seem to notice... or care. He unwrapped the bandana. His touch was gentle, yet his hands were rough. They didn't talk as he cleaned her cut with antiseptic wipes and patted the area dry.

She studied his face as he worked. He had her wound disinfected and wrapped in gauze in a matter of minutes. When he glanced up, he caught her watching him.

"There you go," he said.

"Thank you. You might have missed your calling," Becca said as he was putting things back in the kit. There was something so familiar about his face. Was it his eyes? She shook it off since she was friends with his sister. Of course, he looked like Megan.

"Nah, I don't think so. I can get by. Got basic first aid training in the Marines," he said. He smiled again, and she felt the long-forgotten tingles of attraction deep in her belly.

No, no, no. This was all his fault. If he hadn't given her that stupid ticket, she wouldn't have been here so early this morning and none of this, including injuring herself, would have happened.

Finally, she cleared her throat and said, "Thanks. You did a great job." She tucked the loose strands of her disheveled ponytail behind her ears with her uninjured hand.

"Now that we have you bandaged up, let's try introductions again." He extended his hand to her. "Dr. James, I'm Sheriff Kell Howard."

She sighed. Should she tell him she knew him because of the ticket? Deciding to wait on that bit of information, she said, "Yes, I know. I'm friends with Megan and Chase."

He snapped his fingers. "Oh, you're *that* Becca."

Becca tilted her head. What did he mean by *that Becca?*

"Megan has mentioned you a few times. I'm surprised we haven't crossed paths, what with Lucky being such a small town."

Oh, we have.

"Yes, how surprising," she said.

She picked up the bottle of water he'd brought in, but between her cold stiff fingers and her bandaged hand, she became frustrated after her third attempt to twist off the top.

"Here let me." His hand touched hers as he took the bottle. Tingles again. In one swift motion, he removed the cap and handed the bottle back to her.

Chewing her bottom lip, another habit she picked up in med school, she took the bottle and sipped. "Thanks," she murmured. "Seems like I'm thanking you a lot."

He ignored her comment and walked over to the front desk and picked up a business card. "Dr. Harper James," he read aloud.

"Is that a question, Sheriff?"

"It is. Who is Dr. Harper James? Your husband?" He was back to being all business.

She lifted her brows. "Harper James is my father. We own this building and this medical practice together."

His forehead creased in a frown. "Your father wasn't with you this morning?"

"Wow, you must have gotten straight A's in detective school." Her attempt at humor earned her nothing but a blank expression.

She shook her head. "No, he didn't. On Mondays, he doesn't come in until one o'clock. It's his special grandpa time with my daughter."

His eyes widened. "You have a kid?"

"Yes, Sheriff, that's what I said. Though I prefer the term child instead of kid."

When he said nothing, she figured he was trying to discern the difference between the two terms. He could Google it.

While he was thinking, she checked him out from head to toe. She had to admit; she liked what she saw. He had the whole sexy, tough guy look. Her reaction surprised her. It had been a while since a man had turned her head.

And the badge and gun only enhanced his tough guy persona.

Becca reminded herself of the inappropriate and poorly timed, purely hormonal appraisal of the man. No matter how attractive ... he just wasn't her type. This was precisely why her mother always reminded her not to judge a book by its cover.

Besides, she'd sworn off men. Especially attractive, cocky men.

She cleared her throat. "Most mornings, he and I come in together, usually arriving around seven forty-five."

"So why were you here even earlier than usual today?"

"I have a meeting this afternoon, so I came in early to go over my case files."

He gestured toward the back of the clinic. "If you're ready, I need you to walk me through everything that happened when you arrived this morning."

Yes, sir. Becca felt tempted to salute him, but fortunately, she restrained herself. She wasn't sure what to make of this man. She wasn't a big fan of his bossiness.

Though if she thought about it, shouldn't that attitude go hand-in-hand with a position of authority?

Besides, she wasn't looking for a man in her life. She currently had the perfect balance between work and home. At least, that's what she told herself.

Of course, she noticed him. Who wouldn't?

Chapter 3

"Shh. What was that? I heard a noise," Jodi Riggs whispered to her boyfriend Jimmy and his brother Ben. The trio stood still and listened. They had already cleaned out the medicine cabinet in the storeroom and were in what looked like a small kitchen.

Jodi fingered the framed photograph in her sweatshirt pocket. She hadn't gone looking for it but ended up in the doctor's office, where she'd spotted several photos of a child on display behind the desk. She had snatched a wallet-size photo of the cute toddler posing with a teddy bear. The child had auburn curls and a mischievous smile.

Jodi doubted the doctor would miss this one small photo with all the others left behind. But even if the doctor noticed, she would assume she misplaced it. Besides, what difference did it make if she missed the photo?

"We need to get out of here. Someone came in the side door," Jimmy said.

"Shh," Ben chided.

Jimmy glared at his brother. "Don't shush me."

Then they heard a woman's voice call someone's name.

"Let's go," Jodi urged.

As they exited the room, Ben cut the corner too close and knocked a coffee mug off the counter. The mug shattered when it hit the tile floor. Their presence was no longer a secret. They rushed out the back emergency exit and sprinted down a block where they left their van.

They didn't speak a word until they were in the van and driving away.

"That was close," Ben said as he tried to catch his breath.

"Yeah, thanks to you. You need to be careful!" Jimmy chided. "No one would have known we were still in there if you hadn't knocked that mug off the counter."

"Oh, right. Like the trashed storeroom wasn't a clue? Besides, we should have gone in earlier. We're lucky there was only the one person who came in."

"Chill. We made it out," Jimmy said. "You're such a pain in my ass."

The two Kendall brothers couldn't be more different. Jimmy, older by sixteen months, lived for the adrenaline rush. He took risks that Ben looked uncomfortable with.

"Don't tell me to chill," Ben said. "We would have been there earlier if you hadn't had to get laid this morning. Besides, it was a dumb location. A small clinic like that will not have OxyContin or Fentanyl. We were lucky to get the stuff we got."

Jodi turned away but kept quiet in the back. She wanted to hide the embarrassed blush she knew crept up her neck. Jimmy glared at his brother.

Getting between the brothers would've been a mistake, but she agreed with Ben.

They should have gone in earlier, but Jimmy wouldn't skip sex. The set-up was awkward for Jodi, because Ben was sleeping just a few feet away. Their lack of privacy never bothered Jimmy.

She had been dating Jimmy for six months. In the beginning, she'd thought he was exciting and fearless. His idea of breaking into small town pharmacies and doctor's offices to get drugs to sell seemed like a doable plan. Ben was reluctant, but went along with Jimmy in most things.

Jimmy was edgier than usual during the last two jobs. Taking too many unnecessary risks. Doing a half-assed job with scouting potential targets. What was exciting and fearless before was scarier now.

Especially when they heard the sirens.

They were staying in a house a few miles out of town. Ben had a friend who was letting them crash in the basement until they moved on. If they shared whatever drugs they hauled in, the guy didn't complain.

They'd broken into the clinic, which was the third place in the area, and had grabbed whatever drugs they could find. They avoided national chains, figuring there was too much security, and focused on local small-town pharmacies and clinics.

Jodi was looking at the picture of the child when Jimmy looked over his shoulder. "Whatcha got there?"

She hadn't explained her connection to the clinic. She wasn't sure how or when to tell Jimmy, so for the time being, she said, "Just a photo I liked, so I grabbed it. Figured it wouldn't hurt to take it since we took other stuff, right?"

"Sure."

Chapter 4

Later, as Kell sat at his desk reviewing his notes for the case file, he thought about his early morning encounter with Dr. James. So, this was the woman who his mom had invited to Sunday dinner.

He'd give his mom points for knowing he liked blondes. He didn't know whether to be impressed or scared that his mom knew his type. Because he'd admit the female Doctor James interested him.

The timing of their meeting was uncanny. If he didn't know better, he'd think Mom set up the whole thing.

No way.

Not even Ruby Howard would stoop that low. She wouldn't commit a crime, the speeding withstanding, just to find a suitable wife for her uncooperative son. Would she?

Nah.

He had to admit there was something about Becca James. The pretty doctor with the compelling blue eyes intrigued him more than any woman had in years.

He'd steeled himself, stepping away from her momentarily when he saw the blood smeared on her blouse and hands. He'd taken several deep breaths to get himself calmed down. The sight and smell of the blood took him back in time. The last thing he wanted was to have a full-out panic attack on the job.

Some cop he was. He had moments of doubt about being the Sheriff. But it felt right for his military background and he hadn't had a lot of options, either.

Her father, the senior Dr. James, arrived as Becca finished giving her preliminary statement. The man was a few inches taller than his daughter. He shared her blue eyes, but he seemed much more laid back than the younger Dr. James.

She greeted her father with a hug. "Dad, I'm glad to see you. Where's Emma?"

"I took her over to Esther's house. She'll keep her as long as we need."

Kell saw the relief flash across Becca's face.

Dr. James turned, extending his hand to Kell.

"Sheriff, I'm Harper James. Rebecca's father. Nice to meet you, despite the circumstances." Kell noticed the man had a nice firm handshake and had looked Kell in the eyes as he spoke — two things Kell respected.

He had to admit, if only to himself, he was relieved to find Harper James was her father and not a husband. Not that he was looking for a relationship... far from it... but a man could admire a gorgeous single woman when he saw one.

Kell walked them through the clinic, focusing on where most of the damage had occurred. Deputy Tupper was dusting for fingerprints, but Kell didn't think they'd find anything. Whoever broke in probably wore gloves. He asked Becca and Harper to go over the damages and provide his team with an inventory of what was missing.

"Looks like all the drug samples we kept locked in the cabinet are gone," the senior Dr. James commented. "Our office manager keeps a detailed inventory of the supplies. I'll make sure you get a copy." He motioned to the floor and shook his head. "What a mess."

"Sometimes a lot of the damage happens because the perps can't find what they're looking for. They may have done some of this damage out of spite because they didn't get more for their efforts," Kell explained.

"It's a good thing we don't keep more here. It seems like they didn't have a plan, or they weren't sure what to grab, so they grabbed everything. Some items aren't worth anything."

Kell waited for her to continue.

"We had a fair amount of cough and cold medicine with dextromethorphan. You can mix the cough syrup with clear soda to make something called Lean or Purple Drank."

Kell studied her thoughtfully for a moment, then quirked his eyebrow in question.

"What? I did my residency in emergency medicine and saw too many cases of overdoses. I'm aware of the trends for getting high."

Pretty and smart. Lethal combination.

"You interrupted them, and they ran, or at least they were about to leave when you came in," Kell offered. Becca's face paled. "Are you okay?" He stepped toward her, cupping her elbow.

She shrugged. "It's not like I didn't already consider that possibility, but the outcomes had I been a few minutes earlier are still frightening."

"From what you told me, no one should have been here for at least another half hour. I bet they did reconnaissance on the building and all of your schedules. The MO matches the other recent break-ins we've had in and around Lucky. I'll make some calls to the surrounding towns. In the meantime, I'll need a list of all employees."

"You can't possibly suspect one of our employees?" Becca glared at him.

"Right now, everyone is a suspect. Is that a problem?"

Harper answered as he patted his daughter's arm, "No, Sheriff, we'll give you the list of names. It's a short one since we only have four employees. Six, if you include Becca and me."

"Speaking of employees, Dad, we need to call the staff." She turned to Kell. "What time should we tell them to be here?" She looked at the wall clock. "They are due anytime."

"Not today. You can't open until my team is done inside and has checked the perimeter of the building. I hope we get lucky and find footprints or tire tracks."

Harper took his daughter's arm. "Becca, dear, it's all right. I called Betty before I left home. She has both of our schedules on her laptop and has already started calling patients to reschedule. If anyone has a serious problem, they'll go to the hospital. I will see them later today."

He turned to Kell and continued, "Betty Greene, she's our office manager."

"Do you think we can open tomorrow morning?" Becca asked.

"I believe so, yes," Kell said. "Unless we run into a snag." She opened her mouth, but he raised his hand to cut her off. "Relax, I don't think there will be any issues. When we're done, I'll have someone come in to clean up the broken glass and other damages."

"Thank you." Harper took a business card out of his wallet and jotted something on the back. "Here are our personal numbers if you need to reach either of us." Kell added the card to the one he already had in his breast pocket.

"Now, if you're done with us. I'd like to take Becca home."

"Dad! I don't need any help. I can drive the three blocks."

"Are you sure?" Harper asked.

"Absolutely. Yes. Go on ahead. I'll be right behind you."

"Sir, I'm happy to make sure she gets home safely."

"Thank you." He turned to his daughter. "I'm sure you would be fine, but it's a father's prerogative to worry about his only child, especially after everything you've been through—"

"Dad!" She cut off whatever Harper was going to say, and she glared at both men. Obviously, she didn't like the idea of Kell taking her home. "You can both stop talking like I'm not standing right here."

"You won't indulge your old man and let Sheriff Howard escort you home?"

She shook her head. "Goodbye, Dad. I'll see you later."

Harper kissed her cheek. "All right, I'll stop mollycoddling you. See you later, sweetheart." He shook Kell's hand and shrugged as if he was saying *good luck*.

Kell had watched the exchange between father and daughter. He sure wouldn't have pegged her as a doctor. At least not the doctors whom he knew. She had so much style. Her clothes were feminine, but practical. Simple but sexy, too. Not that doctors couldn't be sexy. He just couldn't picture her in scrubs.

Out of them ... oh, hell, yes.

Nothing wrong with looking and appreciating. He'd been fighting his attraction all morning. His response to her had been immediate. His body had hardened from the moment she'd tumbled into his arms, and he'd caught the fragrance from her shampoo.

Shit, he needed to get laid. What had it been? Six months? Longer?

Her initial shock seemed to have worn off, and she didn't appear to have shaky limbs. He was sure she could manage the drive home alone.

"So?" Kell raised his eyebrows.

"You're not driving me home. I'll need my car later for my meeting."

He held up his hands in surrender. "I wouldn't dare. But before you go, do you have a spare key so we can lock the place up when we get through here?"

She twisted a gold key off her key ring and handed it to him. "Here you go."

"Thanks. Guess I'll see you around."

"Yes, I'm sure you will," she said.

Kell debated telling Becca of his mother's matchmaking ploy. The whole Sunday dinner deal was an obvious setup. Becca was a bright woman. He was confident that she'd figure out what his mother was up to.

He was thirty-three, and he could handle his life without his mom's help, even with the PTSD nightmares and anxiety attacks.

The continued efforts of his mother to fix him up were pointless. He would never commit to anyone, not after all the violence he witnessed during his years in the military. Fighting in Afghanistan and the Middle East, he saw daily malice all around him. The death and destruction of war took a toll and convinced him that bringing children into the messed-up world was a mistake.

He'd sworn off any hope of a family. A wife and kids were not in his cards. An occasional casual, one-nighter took care of the itch. But he hadn't even had an itch in a long time.

That didn't matter. Kell would not go to Sunday dinner. He had a legitimate excuse. He'd be working long hours on the case. Besides, mixing business with pleasure could lead to problems.

That was his story, and he was sticking to it.

He glanced at the wall clock in his office and sighed. It was time to head over to the courthouse. He hated this part of the job.

Why couldn't people admit they were in the wrong and accept their ticket and move on? That way he could stay out of court, but like today's case, people think they don't deserve the ticket.

He shoved his hat on and grabbed his coat, hoping this would be a simple case and he could be back at his desk within the hour.

Chapter 5

As Becca sat on the bench waiting for her case to be called, she thought about the man who was due any minute. Ironically, she'd thought she'd meet Kell Howard on Sunday when she and her dad went for supper at Mrs. Howard's home.

She was looking forward to seeing his face when he put two and two together. After meeting him today, she didn't think he'd give her a bogus ticket. That didn't square with the person she met earlier. Yes, he was intense and didn't smile much. But that is a long way from giving out wrongful tickets.

He clearly thought he was justified in issuing her the ticket, but he was mistaken, and that's the reason she was in court.

She'd been keeping her eye on the door, so she saw when he entered the courtroom. He removed his hat and moved down the aisle. Seconds later, the bailiff called, "The People versus Dr. Rebecca James."

He didn't disappoint. His head shot up, and his gaze locked on her with a quizzical expression.

She stood, gave a nonchalant shrug, and moved to the table in front of her while he walked to the other table. They were side-by-side for a split second. Long enough for him to whisper, "Well played."

She gave a slight nod of her head to acknowledge she heard his comment.

"The Honorable Judge Franklin is presiding," the clerk announced.

The judge asked the prosecution to present their evidence first.

"Your Honor, I issued the ticket to the defendant on January fifth. The individual did not make a complete stop at the stop sign at the corner of Elm Street and Rose Avenue; therefore, I issued the ticket."

"Thank you, Sheriff Howard."

The judge looked over at Becca. "You may present any evidence you have now."

"Thank you, your honor. I've brought photos of the corner where I got the *failing to stop* at a stop sign ticket. May I show you, your Honor?"

"Yes. Please approach the bench."

Becca walked to the judge's bench and removed the photos from a manila envelope. She laid the photos out in front of the Judge.

"As you can see, your Honor, there is a stand of evergreens at the corner of Elm Street and Rose Avenue. I was driving east on Elm Street, and I stopped to turn left on Rose Avenue, but I had to stop, then inch my way forward so I could see around the evergreens. It's a difficult intersection." She spread the photos out for the judge.

"Sheriff Howard assumed I ran the stop sign, but from his vantage point, he couldn't see my car had stopped. His vehicle was facing south on Rose Avenue." She showed the judge where Kell's car had been parked. She glanced over to where Kell sat. He was grinning at her.

She took a deep breath and continued, "It's not the fine, or the points on my driver's license, it's the principle of the thing. Paying the fine is the same as pleading guilty, and I did not run or make a rolling stop at the stop sign." She inhaled, then blew out her breath.

The judge adjusted his glasses and peered down at the photos. "Thank you, Dr. James. May I keep these?"

"Yes, Your Honor." Becca returned to her table.

"Sheriff Howard, what do you have to say?"

Kell gave a quick look at her. A smile was still on his face. "I stand by the ticket I issued."

She started to roll her eyes, then remembered where she was and hoped the judge hadn't seen.

The judge drew himself up, sitting straight and tall in his chair. He cleared his throat and said, "The evergreens on that corner are a hindrance. They never should have been planted so close to the intersection. Dr. James is correct. Cars do need to inch forward to look for traffic."

Judge Franklin shuffled the photos in front of him. "Sheriff, from where your vehicle was parked, I agree with Dr. James. You would have had a difficult time seeing. So, I'm going to throw out the ticket." He paused as he shuffled the photos into a pile. "Lucky will survive without the seventy-five-dollar revenue. I'm going to have a chat with Bert Fellows over in the township road commission office to see what we can do to make visibility better at that intersection."

Becca sighed, feeling vindicated. "Thank you, Your Honor."

"Oh, Sheriff, please say hello to your mother. I expect I'll see her at Bingo before too long."

"Sure thing, I'll tell her."

Judge Franklin hit his gavel. "Next case."

Becca hurried down the aisle into the outer hallway, with Kell on her heels and what felt like a victory a moment before now felt awkward.

"Congratulations, Doc."

She studied his face. "Are you being sarcastic?"

"Not at all."

"All right then, thank you."

"Look, we got off on the wrong foot this morning. I don't understand how I didn't make the connection. How I didn't recognize you."

Shrugging, she said, "Oh, I'm sure you see so many women during your busy day of writing up tickets. It's probably difficult to tell us apart."

Okay, that was a little too snarky. Dial it back.

"Or could be that it was one of my first weeks on the job," he said.

"That's true." She acknowledged. "Anyway, I'm glad to put this behind us. I mean, with me being friends with your sister."

"Agreed."

"I better get going. I need to stop at the grocery store on my way home."

"I'll keep you posted about the investigation."

"Oh, yes, thank you." Becca paused, then added, "Will I see you on Sunday?" She only asked to be polite. She didn't care one way or another if he came.

"No, I have too much work to get done."

"Oh, I see. All right, goodbye."

"Bye, Doc."

☘

Late that afternoon, Becca and Emma had just settled on the sofa to watch *Finding Nemo* for the umpteenth time. She didn't mind the repetition. Cuddling with her daughter on a wintry afternoon was no hardship. The movie became background noise, though, as her thoughts wandered to her interactions with Sheriff Kell Howard.

Becca was sure Kell picked up on her dad's slip-up that morning. As soon as he'd said, *after everything you've been through,* Kell's brows had lifted. That man didn't miss much.

She wasn't sure why she wanted to keep her past a secret. But it was personal, and she liked to keep her personal life private. He was a cop, so if he wanted to dig into her past, he could.

She didn't feel comfortable discussing that chapter of her life. There was not a day that passed that she didn't think about the child she miscarried or the other details of that night. The fight. The crash. Her baby.

But thinking about Josh and his betrayal and everything that led up to the accident was useless. She'd put that man out of her head years ago.

She was happy with her life here in Lucky.

Adopting Emma had been a big step toward healing herself. She'd wanted to be a mother for as long as she could remember. How could she raise such a happy, spirited little person and not see the beauty and humor in life? Emma represented everything good in the world and, as her mother Becca would do everything she could to protect her daughter.

As the movie continued, Becca thought about texting Megan. But what would she say? Megan certainly hadn't mentioned that her brother was hot. But of course, she wouldn't think of her brother in that way. She chuckled quietly, but Emma still heard.

"Mommy, this isn't the funny part."

Uh-oh. "Oh, sorry, Mommy was thinking of something else."

"You gots to pay attention. Nemo meets Dory soon," Emma said.

"You're right. Sorry." She zippered her finger across her lips.

Only a few minutes went by before her dad walked into the room and said, "Becca?"

"Yeah, Dad." She held up a finger. "Just a sec." Becca paused the movie, noticing her daughter's grumpy face. "Let me talk to Grandpa for a minute." Becca laughed when Emma gave an exaggerated sigh. Already a little drama queen at three.

"Yes, whatcha need?"

"I'm headed over to the hospital. There are a couple of my patients I need to see today rather than having them wait until tomorrow."

"Okay, thanks. Anything special you want for dinner?"

"Whatever you feel like is fine with me."

"Cheesy noodles," Emma shouted.

Becca tickled Emma. "Silly, you'd eat that every day if we let you."

"Yep," Emma said, between giggles.

Her dad chuckled and waved. "I'll leave the menu up to you, ladies. Let's see if you can sneak a vegetable into the meal."

"Oh, this from the man who often takes his granddaughter to McDonald's."

Emma bounced, "Yay. Mickey Ds."

"I agree with you, Sweet Pea. I'll see you beautiful ladies later." He blew a kiss to Becca and Emma.

"Bye, Dad."

"Bye, Gampa."

Chapter 6

The next few days flew by. Things had gotten busy at the clinic because of the rescheduled appointments, and Emma had run a low-grade fever over the last twenty-four hours, so Becca was putting in double duty as a doctor.

Finished with her patients for the day, Becca made a quick stop at Espresso Yourself for a latte, hoping to catch Megan for a visit since they hadn't talked since before the break-in.

Megan had kept her up-and-coming music career going strong. No longer based in Nashville, she'd moved back to Lucky and was engaged to a hunky firefighter, Chase Devine. Becca smiled when she thought of the happy couple. Her friend would make a beautiful summer bride.

Megan greeted her with concern etched on her face. "Oh my God, I heard about the break-in. Are you okay?"

"I'm fine now. It was scary. I won't lie," Becca said.

"I should have called, but I didn't want to bother you since I knew you were busy catching up with patients after being closed."

"That's okay. No worries. My week got complicated. More so when Emma got a fever."

"Oh, no! I'm sorry. Is she doing better?"

"Fever broke yesterday. I didn't even realize you knew about the break-in."

Megan gave her the *oh-come-on* eye roll.

"Oh, right, this is Lucky, and your brother is the sheriff."

"Correct on the first count. Small town and all. Wrong on the second. My big brother hasn't said a word."

Becca frowned. This information disappointed her. She couldn't explain why. Perhaps because she'd couldn't get the overbearing sheriff out of her mind. Apparently, he didn't have the same problem. Becca shook that thought right out of her head. It was more likely he wouldn't discuss police business. "Well, it's not something I ever want to repeat." She brushed a stray hair behind her ear.

"What can I get you?" Megan held up her hand. "Wait, don't tell me. A latte with an extra shot of espresso?"

"Perfect. Thanks."

"Got it. Go. Sit. It's on the house."

"No, Megan, that's crazy. You'll never make a profit by comping all your friends."

"Let me worry about that."

Becca sighed. "Okay, thank you." She took a ten-dollar bill from her purse and put it in the tip jar. "For your crew." She took a seat by the window to wait for her order.

She loved the eclectic feel of the place. A twist between a soda fountain from the 1950s and an old-fashioned diner and bakery, like Lulu's from the movie *Waitress*. A black-and-white checkered tile floor set off a mix of bright-colored retro tables and chairs Megan had found at yard sales. She repurposed them to fit the look she was going for in the café. Artwork by local students hung on the walls.

Espresso Yourself, in a town with no Starbucks, was just what the doctor ordered. Except for the chocolate treats, because those were definitely not.

Since moving to Lucky five years ago, Becca had been busy getting her practice going and then adopting Emma, leaving her too preoccupied to put much effort into socializing. She had left a group of friends back in Cleveland where she'd grown up, gone to school, and worked. Becca chose a local college to be close to home after her mother's death. Then she attended her dad's alma mater, Case Western Reserve, for medical school.

When Megan came to Lucky last summer to recuperate after an assault, the two women became friends. When Megan fell in love, she left the bright lights of Nashville to move back home. She still sang and recorded music, but opening Espresso Yourself was a labor of love. Becca was grateful their friendship continued to grow.

"Here you go." Megan set the drink and a small bakery sack on the table.

"Wow, this is service. Delivered by the proprietor herself." Becca grinned.

"But of course. You're one of my best customers."

"Not if you keep comping my orders." Becca scoffed good-naturedly. "What's this? I only ordered the drink." She peeked in the sack and her mouth watered at the sight of the chocolate muffin sure to ruin her appetite for supper. She pinched a sampling of the warm, gooey taste of heaven. "Oh, my God. This is sinfully good."

Megan smiled. "You're welcome. I know you love chocolate as much as I do. This is our new double chocolate muffin."

"Do you have time to sit and visit for a few minutes? Seems like forever since we chatted," Becca asked.

"Sure." Megan nodded. "Let me get Brianna from the back room. I'll be back in a sec."

As Becca sipped her latte and waited for Megan to return, she thought it might be nice to invite her cousin Lori and Megan for another girl's night out. They'd had so much fun the night they went to the library for the book talk and then on to Joe's Bar and Grill for drinks. It was the happening place to be in Lucky. Typical bar food, but the beer was cold, and the burgers were hot and tasty—the best around.

She was still mulling over the possibilities when Megan scooted into the chair beside her. "I feel like all our chats have been one-sided... all about me because I've been so busy getting this place up and running. If I've neglected our friendship, I'm sorry. Have I been a crappy friend?"

"Don't be silly. Of course, you haven't been a crappy friend. Not at all. I know you've been busy. I'm happy for you and Chase."

"Thanks. We've only touched on your life briefly in our conversations. I know that you're an exceptional mother and doctor."

"Aww, that's sweet of you to say."

"Oh, and you have a sweet tooth for chocolate."

"Doesn't everyone?" Changing the subject, Becca asked, "What time do you want me here to help on Saturday?"

Becca planned to host a support group for victims of crimes. Sam Winston, a friend from medical school whose focus was mental health, had moved to Lucky to work at the hospital and consented to run therapy sessions. But the project needed funding, so Megan and Becca put their heads together and developed the idea of hosting a bachelor auction.

"The festivities kick off at six. We'll serve wine and some appetizers before the auction starts at seven. If you can, come in the afternoon to help with the set-up. You can bring a change of clothes."

"Sounds like a plan. My dad's not on call, so he agreed to watch Emma. He was relieved he didn't have to take part in the bachelor auction." She laughed.

Megan not only purchased the coffee place but also the vacant building next door, and, with Chase's help, had renovated it into a multi-functional facility. The first floor held a small stage. On Thursday nights, they served beer and wine, and karaoke was a big hit. There was a large room on the second floor that the community could use for meetings and private gatherings.

The idea of a bachelor auction was just off-the-wall enough to appeal to Megan's sparkling personality, and she was the perfect choice as the Master of Ceremonies. Shining in the limelight was nothing new for that girl. Thank God Becca didn't have to be center stage. She'd leave that honor to her friend.

"I have a few more flyers left," Megan said. "Everyone in town knows. But I'll drop them off at Joe's. He said he'd keep a few on the bar for us."

"I still can't believe you signed Chase up. Poor guy," Becca said with a chuckle.

"Oh, he'll have fun. I was thinking of asking someone to get into a bidding war with me. That way I can inflate the bid. It's all for a worthy cause. If nothing else, it will create excitement, right?" asked Megan.

"But won't Chase mind if someone outbids you?" Becca asked.

"I *will* mind. I don't plan on anyone outbidding me." Megan smiled, looking every bit the chart-topping country singer she was.

"So, who else did you get to take part?" Becca asked, sipping her latte.

"We have four firefighters, including Chase. There are three guys from Devine Construction, the new high school football coach, our good Dr. Winston, agreed earlier today. He said he figured since he has moved here, he might as well immerse himself in the craziness that is a small town," Megan said.

She looked over to the counter and saw there were a few people in line. She held up a finger before she stood up. "Hold on, I'll be right back." She hustled over to the counter to help Brianna.

When Megan returned to their table, Becca said, "I'm glad Sam is getting more acclimated to Lucky." She pinched off another bite of the muffin.

"Me too. His group counseling helped with my emotional healing after everything I went through last year," Megan said.

Becca smiled. "I'm glad you're doing so well."

"Thanks." Megan grinned back at her friend. "Let's see ... who else? Bruce Kincaid called me this morning. He's in."

"Bruce is the realtor, right?"

"Yes, and he's a family friend. A little older than Kell and Chase." She clapped her hands. Becca could feel the excitement coming from her friend.

"Let's see who else. Oh, Judge Franklin called right after I hung up with Bruce and asked to be added. I didn't know he was single."

"Wow, that's wonderful." Becca was content to help behind the scenes by distributing flyers. She wasn't even sure they needed to do that, since word-of-mouth was the best way to communicate around town.

A movement across the street caught Becca's gaze. When she saw who it was, her pulse quickened.

"Hey." Megan snapped her fingers. "Did I lose you?"

Feeling breathless, she replied, "No. I'm right here."

Megan followed Becca's gaze out the window. "Oh, there's that brother of mine. It looks like he stopped to chat with John and Margie."

The McHales owned the sporting goods store down the street, and they lived next door to Becca's great-aunt Esther. She'd exchanged a passing greeting when she saw them in their yard or driveway. John McHale had helped to save Megan when her stalker tried to kidnap her last fall.

Becca snuck a quick glance out the plate-glass window to the sidewalk. Megan noticed and asked, "So, what did you think?"

"About what?"

Megan cocked her head. "Not what, who. I wanted to know what you thought about Kell. I guess I have my answer."

A flush crept across Becca's cheeks. "What? No, I found him to be very bossy.

Megan quirked a brow as if she was humoring Becca's protest, which was confirmed with her comment, "The lady doth protest too much, methinks."

"Hardly," Becca huffed.

When Megan gave her an *oh come on skeptical look,* she said, "Oh, all right. He's a twelve, on a scale from one to ten." Laughing, Becca continued, "Okay, he's good-looking."

Megan smirked. "So, are you interested?"

"What? No!" Becca said, louder than she intended. Lowering her voice, she tried to explain. "I'm not. I would never get involved with a guy who looks like him. But there is no law against looking, is there?"

Megan shook her head. "I'm confused. Girl, you're shooting out mixed messages. You clearly think he is good-looking. Why is that a bad thing?"

Becca held up her hand to stop her friend. "He's bossy."

Megan waved away Becca's hand. "Yes, you already said that. You're repeating yourself."

Becca sighed.

"You know he comes from an excellent family, if I say so myself." Megan shined her fingers across her shoulder.

Becca laughed. "All of that doesn't matter."

"Sounds to me like you're discriminating against him because he is attractive." Megan crossed her arms and stared.

Megan would not let the topic go, so Becca confided in her friend.

"Here's the deal: my ex-husband was really handsome, too. I've learned the hard way to avoid hot guys. And I'm busy with the clinic and Emma, so I'm good."

Josh was the last person Becca wanted to discuss. She wished she could rewrite her history with him. So, she tried to avoid the topic. The humiliation and anger had faded away some with time.

"Your ex must have done a real number on you."

"Yep, he did."

When Becca said nothing else. Megan asked, "Are you going to share with the class?"

It would be a relief to talk to a friend about what happened. Taking a deep breath, she explained, "He's a doctor, too. We met in medical school, though he was a year ahead of me. We both worked at Mercy in Cleveland." She paused and took another deep breath, as if each word she spoke drained her body of air. Even now, years later, she felt a pain in her chest.

"We hadn't even celebrated our third anniversary before I learned he was dubbed *Doc Juan* by the female nurses and interns. The kicker was I could have ignored the gossip, and I might have if I hadn't walked in on Josh and one of the first-year interns in our bed when I came home early from my shift. I was six weeks pregnant, and I was dealing with all-day morning sickness."

Megan shook her head. "Wow. He sucks. I'm sorry. I didn't mean to pry."

Becca shrugged. "Long time ago, and I'm fine now. It's good to talk with someone. The hardest part wasn't Josh and his cheating. I miscarried."

"Oh no, I'm sorry. I reiterate, he sucks."

"I try not to talk about Josh, the baby, or our life. It's all jumbled together. We were driving and arguing about his cheating. It was raining, and we were distracted and didn't see a car run the red light. We were T-boned. Josh was on the side that the car hit. It all happened so fast. Josh was bleeding, and I tried to help him, but my seatbelt wouldn't release." Becca paused long enough to take another drink.

"The fire crew finally got us out, but it was awful. Josh was lucky. His injuries weren't life threatening, but he has a limp from the damage to his leg. I started cramping and bleeding that night and I lost the baby. The doctor didn't think the accident caused the miscarriage. One of those awful, unexplained things. But I didn't believe him. We divorced a few months later, and my dad and I moved here to start over with the clinic. My dad grew up here."

"There are no words. Sorry sounds totally inadequate," Megan said. "Where's your ex now?"

"Oh, I imagine he's still in Cleveland. Screwing his way through more first-year interns." Becca laughed half-heartedly. "When I moved, I left my old life behind. I haven't looked back."

"So, not to be indelicate, but Emma isn't his child?"

Becca shook her head. "No. I adopted Emma after I moved here."

Megan nodded. "Oh, well, I'm very happy you've made a life here in Lucky and feel so fortunate we met. You've become a good friend."

"I feel the same." Becca reached across the small table and squeezed her friend's hand.

"You know, I sure hope karma has bitten your ex in the ass by now," Megan said.

"If only." They laughed.

Their conversation ended when the bells on the door jingled and in walked Kell.

He surveyed the room and smiled when he spotted Megan and Becca together. "Ladies." He tipped his hat. "How are you on this beautiful, but cold, afternoon?"

Becca wished she could climb under the table. But the tiny bistro table she usually found so charming barely accommodated her knees. She avoided facing him, since they seemed to antagonize each other.

As usual, Megan jumped in. "Kell, you remember my friend Becca James from Monday?"

He removed his hat. "Nice to see you again. At least under better circumstances today."

"Yes, it is. Any progress on the case?" Becca asked.

"Not yet," he said.

"What can I get you, bro?"

"My usual."

"Gotcha. One boring black coffee coming up. Be right back." Megan stood and moved to the counter.

Becca scrambled to stand too, then realizing too late that it left her standing awkwardly next to Kell.

Before she could stop herself, Becca asked, "Write any traffic tickets today?"

He grinned. "As a matter of fact, I did."

"Oh, no. I hope you don't end up back in court."

"Don't worry. It's all part of the job."

She still held her drink, but her mouth got too dry to continue a conversation. That was her cue to leave. She eyed the exit. Escape was only a few steps away.

She licked her lips. "I better run. Megan, thanks again for the latte and muffin," she called over her shoulder. "I'll see you at your mom's house on Sunday."

"You're welcome. Yep. See you then."

Becca turned to Kell. "Goodbye."

"Here, I'll get that," he said, as he stepped to the door and opened it for her.

"Thanks."

"Sure, no problem." He pointed to her bandaged hand. "By the way, how's the injury?"

"Ah, getting better. Thanks."

"Bundle up. There's an icy wind this afternoon." He looked like he had something else he wanted to say.

She hesitated for a second, dancing from foot to foot. Not only were there high winds, but it was cold, and light snowflakes fell, sticking to the sidewalk.

It was silly to stand there freezing, so Becca said, "Goodbye, Sheriff."

"Bye, Doc."

Chapter 7

Was it just him, or did Becca scramble out of there in a hurry? So when Megan brought his coffee over, he asked, "What was that about? Did I interrupt something?"

"Not really. We were having some long-overdue girl talk."

He wasn't sure if he bought the innocent explanation. But it wasn't any of his business.

"Did you know Mom invited Becca and her dad for dinner on Sunday?"

"Yes. Mom told me on Monday morning when I pulled her over for speeding again."

"Again?" Megan put her hand to her forehead. "I'm sorry, Kell. She can be outrageous at times."

"Try all the time."

His sister had experienced her own battles with their mother.

In her sweetest sing-song voice, she said, "So about dinner on Sunday, Mom wants you to be there."

"Yeah, I know. I got her message loud and clear. She refuses to respect my answer."

"Here." She tugged on his arm, pulling him toward the ridiculously small table where Megan and Becca had been sitting. "Sit." From the determined look on her face, Kell feared he was about to get lambasted by his sister, who inherited not only their mother's red hair but her quick-to-spark Scottish temper.

He arched a brow. "You don't expect me to sit there. My knees will topple it."

"Don't scoot in. Just sit."

Sighing, Kell sat, angled away, and waited for the lecture he knew was coming. He scrubbed his hand over his face, scratching at his beard. It had been a long day and wasn't over yet. There had been a time when he would have walked away. Kell didn't have to listen to his little sister or his mother. He was a grown-ass man.

He took a big gulp of his coffee and burned his mouth. "Damn. That's hot."

Shaking her head, Megan laughed. "Yeah, dumbass, coffee's hot."

He glared at her.

"What's your problem?" she asked. "Why won't you come to dinner? I don't get you. You've been gone for years. You're finally back home, but it feels like you're avoiding us. We want to spend time with you."

"You know why I don't want to go. Mom is unrelenting. She wants to play matchmaker." Megan didn't respond. "See, you can't defend her."

"You're right, but she has been better toward me now that I'm engaged to Chase. She knows a wedding and a grandbaby are imminent." Megan grinned.

"I'm happy for you and Chase. But I'm not interested in finding the one and producing a half dozen rug rats for her to granny. I'll leave that to you."

It's not like he hated sex. But in a small town, you had to be careful when dating. Discretion was the key. For now, his fist was handling the situation until he could find a discreet alternative.

The decision to return to his hometown of Lucky, as sheriff, put him smack dab in the middle of the community's grapevine.

It was nobody's business who he had sex with. But he wasn't naïve enough to think in a town the size of Lucky there wouldn't be gossip. And if there was gossip, his mother was bound to hear. Hell, she'd be the one spreading it.

That was the last thing he needed. Sex did not equal love, marriage, and a happily ever after, and finding a woman to accept those conditions wasn't easy. What harm could come of it if he was forthright and set the ground rules from the beginning, if the woman felt the same? Nothing serious. Nothing permanent. Besides, what woman would want to take on his PTSD issues?

Megan changed her tone. Somberly, she said, "Listen, Kell, I can't even imagine what you went through over there or the horrors you witnessed. I'm sure you're dealing with a lot of crap, but if you need to talk, Chase and I are always here for you. Plus, you might see a professional."

"I'm fine." Kell regretted his short, gruff response immediately.

"Okay. Okay." She held up her hand. "I'll change the subject. Are you going to sign up for the charity auction? We could use a few more guys."

He shook his head. "Not happening."

She frowned. "Oh, you're such a grump."

Kell was grateful when his radio interrupted.

"Look, sis, I've gotta run. You enjoy your dinner at Mom's place. I will be working."

He could at least admit, to himself, his attraction to the doctor with the long blonde hair and sparkling blue eyes. Sunday dinner did sound a bit more appealing.

His excuse that he had to work wasn't a total lie, though. They had all been working overtime to solve the burglary cases. Kell stood and his leg knocked into the table, causing it to wobble. He righted it, then gave her a peck on the top of her head. "Stay out of trouble, Little Red."

She swatted him away. "Don't call me that."

He cocked his head and gave her a wicked grin, then opened the door.

Before he could escape, she said, "You need to stop being a dumbass and open yourself up a little to someone." When he didn't reply, she continued, "It's not a crime to ask for help."

"Duly noted," he said, for no other reason than to get her to shut up.

He didn't turn around. He simply closed the door and walked away.

Kell spent the next few days wrestling with his superfluous thoughts about Becca. By Sunday afternoon, he'd given up his resolve to boycott the family dinner with their special guests, Dr. Harper James and his daughter, Dr. Becca James.

He'd survived worse. Much worse.

There were five of them. Megan had come, but Chase was on shift at the fire station. A fact that might have helped Kell decide to skip the meal, had he known. He had counted on his best friend to be there. But so far, Harper and he were holding their own.

The meal was uneventful. It was actually pleasant. Harper and he discussed the football playoffs, and the women talked about some new reality show. They were just finishing up when the topic of the auction fundraiser came up.

He stood and said, "I'll get a fire started in the other room."

Harper looked like he would gladly go with him, but Megan spoiled his escape when she said, "Too bad you're on babysitting duty, Harper. I'm pretty sure you'd have lots of women bidding on you." While Kell took pity on the man, there was no way he'd stick around to be grilled about the auction.

After he set the fire, he returned to the group. He took a second to appreciate how pretty Becca looked. Her hair was down, and it curled at her shoulders. Her cheeks were pink, and he wondered if she had put on some kind of make-up because her eyes seemed bigger and brighter.

"That was, without a doubt, one of the best dinners I've ever had. The roast was delicious, Ruby. Would you be willing to share your recipe with us?" Harper said as he wiped his mouth with the cloth napkin.

His mom was all about impressing someone. He wasn't sure if Becca was the target or had his mom set her sights on poor Harper?

"We appreciated your invitation, Ruby," Becca said.

"Yes. Thank you," Harper said with a smile. He stood as Mom began to clear the table. "Let me help."

"No, please sit. You and Becca are our guests."

Kell scooted back from the table. "How 'bout you both sit and relax? I'll manage mess duty."

"Oh, thank you, Kell. You're such a helpful young man." She smiled.

It was all he could do not to shake his head at his mother's lack of subtlety.

"Megan, would you mind lending your brother a hand in the kitchen and start the coffee? I'll serve dessert in a few minutes."

"Sure, of course." In a dramatic stage whisper, she added, "Once a barista, always a barista. My work is never done." Laughing, she brushed the back of her hand theatrically across her forehead.

"Drama Queen," he muttered just loud enough for his sister to hear.

She curtsied with a grin.

"Do you need an extra pair of hands?" Becca must have considered her offer to be extraneous, because she didn't wait for him to respond before she stood and picked up her plate and a few other dishes within reach.

Kell would not complain. "Sure. Many hands. Light work." He held the door for her.

While Megan made the coffee, he rinsed the plates and handed them to Becca to load into the dishwasher.

"I think I ask you this every time I see you, but is there any news about the burglaries?"

"Nothing helpful. There have been two other similar break-ins within sixty-five klicks of Lucky," Kell said.

Megan wrinkled her nose. "Klicks? What is that in miles? For us civilians."

He chuckled, but before he could answer, Becca said, "Klicks stand for kilometers."

Kell arched his brow, impressed that Becca knew the answer.

She shrugged. "I worked for Doctors Without Borders for a year."

Did she, now? Impressed, he nodded his head in approval. Then turned to Megan, "About forty miles, Sis."

"Gotcha," she said, giving him a mock salute.

Turning back to Becca, he said, "We're evaluating notes on each of the cases. I'll let you know if anything develops."

"Thanks."

Megan interrupted them. "Look at that. You two got all the dishes loaded."

"Yeah, thanks for your help," he said, snapping the dish towel at her.

Megan laughed and danced away. "Come on, you two, let's get back in there and save poor Harper from Mom."

When they went back to the dining room, Becca smiled when she saw her dad patting his stomach. He was still talking about the delicious meal.

"If I ate like this every day, I'd have to increase my daily run." Chuckling, he turned to Kell and asked, "How do you stay in shape?"

Yes, what do you do to keep that body looking so good?

"Good genes, I guess." He smiled.

"Oh, Kell, you're too modest," Ruby chastised. "Did you know he's a former Marine? He's in tip-top form—"

"Mom," interrupted Megan, "they know. There are pictures all over the house dedicated to his years in the service."

"Oh, hush, a mother has a right to be proud of her children. Don't you agree, Harper?"

Her dad blinked in surprise, not keen on having to take a side. "Yes." He cleared his throat. "Kell, how long have you been out?"

"Seven months." He ran his hand along his jawline. "At first, the Marines got me in shape, of course. Mom is correct on that point. Now I try to run every day, if I can. As sheriff, I'm on call, so I can't always get a run in, but I try."

"Where did you serve?" Becca asked.

"Iraq, Syria, and Afghanistan. Most of my time was in Afghanistan."

"How long were you over there?"

"Four tours."

She shook her head. "Wow. Just one year with Doctors Without Borders seemed like forever. Though the work was rewarding."

Ruby stood up. "I'll get the dessert. Why don't we all go into the family room?"

A blazing fire warmed the room and gave off a soft glow, which was a welcome reprieve from the snowy cold outdoors. The shadow of the flickering flames danced on the walls.

Megan was right. Family photos filled the room. There was this super cool wall with a bunch of frames that told the family's story. Becca wandered over to the wall of photos.

A particular photo caught her eye: three little boys dressed in baseball uniforms, each holding a small trophy.

She smiled at the boy's big grins. The boy on the left was missing a front tooth, and freckles dotted his small face. Hard to believe that Kell was ever that small.

He startled Becca when he came up behind her and said, "My two best friends." He pointed to the boy on the right. "That's Chase." And then pointed to the boy in the middle. "And that's Johnny Martin. Don't know if you follow big league baseball, but Johnny's a pitcher for Cincinnati." He stood so close she could feel the heat from his body. Her pulse quickened.

She nodded and cleared her throat, pretending not to be affected by his nearness. "Johnny and my cousin Lori were..." She hesitated, not sure what to say. "They were something in high school."

"Aha. I thought there might be a connection between your families. Small town, same last name and all."

"Oh, yes. This is my dad's hometown." She gestured back to the photo. "Cute picture."

He shrugged. "If you say so." He gestured toward the fireplace. "I've got to stoke the fire."

"Sure."

Megan came over to join her. Becca gestured to all the frames. "I love all these photos. They tell your family's story."

"Yes, they do," Megan replied.

Farther along the wall, there was a picture of a little girl with a microphone. No, wait. Becca leaned in closer. It was a hairbrush, not a microphone. It was a younger Megan. So cute. Even if the two women hadn't become friends, she'd have recognized Megan. The hair gave her away, such a beautiful shade of red. "Looks like you aspired to be a singer, even at a young age."

"Well, I didn't get far with a hairbrush as my microphone." The two friends laughed.

Becca stopped in front of a snapshot of Kell and Megan. The siblings stood at the edge of a body of water. Was it Lucky Lake, perhaps? Again, she leaned in to get a closer look.

Kell had his arm protectively tucked around Megan. She gazed up at her big brother with the sweetest expression, as if he'd just invented the peanut butter and jelly sandwich. Becca knew Kell was eight years older than Megan.

Becca bit her lower lip as she studied the photo. What caught her attention was how much Emma resembled Megan. Becca guessed Megan was three or four in the picture. She blinked a few times. The resemblance was uncanny. Curly red hair. Small button nose. Chubby cheeks. "Oh my God, Megan, Emma looks so much like you as a child. She could be your daughter."

Megan studied the photo. "Yeah, she does. Cool, I have a mini me."

"Yes, I guess you do." The two women moved back to the sitting area with the others. Becca turned her head to look back at the photo of Kell and Megan. She couldn't quite put her finger on what made that photo stand out.

"Mom loves her photos. She calls it her bragging wall," Megan said.

"Whatever it's called, I love all your family pictures. When I move into my new place. I'd like to have a display of photos on the wall going up the stairs. I'm still in the planning stage. There is so much to do first."

Ruby walked in carrying the dessert. Never missing a beat, she jumped into the conversation. "Megan told me you bought a house," she said to Becca. "What street?"

"It's a cute little Cape Cod, a fixer upper over on Elm. I'll be a block from my great aunt Esther's house."

Ruby nodded. "I know the one. Brick and with white siding?"

"Yes. I'm really into the older homes in the neighborhood and eager to get started working on the updates. I don't plan to move in until most of the work is done."

Becca felt a sense of satisfaction and was eager to start some of her DIY ideas. She hoped the room she pictured for Emma would turn out as cute as it did in her mind. Painting it pink and purple was a sure bet for her little princess. She smiled, thinking of Emma's face when she saw the result.

"I closed last week, so now I have to get to work." Turning to look at her dad, she said, "I'm sure my dad will enjoy his privacy when we finally move."

"Sounds like you'll have your hands full," Ruby said.

"I have a to-do list so I can check the jobs off as I go. I hope being organized will help the process get done faster."

"Oh, don't let her fool you. There are so many projects that need doing in that place. Wallpaper from the seventies, in more than one room. The kitchen and bathrooms need updating. I won't elaborate further, since my daughter is giving me the cross-eyed, how-can-you-say-that expression." her dad chuckled.

"Oh, hush. I am not, and it's not that bad," Becca chided.

"Oh, no? I break out in a sweat thinking about all your home improvement projects." His hand glided over his forehead.

"I'm sure you'll turn the place around in no time," said Ruby. "Kell is mighty handy with a hammer and paintbrush. Kell, you wouldn't mind giving Becca a hand with her renovations. Would you?"

"Oh? That's unnecessary, but thank you," Becca quickly responded.

Ignoring her response to his mom's comment, Kell looked over to Becca and said, "You've got my number on the business card I gave you. Call me if you need a hand."

Becca blushed at the blatant attempt Ruby made to coerce Kell into helping her.

The two of them got off on the wrong foot to use one of her dad's expressions. Today had been the first time she'd gotten through their conversations without snark and sarcasm.

Most women would love a chance to work side by side with that man. Thinking about being alone with Kell in her little house caused her belly to do calisthenics. But the last thing she needed was to get involved with Kell Howard.

🍀

Kell watched as Becca blushed and ignored his mother's suggestion.

Sure enough, Becca said, "Oh, I'm sure I will be fine. But thank you." Changing the subject, Becca turned her attention to the dessert on the coffee table in front of her. "You're going to kill my diet. Look at this extravagant dessert. It must have taken hours."

"Yeah, way too pretty to mess up by sticking the serving spoon in the bowl," said Megan. "But it's chocolate, so that's not happening."

"This is the dessert I make for the senior center. It's easy, a little pudding, whipped cream and graham crackers. The old men get a kick out of the name." Ruby took a pregnant pause. "It's called *The Next Best Thing to Sex.*"

"Mom!" Megan shook her head in exasperation. Becca felt her cheeks color, but she laughed. Her dad ducked his head, but she caught the smirk he hid.

Ruby chuckled. "What? That's the name. I swear on your grandma's grave."

"Mom, we might believe you if you didn't have Grandma's ashes in an urn on the mantel."

"On that note, I'm out of here." Kell stood. "Thank you, Mom, for the great meal."

"Kell, you're leaving now? But you haven't had dessert."

"That's okay. I don't need the next best thing..." Becca met his gaze, her eyes widening. Apparently, she was the only one who caught his inference. "It was nice to see you again, Becca, Harper."

Harper stood to shake Kell's hand. "Good to see you."

Megan shouted a "Bye, Bro."

"Bye, Sis."

At the door, he turned toward Becca, and he tipped his hat. "G'night." She responded with a small frown. She was doing a decent job of keeping her walls up. But all that did was give him more of an incentive to see if he could wear them down.

Damn glad he'd gone to supper, and he started his SUV with a smile on his face.

Chapter 8

Kell looked around his tiny studio apartment. Only five hundred square feet, if that. It had a basic kitchen and bathroom. And the second-hand furnishings worked fine for him. The location couldn't be better. It was above the Espresso Yourself, and close to the sheriff's office.

All the DIY talk had Kell paying closer attention to the preparations Megan had made to update the apartment for him. She'd painted and put her girly touches on the place. Even though he'd thought the plain beige walls matched his overall mood, he hadn't objected when she'd painted the place a light gray.

Truthfully, he saw little difference between beige and gray. But he humored his sister. He hadn't wanted to rain on her happy parade, but honestly all he cared about was a toilet and a fridge.

She hung up shades and curtains with a black geometric pattern that came from some place online. She must have liked the place, because there had been other deliveries with boxes from the same place. Like every day for a week, he'd find boxes in the hallway outside the apartment.

New towels, a bath rug, and a shower curtain arrived in one box, while an array of dishcloths, a kitchen rug, and an oven mitt came in another. He laughed when he opened a box with a kitchen wall clock with spoons and forks poking out. Hey, at least he knew where to find clean utensils if he didn't feel like doing the dishes.

She didn't stop with the kitchen and bathroom. She bought him new bedding, which he would have appreciated more if he were sleeping in the bed. But he couldn't tell her that. The recliner and the TV were all he needed. They helped keep the nightmares to a minimum.

The place worked for him. Low maintenance, convenient location, and the price was right. He could walk across the road and down a block to Joe's Bar & Grill for supper most nights, since cooking wasn't in his skill set. He often would take a book with him and grab a booth in back where he could lose himself in the intrigue while chowing on a burger.

He especially avoided being home on Thursday nights because his sister hosted karaoke on the ground level next door. The music and often off-key singing carried up to his apartment. So, he often stayed late at his office. It was the perfect time to get caught up on paperwork.

The Sunday supper earlier at Mom's hadn't been so bad. He'd actually enjoyed himself because Mom had been on her best behavior and had kept her meddling to a minimum.

After such a nice day, he decided instead of sitting up all night with the TV tuned to some West Coast game; it was a safe night to sleep in his bed. Kell was long overdue to have a peaceful night's sleep, so he laid down and closed his eyes.

He was on patrol, bouncing along the streets in the Humvee.

An Afghan woman clad in a traditional burqa walked through the marketplace. Her arms were full, laden with her purchases and a small child on her hip.

Kell had a clear view of her. They'd only been out on patrol for a few hours. It was late afternoon, hot as hell, and so far, they hadn't run into any problems. But there'd been an escalating string of car bombings.

Out of nowhere, a rusted-out Corolla zoomed past the woman, stopping on the side of the road not ten feet in front of the woman. The car blocked the bus stop.

The hairs on the back of his neck prickled, warning him of impending danger. His sixth sense had kept him alive so far, so he wasn't about to ignore it.

"Hold up," he shouted to the Marine at the wheel. Seconds later, a bus pulled up behind the car.

The Humvee stopped. But before Kell could voice his concerns, an Afghan man jumped out of the car and sprinted down a side alley.

"What the fuck?" Kell said.

He was stepping down when the car exploded. The horrific scene happened so fast. Copious flying debris blew in all directions, hitting innocent bystanders. The bus, the people on it, and other surrounding vehicles and buildings took the brunt of the blast.

He was cognizant of the other Marines following as he ran toward the flames and wreckage and heard the cries of anguished pain all around him.

Kell saw the woman and her child lying motionless on the ground and knelt to check for a pulse. Nothing. The smoke and fire engulfed the area. The Afghan woman's blank eyes stared up at him.

Kell jerked awake. Sweat covered his body. He reached to flip on the bedside lamp, but it took a couple of tries before he could control the tremor in his hand.

"Fuck," he muttered. This was why he didn't sleep. Why he spent most nights in his recliner, avoiding sleep. Anything to keep from reliving the real-life nightmares he'd seen during his tours in the Middle East.

Late night television was a poor substitution for self-medicating with booze. But he valued his job as sheriff and respected the men and women he worked with too much to show up hung over. He'd weaned himself off the late-night painkilling shots months ago. So, now he stuck to watching mind-numbing television and forcing himself to stay awake.

❧

The following Friday afternoon, Kell exhaled a sigh of relief. Lucky hadn't had any more break-ins. However, it was his experience in life that when he managed one problem, another seemed to pop up.

This time it was with his deputy, Paul Gibson.

When you worked alongside someone every day, it was easy to pick up on their mood. Sideway glances from the passenger seat. Subtle fidgeting. So Kell needed answers. He had wanted to give the man time and hoped Gibs would come talk to him on his own. He hadn't. So Kell called the young man into his office.

Kell looked up from his desk when there was a rap on his office door. "Sir, you wanted to see me," Gibs said.

"Yes, come in. Let me just turn off the music." Kell twisted in his seat and hit a button on his Bluetooth speaker that was playing "Strawberry Fields Forever." When he turned back around, he shrugged with a chagrined expression. "One of my Marine buddies got me hooked on the Beatles."

"Oh, my mom loves their music," Gibs said.

Kell nodded. He wondered how many people of this younger generation truly appreciated the talent of the Fab Four.

"Would you like coffee?" He held up his cup to show he had gotten himself one. "Not as good as Megan's, but it'll do."

"No, sir, but thank you." The young deputy was tall and slender. Gibs was at least a head taller than Kell. He wondered if the man played basketball in his youth.

"Have a seat. You know I've told you before, you can drop the *sir*. There was enough of that in the military." Gibs took the chair in front of Kell's desk.

Kell didn't want to put the guy on the spot, but if there were problems which could affect the man's performance, it was Kell's duty to find out.

Yeah, right, what about your own issues?

Shoving his thoughts to the back of his mind, he ripped the bandage off, and asked, "The last few days, you've seemed preoccupied. Whatever it is, I hope you know you can talk to me. Is something on your mind?"

Gibs removed his hat. Brushing his hand through his wavy hair, he took a deep breath. Still stalling. "Spit it out, Gibs."

"Umm, not that it matters ... sir, and it's none of my business ... what you do in your private life—it's just that Lucky is such a small town."

Kell's curiosity was piqued. He fought the impulse to tap his foot. "What's this about?"

"Well..." He pulled his phone from his pocket and scrolled. He sighed, resigned at that point. "I'm not the only person who has seen this." Gibs stood and handed Kell his phone. "It's about your Swingr account."

"My what?"

Kell glanced at the phone as he took a sip and his hot coffee spewed onto his desk and shirt. "Shit!" He set the coffee down.

Gibs scrambled to grab some tissues from the box that sat on the credenza beside the desk. "Here."

"Thanks." He dabbed at his shirt. He scanned the phone and saw his picture. "This is insane." Kell shook his head in disbelief. "Why? How?" He did not know what to say. "This is a joke, right?"

"I don't think so."

He didn't like that response. "This makes no sense. I don't have a ..." He looked at the phone again. "A Swingr account. I'm not sure I even know what it is. Do you?"

Gibs stood beside the desk and cleared his throat. "It's an app for couples who want to find other couples to ... uh ... swing with."

Kell put his head in his hands. "Oh, my God. You've got to be kidding."

"Sorry, Sheriff, I hated having to be the one to tell you. I thought you'd want to know. Could be a bogus account? Identity theft or something?"

Gibs reached for his phone. "Here I'll show you. The young man typed and scrolled, then he showed Kell the phone. The screen showed exactly what the site was all about. There was even an upside-down pineapple as part of the logo.

"Wow, I thought I'd seen just about everything," Kell said. He shook his head. "Can you get back to my photo?"

"Sure thing," Gibs said.

Kell inspected the photo. The frightening answer suddenly dawned on him. "Son of a...." It was a photo his mom had taken the last time he'd been home on leave.

Mom! She was at it again. "My mother set this up. It shouldn't surprise me. It's exactly something she would do."

"I don't know, sir. She must not understand the app's purpose," Gibs said.

"Obviously not."

Gibs cleared his throat. "This doesn't seem to be the best approach for her to take if she wants you to get married and settle down with a family."

Shit, did everyone know Mom's endgame? "Good point."

"You need to talk to her, huh?"

"You've got that right." He stood and grabbed his coat and hat.

"Want me to come along?"

"Nope. But thanks. Best not to have a witness."

Gibs blinked in surprise. "Got it."

"Thanks for the heads-up, Gibs. I appreciate you coming to me. I'll be back shortly."

❧

It took Kell three and a half minutes to get from the station to his mother's house. He slammed on the brakes and turned into the driveway. Mom came to the front door before he even reached the stoop.

She opened the door. "Kell! This is a pleasant surprise. What brings you home?"

He stepped into the house and removed his hat. "You know exactly why I'm here. Drop the innocent act."

She ignored him and pointed to his shirt. "What happened to your uniform?"

"Coffee," he growled.

"Oh dear, would you like me to throw the shirt in the wash? I don't mind a bit."

He didn't budge and continued to glare.

"Why don't you come into the kitchen and sit down? I've got a pot of chili on the stove."

"No. Thanks. I already ate." But he followed her into the kitchen.

"Sit down." She poured another cup of coffee and set it in front of him. "Now be careful with this one."

Kell pinched the bridge of his nose. He couldn't believe he even had to have this conversation with his mom.

"Oh Kell, you and your sister always had a flair for the dramatic. So, are you going to tell me what's got your panties in a bind?"

He cringed at her word choice.

"Really, that's how you're going to play this?" Sighing, he continued, "My *panties* are in a bind because you opened a Swingr account in my name."

He could see her wheels turning, contemplating her options. Finally, she sputtered, "Since you don't seem able to find a girl on your own, I thought the app might help."

He moved his thumb and forefinger from the bridge of his nose and massaged his forehead. "Mom, this app is for couples who want to swap partners."

Mom's eyes widened. "Oh goodness. They should make that clearer in the sign-up process."

Losing control, he raised his voice. "The app logo is an upside-down pineapple, for God's sake."

"Don't you raise your voice to me and use the Lord's name in vain, Kell Jamison." She brushed her hair out of her face. "What does a pineapple have to do with anything?"

He shook his head. "Never mind."

"I want to find you a nice woman so you can start a family. Your biological clock is ticking."

God, give me patience.

"Men don't have biological clocks."

"Well, my *grandma* clock has been ticking for a long while now." She sighed. "Kell. I think at your age—"

"It doesn't matter what you think. It's my life. My decision." He paced the small kitchen. "Mom, I need you to hear me. I do not need your help to find a woman."

"But—"

He held his hand up. "Don't you care what I want? Or in this case, what I don't want?"

He must have gotten through to her.

"I can only imagine the horrible things you saw. That you had to do. But honey, there's so much good in the world, too." She wrapped her arms around him. Despite him being a head taller, she could still wrangle him into a hug now and then.

He stepped back and relented, returning a quick hug. "Stop railroading me into your way of thinking."

She frowned. "All right."

"So, you will fix this mess you made?"

She hesitated a tad longer than he was comfortable with. "Mother? Promise me."

"Oh, all right, I promise."

"Okay, I have to get back to work." He walked to the front door, turned, and shook his head as he said, "I'll give you a point for creativity."

"Desperation breeds creativity," she snapped.

"Let's see that it doesn't."

Back at the station, he called Gibson back into his office.

"Hey, listen, I want to apologize for my abrupt behavior earlier. You shouldn't have to be in the middle of the Howard family drama."

"Don't sweat it. I have a mom, too, you know. She's pulled a few stunts over the years."

Kell scratched his head. Suddenly, it occurred to him he may have given the wrong impression.

"Listen, I don't have an issue with anyone who wants to swing."

The young man's eyes widened as his face blushed. "No, sir, I mean, I'm not on the app. That isn't my thing. But if I tell you who showed it to me..." The poor guy looked like he'd swallowed rotten sardines.

"I understand. Can you do me a favor? Let whoever the person is on Swingr know my account was bogus."

Gibs nodded. "Yeah, sure thing, Sheriff."

"Thanks." He gave Gibs a manly pat on his shoulder. "All right, consider the subject closed. How about we both get back to work?"

Chapter 9

On Saturday, Becca was over at her newly purchased house to remove the awful kitchen wall covering. The fruit montage was just plain awful. One of Emma's favorite songs, "Apples & Bananas," came to mind.

According to the DIY YouTube video she'd watched, she felt confident she'd be able to tackle the project by herself. She laid out the tools she'd picked up yesterday at the hardware store and got to work.

To make it easier to remove, she'd make cuts in the wallpaper with a scoring tool and then spray it with a liquid stripper. According to the nice people on the YouTube video, the wallpaper should come off easily, but she might need to use a scraping tool,

This would be easy.

An hour later, she'd made a big, wet mess in the kitchen. The bandage on her hand had gotten soggy very quickly, and it hindered her progress, or lack thereof.

She'd given up for the day when she heard her dad and Emma come in from the garage.

Emma came skipping into the kitchen. "Mommy!" She stopped and pointed. "Why do the walls look funny?"

Funny was one word for the clumps of wet wallpaper that stuck to the wall.

Becca grabbed a towel to dry her hands. "I was removing the fruit wallpaper."

"And doing an excellent job, by the looks of it," her dad said, chuckling, as he strolled in after Emma. "We thought we'd stop by to check on your progress."

Becca frowned. "As you can see, I didn't get far. It's harder than the video made it look." If she thought her dad would take pity on her and offer to help, she was mistaken.

"Please don't look at me with your pleading eyes. Your mom took care of all the decorating. She knew I was useless with a tool, but wicked smart with my stethoscope." He chortled. "What she couldn't do herself, and there wasn't much, she would hire a handyman for the job."

"Hmm, that's what I should do."

"Why don't you ask Kell?"

"Not you too, Dad. Matchmaking doesn't look good on you."

He shook his head. "Don't be ridiculous. Ruby told us he had experience in this kind of thing, right?"

"Yeah, but the man is busy."

"What can it hurt to ask? Whether he's too busy or simply not interested, he's a big boy. He can always say no."

"I'll think about it," she said.

"Mommy, what's in this bottle?" Emma asked.

Becca looked over at her daughter, who was holding the spray bottle.

"Honey, please put that down. It's a special soap to remove the wallpaper."

Emma did as her mom requested, and then with her hands on her hips, she looked from one wall to the next and said, "It's not good soap, Mommy."

Becca giggled. "You're right, sweetie." She glanced down at the time on her phone. "I'll need to finish this next weekend because I promised Megan I'd help with setup for tonight. I need to swing by home to change out of these damp clothes."

"All right, we'll see you at home," he said. He took Emma's hand. "Come on, kiddo."

"I'll be right behind you." She turned to Emma. "Come here, my pretty..." she said, in her best imitation of the wicked witch. Emma squealed in delight and ran after her gampa. "Bye, you two, love you."

They responded in unison. "Love you, too."

That night, Kell offered to take the on-call shift. Gibs and Tupper had volunteered for the bachelor charity auction, which was apparently a new addition to the line-up of fun activities during the annual Winter Festival. Why couldn't they just ask people for donations? Why did they have to come up with such an asinine idea?

He'd picked up chili and cornbread over at Joe's so he could get a quick bite before heading out. All he had to do was pop it in the microwave. His kind of dinner.

Since he was only on call, he could stay home if he wanted to, but he planned to patrol the downtown. He could hear the music blasting and the rumble of conversations spilling out of the building next door.

On his way out, he stopped in the interior archway that connected the two buildings and watched. Megan had a sizable crowd. A lot more females than males. His cue to leave.

"Kell?" called Megan.

Damn. So close.

He turned when Megan called his name again. Becca was standing beside her.

Megan clapped her hands. "Thank goodness. It's about time you got here. I'm glad you changed your mind. You're up next."

Squinting at his sister, he scoffed. "You're hilarious." When she gave him one of her *come on, dumbass* looks she'd perfected over the years, he added, "I don't know what you're talking about. I'm on call, and I'm heading out on patrol."

"Why'd you sign up if you weren't planning to follow through?"

He spoke through gritted teeth. "What the hell are you talking about? I didn't sign up for anything."

He didn't miss Becca's head as it ping-ponged back and forth to keep up with the conversation.

Megan tilted her head. "You didn't?"

"No! Of course not."

"But who would..."

They looked at each other, then chorused, "Mom!" Megan laughed, but Kell glowered and shook his head.

Surprise registered on Becca's face. "What? Your mom?" she asked.

Ignoring Becca's question, he said, "I don't have time for this. I gave Gibs and RT the night off so they could take part. Like I said, I'm on call." He took a step toward the doorway.

Megan skirted around him and blocked his exit. "Come on, it won't be so bad. You know it's for a worthy cause, right?"

Kell's resolve weakened slightly.

"Dr. Winston helped me so much last summer, and now he's moved to Lucky and plans to make therapy sessions available to the community."

Becca nodded. "All the money we make tonight will subsidize the programs."

He didn't like to think about last summer and the ordeal Megan endured because of her stalker.

Tugging on his arm, Megan whined, "Come on. It will be quick and painless, I promise."

He rubbed his jawline. His sister glared at him with her arms folded across her chest.

Finally, he said, "All right. All right. But only because the money is going to a good cause and Lucky will benefit."

"Don't worry. I overheard a couple of gals who are interested in bidding on you," Becca offered.

He turned to her. "Becca, you bid on me. Please."

"What? You can't be serious?"

"As a heart attack. Ruby strikes again. She signed me up without my knowledge. I'll deal with her later. But right now, I need you to bid on me. I'll pay you back, whatever the amount."

Becca bit her lower lip. "Hmm. I don't know."

Why did he get the impression she was enjoying this?

Kell snapped his fingers. "What if I agree to help you with whatever projects you have at your house? Didn't your dad mention you needed to take down wallpaper?"

Interest sparked in her eyes. But she didn't answer immediately, and he was about to beg, when she asked, "You'll really help me with the wallpaper? And if there are other jobs...."

"Yes. So, do we have a deal?" he asked.

She put her hand out to shake. "Deal."

Then he heard Megan's voice over the crowd. "Sheriff Kell Howard will be our next bachelor."

"Because this is so weird, for obvious reasons." Megan scrunched her face and shivered dramatically, playing to her audience. In a stage whisper she said, "Duh, because he's my brother."

She paused for the laughs, then she continued, "My dear friend, Brenda will handle the auctioning of Sheriff Howard." She handed the microphone over to Brenda and stepped back and to the side.

"All right, thank you, Megan. Our next bachelor was born and raised in Lucky, and that makes him a lucky guy," Brenda deadpanned, and the crowd laughed. "He's also, as you know, the big brother of our favorite country singer, and the sheriff of Lucky." A raucous cheer burst through the crowd. "Kell, come on up here!"

He made his way through the throng of women and stepped up on the make-shift stage.

"Here he is, ladies."

Under his breath, he muttered, "Can we hurry this up?"

"First you have to take off your coat and play nice or we won't make as much money," Brenda said to him, then turned to the crowd. "Can I get a starting bid of twenty-five dollars?"

"Twenty-five," a brunette from the back shouted.

"Do I hear thirty dollars? Ladies, check out these biceps." Brenda squeezed his arm.

Kell twisted around and pinned his sister with a glare. He mouthed "Paybacks, sis."

Someone to the right bid thirty. And before Brenda could up the next bid, someone else yelled, "Thirty-five."

"We have thirty-five. Just a reminder that the winning bidder not only gets a lunch or dinner date with their handsome bachelor but will also get a twenty-dollar gift card to Espresso Yourself."

"Forty." Kell thought the bid came from the same woman in back. Where was Becca? Why hadn't she started bidding? He glanced around and spotted her leaning against the wall. Smiling. She was enjoying watching him sweat.

Finally, Becca stepped forward and raised her voice to be heard over the crowd. "One hundred dollars."

Kell's brow lifted in surprise. *The doctor has spoken.*

An enthusiastic cheer came from Megan. Brenda said, "One hundred dollars. Do we have another bid? Going once, going twice… congratulations, Dr. James."

Kell grabbed his jacket and slowed, only to hook Becca's arm and drag her along with him. "Enjoy yourself?" He asked on his way to the door.

"I don't know what you're talking about," Becca said.

Kell stopped. He wiped the sweat from his forehead with his sleeve. "Uh-huh, the smirk on your face tells a different story."

She laughed. "I couldn't resist. You should have seen your expression." She scanned his face with her doctor's eyes. "Wait, you're sweating. Are you okay? Oh, Kell, I'm sorry. I didn't realize this was truly stressing you out."

"Forget it. Call or text me to set up the date."

He exited the building before she could respond.

❧

The next night, Kell questioned his decision to take the sheriff's job … again. As a kid, Kell remembered Sundays in Lucky as peaceful.

But when he took the call from his deputy alerting him of another break-in, Kell thought, at the very least, it might have been too soon. He hadn't given himself any time to acclimate to civilian life before jumping headfirst into this job.

When the mayor had offered Kell the position, it was with the assurance that Lucky was a quiet little town with law-abiding citizens. Kell wouldn't have much to do other than traffic violations, neighbor disputes, and breaking up of the occasional bar fight.

So far, that hadn't been the case.

Tonight, a call came in reporting a suspicious beam of lights in a refurbished warehouse on the outskirts of town. It came in seconds before a silent alarm alerted the sheriff's office. It was unlikely that anyone with authority would be in the building at this time of night on a Sunday. A legit employee wouldn't trip the silent alarm or use a flashlight instead of turning on the lights.

Kell ordered a silent approach and was now on his way to the location. He ignored the typical warning signs he knew well and white-knuckled the steering wheel, as his chest constricted. He had a job to do, and he wouldn't let his men down.

What about Leaks? You let him down.

This was not Afghanistan. Not the same thing at all.

Kell pulled into the lot and shut it off. Deputy Paul Gibson and Deputy Rick Tupper were already out of their car and waiting.

He shook all the self-doubt and negative thoughts from his mind. "Focus," he muttered as he got out of his vehicle.

"What's the situation, Gibs?" He directed his question to the man with more seniority.

Apparently, Gibson was familiar with the building. He filled Kell in on the layout and the situation. "The first floor is vacant. They are still leasing the office space. But the second floor houses several businesses, including the medical office with the silent alarm."

"Access points?" Kell asked.

"Two exits flank the building on the east and west, with stairwells at each end."

Without warning, Kell's vision blurred, and he had to lean on the hood of his SUV for balance. The cold, dark winter night disappeared, and he was back in the miserable arid heat of Afghanistan, in the dark stairwell where they were ambushed by the sniper.

He swiped at the icy sweat beading on his forehead. His pulse raced, and he inhaled and mentally counted to three, then exhaled. A panic attack was not acceptable.

Kell shook off the black memory and asked, "Has anyone come out of the building?"

"Hard to say for sure, sir. Rick and I pulled up seconds before you." Gibson's eyes narrowed. "Are you feeling okay, Sheriff? No offense, but you look like shit."

"I'm fine." *Bullshit.* "You and RT cover the west exit. I'll cover this one. Radio me when you're in place. We'll synchronize and enter together."

"Yes sir. Give us two minutes to get in place. Come on RT."

"On it," RT replied. The two men hustled off to the far side of the property. Kell assessed the building. He swallowed a few times to keep his mouth from drying shut. Why was this happening tonight? There didn't seem to be a common denominator.

"Fuck." Sweat dripped down his face. *Get your shit together.*

Kell took a step towards the door, and his knees buckled as dizziness swamped over him. He fell to one knee and clenched his jaw, hoping he could keep the nausea that churned in his gut from erupting. He staggered up and took slow, deliberate steps toward the building.

No fucking way could he go inside. Leaks was in there.

The tinny smell.

The screams.

Death.

He would die if he opened the door.

"Move your ass, Marine," he commanded. Relying on his years of training, he yanked the door open and stepped into the stairwell with his gun drawn. Tightening his grip, he froze.

He listened for sounds from the intruders, but all he heard were the screams that echoed from the landing above. Blood seeped down the graffiti-covered cement wall and the memory paralyzed him. He couldn't move up the stairs. He couldn't face his friend's dead eyes.

Gibs whispered over the radio. "We're in place." A half a beat later, he said, "Sheriff? Are you there? Come in."

Hearing the man's voice jerked him back. He blinked, and took in his surroundings, focusing on the present instead of the past.

No screams. Only silence.

Drywall, not cement.

No dripping, wet blood.

No metallic smell.

No Leaks.

"Go," he whispered into his radio. Kell charged up the stairs and burst through the upper door. Gibs motioned. "Sheriff. Over here." Kell met his men at the door to the medical office, which was closer to the west end of the building. RT pointed to the jimmied door.

After a thorough search of all the rooms and closets, Gibs said, "Damn, they got out before we got here." His frustration came across in his tone. "Looks like they went out a window." He pointed to the broken pane. "They used a rope and shimmied down."

The burglars had left a scene similar to the one at Becca's clinic. Ransacked. Cabinets raided. Kell looked at a pile of trash where the burglars had emptied what looked like a medicine cabinet. "Won't know for sure until we get forensics in here. I'll head over to the station to make a few phone calls and get things started. Secure the site, then both of you go on home."

RT nodded. He was already halfway down the hallway when Gibson said, "Sure thing. Sheriff, I —"

It looked like Gibson was going to argue. Kell cut in. "It's been a long day, Gibs. I'll see you both tomorrow." When Gibs was slow to respond, he added, "That's an order."

"Yes, sir." Gibson jogged to catch up with RT.

Kell walked bristly to the stairs, haunted by the ominous reminder that his PTSD was not going away with time, as he had hoped. It was getting worse. Ignoring it hadn't helped, and he knew it was affecting his job. What he didn't know was what he was going to do about it.

Chapter 10

"Ow!" Jodi cried.

Ben slowed. "What's wrong?"

"I scraped my shin, and it's bleeding." Shimmying down the side of the building hadn't been part of the plan. "No one said anything about using a rope and a window for our exit. In and out without a problem, that's what you said." She directed her comment to Jimmy.

"We didn't know about the silent alarm," Jimmy said.

"No shit, really?"

Jimmy glared at his brother.

"This is bullshit. There has to be an easier way to make a buck," Ben said. "We found nothing of real value."

How 'bout real jobs?

Jodi kept the thought to herself. How much longer was she going to stick around? Their life had been fun and exciting at first, not so much now. They were taking more chances with each job.

Jimmy didn't love her. She knew better. And she sure didn't love him. When they got back to the hovel where they were crashing, she headed to the makeshift bedroom to lie down. It had been too much excitement for her, and she didn't want to listen to the brothers fight.

She stopped first in the bathroom to clean her scrape. Now that she could see the cut, it looked worse than she first thought. She wrapped a towel around her leg to keep the wound clean.

In the bedroom, she pulled out the photo from her back pocket. Rubbing her thumb across the little face, she closed her eyes for a second.

She jumped when Jimmy came up behind her and asked, "What are you looking at?"

"Damn it, Jimmy. You scared me."

He ignored her and asked again, "What are you hiding?"

"Nothing." She tried to stuff the photo back in her pocket, but he was quicker, and he grabbed it. She let go so they wouldn't tear the photo.

"Who's this?" he asked.

"No one," she said.

"Don't look like no one to me."

"It's the picture I picked up at that clinic. I just thought it was cute." No way would she let Jimmy know anything about the child.

"Don't go getting any ideas about getting pregnant."

Don't worry, I won't. She tried to grab the photo. "Give it back, Jimmy." But he held his hand above her head, out of her reach.

"What's so special about this picture?"

She shook her head. "Nothing, I told you."

His eyes narrowed. "So, I could tear it up and you wouldn't care."

"No."

"Yeah, right?" He held the photo with two hands, and it looked like he would tear it in half.

"Jimmy!" Her voice wavered. "Why would you do that? That's a dick move."

He backhanded her. "Watch your mouth."

She gasped and covered her stinging cheek with her hand. Shocked by his violent response, she backed away from him. He'd never hit her before.

Ben stepped into the room. "Give it back to her."

Jimmy swung around. "Mind your own business."

Jodi sighed. "Please give it back to me, Jimmy."

He glared at her for another second, then said, "Sure. Since you asked nicely. Here you go." He tossed it so she had to scramble to the floor. She smoothed out the ruffled edges before tucking it into the back pocket of her jeans.

Jodi didn't understand why the photo was so important to her. When she'd seen the photo in the doctor's office, she'd grabbed it. Being back in Lucky brought back the memories. That's what it must be. Being this close was causing her to rethink her decision. She had a serious case of the *what-ifs*.

What-ifs were a ridiculous waste of time and energy. She couldn't support herself. She'd never be able to support her child or provide the security of a home. It had been for the best to give her up for adoption.

Jodi sat on the threadbare sofa, as far away from Jimmy as she could get. He flipped on the old RCA television. Ben took a chair and pulled out a book. She'd heard Jimmy complain numerous times what a nerd his brother was for always having his nose in a book.

"You know I've been thinking," Jimmy began, but waited for Ben to look up from his book and pay attention.

"Oh, boy," Ben said,

"What's your problem?" Jimmy asked.

Ben sighed. "Nothing, Jimmy." He put his bookmark in the book and closed it in his lap. "What have you been thinking?"

"We had a solid run at breaking into pharmacies and clinics. But the last few have been close calls. Cops were on us too quick."

"True. I'm glad you have realized that. It's time for us to look for jobs. Actual jobs," Ben said.

"Jobs? What the fuck for? I was thinking maybe heading south. This winter weather sucks."

Jodi agreed with Jimmy about the weather, but Ben was right about them finding paying jobs.

"Oh, I don't know. For an honest living. So, we can get out of dumps like this for a change." He spread his arms, showing their living space.

Jimmy stared at his brother.

"Obviously, that's not what you were thinking," Ben said.

"Hell no!" Jimmy scoffed.

Ben sat up straighter. Setting the book aside, he said, "Depending on what you come up with, you may be on your own."

Jimmy narrowed his eyes at his brother. "What are you saying?"

"I'm saying I'm considering going back to Indiana."

"But Ma wanted us to stick together. She begged me to take care of you."

"Do you think this is what Ma had in mind?"

Jimmy jumped up and glared at his brother. "You think you can do better?"

"Calm down, Jimmy," Jodi said. "Ben is just telling you how he feels."

Jimmy turned his attention to her and pointed. "You shut up. This is between me and my little brother."

Jodi didn't dare roll her eyes in fear of another backhanded slap. What plan could Jimmy be working up in his head? No matter what happened, she didn't think Ben or she would be happy.

Her cheek still stung. Jodi thought about what she would do if Ben left. She definitely didn't want to be alone with Jimmy. If he hit her once, she was smart enough to know he'd hit her again. She needed to be ready with a plan of her own.

Chapter 11

On Monday, when Becca's two o'clock canceled, she took a few minutes to herself in her office. Her morning had been jam-packed with seeing patients, updating charts, and having her weekly meeting with Betty.

Yesterday had been a fun day with Emma. They'd gone to the movies and out to lunch. *Like the big girls do*, her daughter had happily announced.

She had been too busy to think about her bargain with the sexy sheriff. But in the solitude of her office, she thought about the man.

Which irritated her. There was something about the guy. Should she reach out to ask if he'd be free on Saturday to tackle the wallpaper? She picked up her phone.

No, she shouldn't hold him to the agreement. Truth be told, they'd coerced the poor guy into the auction, thanks to his mom and even Megan. He must have more important things to do on his day off than strip fruity wallpaper from the seventies. She put her phone back down on her desk.

She shook her head. This was ridiculous. She grabbed the phone again and started typing. If she sent a text, she hoped he wouldn't feel put on the spot. It would give him the chance to say no.

Becca: *Hi Kell. This is Becca James. Wondering if you would like to have drinks tonight?*

Where the hell did that come from? Going from stripping wallpaper to drinks was quite a leap. She got a response within seconds.

Kell: *Hello, Becca James. Is this the auction date?*

She sighed and typed.

Becca: *Sure. We can discuss our deal. But I also want to apologize.*

Kell: *For?*

Becca: *The other night at the auction. I may have enjoyed your discomfort a bit too much.*

There was a long pause before the typing bubbles appeared.

Kell: *When and where?*

Becca: *How about eight? At Joe's?*

Kell: *Works for me. See you tonight.*

Becca: *All right. See you later.*

Usually there was a crowd at Joe's Bar & Grill on Monday nights for football, but because of the upcoming Super Bowl, there wasn't a game. The place was pretty empty and without the football fans, they wouldn't have to shout to be heard.

She glanced around and immediately spotted Kell in a booth in the back corner. The man was hard to miss.

He held a book on the table in front of him. *The man reads.* Okay, he got points for that. She loved to read. Though with her busy life, she had fewer opportunities.

She did not know why she was nervous, but she was. *You can do this. Take a deep breath and exhale.* This isn't a date. We are simply getting together to discuss how and when he can help me at the house.

Kell spotted her, closed his book, and stood up as she reached the booth.

"Hi. Thanks for coming." She took her coat off and placed it on her side of the booth.

"Sure thing." He smiled, showing off his bright white teeth. It seemed forced, though. She squinted, looking closer at his face. He looked tired. But that didn't diminish his appeal at all.

Focus on something other than his smile. Thankfully, the server arrived and provided a distraction.

Kell asked, "What would you like?"

"I'll take a glass of Pinot Grigio, please," she said with a smile.

The server looked back at Kell, who said, "I'll have whatever stout you have on tap."

"Got it. How 'bout an appetizer?"

"I'm good with just the wine," Becca said. She cocked her head toward Kell. "What about you? Have you eaten dinner yet?"

"I'm good with the stout. Thanks, Wendy."

"All righty then, back in a jiffy."

The doctor in her took over. She leaned across the table and said, "You look tired. Didn't you get a good night's sleep last night?"

He looked surprised. She knew her directness might not be well-received, but why not be straight-forward?

He hesitated, then shook his head and said, "No, I didn't sleep. We had another break-in last night."

"Oh no. I'm sorry. Was anyone hurt?"

"No, none of my men. Don't know about the perpetrators."

"May I ask where?"

"There's a refurbished warehouse that has office space on the outskirts of town. They broke into a medical office."

"I'm sorry. Still no leads?"

"Not yet. My deputies went over the place this morning. Hopefully, they found something that will give us a lead."

"I hope so."

"Your suggestion to have drinks was a welcome reprieve for me. And before I forget." He pulled his wallet out and counted out twenty-dollar bills. "I told you I'd cover the bid."

Becca put her hand up. "No, please, that's unnecessary. I've got it. I planned on donating, anyway."

Kell's eyebrows knitted together.

"I'm serious, Kell. You can pick up the tab tonight, if you like." Becca reached across the table and stayed his hand.

He nodded.

"So, I bet you're wondering—" Becca barely had time to bring up her reason for asking him out because true to her word, Wendy the server was, indeed, back in a jiffy.

"Here you go. I brought some pretzels to nibble. On the house, Sheriff."

Becca watched as the server batted her eyelashes at Kell and had to stifle a scoff. The man was a chick magnet. So like Josh.

"Thanks," Kell said.

"Sure thing. Holler if you need anything else." The young server headed back to the bar.

Kell lifted his beer. "To new friendships."

"Between you and, er ... Wendy? Or you and me?" An awkward sound, something between a snort and a scoff slipped out.

He frowned, setting his beer down on the table.

"I'm sorry. That was a juvenile thing to say. I don't know why I said it. We aren't even on an actual date. So, if you're interested in —"

He counted on his fingers. "One, she's harmless. Two, she's far too young. And three, you know very well who I was referring to."

She nodded as she raised her glass. "To new friendships."

He lifted his beer and clinked her glass.

"I want to apologize for giving you a hard time on Saturday night. But I'll admit I hesitated to call you."

"Why is that?" he asked.

"I was afraid Ruby might get the wrong idea. I got the impression she may have an agenda where we're concerned."

He let out a sharp guffaw. "What was your first clue?"

"Her subtle hints weren't so subtle."

"No kidding." His face turned serious. "I'm sorry about that," he said.

She waved off his apology. He wasn't responsible for his mother. "Speaking of Ruby, are you as handy as she claimed?"

"Keep in mind my mother tends to, uh, embellish. But, in this case, yes, I am *handy.* I've worked on construction crews and during high school, Chase and I worked for his old man at Devine Construction."

She took a sip of her wine, and asked, "How are you at stripping, um ..." She stumbled over her words, and he gave her a wicked grin. "Wallpaper. Stripping wallpaper, Stud."

He laughed. "Ah, wallpaper. Gotcha. Never have, but I'm a fast learner."

"I bet you are. If you're free on Saturday. I was thinking about trying it again. I started it last weekend and made a mess of it."

"Sure," he said.

"It's not a problem if you're busy or have other plans."

He grinned. "Becca, I said sure."

"You'll do it?"

"Yes, were you expecting me to say no? A deal's a deal, right?"

"Right."

He leaned forward, putting his elbows on the table. "Besides, this is Lucky. We help each other out."

"Thanks. Tell you what, would you be able to meet me at my house on Wednesday night? I can show you around and we can assess the work."

"What time?"

"After dinner. Say half past seven?"

"It's a date." He chuckled when she shook her head at him.

Becca and Emma stopped at Espresso Yourself on their way home the next day. Checking out the different bakery treats had become a fun mother-daughter outing. By offering a limited selection of baked goods each day, Megan kept her clientele guessing. A devious plan, Becca thought, since it kept those with a sweet tooth and no willpower hooked. She knew the dangers of too much sugar, so she limited their outings to once a week.

"Mommy, may I puh-lease have a pretty pink cupcake," Emma whined as she tugged on Becca's hand. Usually, her daughter would go for anything chocolate, but she had to agree the cupcakes were pretty.

"Those do look yummy. Hmm, because you used manners, why don't we buy a couple for dessert?"

"Yay!" Emma clapped her hands. "Gampa loves pink."

He does?

Becca ordered her usual latte and a cup of hot chocolate with extra marshmallows for Emma.

"Hi, you two," Megan called out as she came into the cafe from the backroom. She headed straight for them. Kneeling in front of Emma, she asked, "What did you order? Oh, wait. I know. You ordered a large black coffee."

"Nope." Emma giggled.

"No? Hmm, let me think." Megan tapped her finger to her chin. "Oh, I know. You ordered an espresso macchiato?"

Emma scrunched her little face like she tasted something bitter. "No. I don't know what that is. I gots hot chocolate with extra marshmallows, silly."

This had become an amusing game between the two of them. Megan was a natural with Emma.

"Mommy and me—" Emma began.

"Mommy and I," Becca corrected.

Sighing as if the weight of the world hung on her tiny shoulders, Emma tried again. "Mommy and I are buying the pink cupcakes for dessert. For Gampa."

Becca winked. "Because you know how much my dad loves a pink cupcake."

Megan smiled. "Don't we all? What a wonderfully yummy idea."

"Sweetie, why don't you go sit at your favorite spot?" Becca said. "I'll be there in a minute."

Emma's favorite place to sit was a small round bistro-style table with colorful mosaic tiles of different shapes and sizes set in a swirly design. Emma loved to follow the design with her finger.

"So, I hear you had drinks at Joe's last night? With Kell ...."

"Where did you hear—oh, never mind, it's Lucky."

"Yes, it is." Megan folded her arms across her chest. "And... my inquiring mind wants to know."

"And nothing. Kell and I met for drinks. He agreed to help me with some of the work I have at my house since I saved his butt at the auction." She shrugged with a laugh.

"That's it?" Megan asked as she handed Becca the pastry box. She nodded toward the table where Emma waited. "I'll bring your drinks over."

"Thanks. And no, I have nothing to report. But—"

Megan's head jerked up. Her eyes were alert. "But?"

"I might as well tell you now, since it seems there are eyes and ears everywhere in this town." Becca laughed. "Kell is coming over to my house tomorrow night." She held up her hand when Megan gave her a knowing grin. "I'm going to show him the house and talk about the things I want to do...."

Megan's eyes widened and she didn't try to hide the smirk on her face.

"What I want to do to my house." She laughed, shaking her head. "Really, Megan."

"All righty," Megan said, sweetly.

When it was time to go, Emma scooted her chair back, but her finger got pinched between the chair and the edge of the table.

"Ow." Emma squealed in pain and tears followed.

Becca quickly pulled her onto her lap. Hugging her tight, she whispered, "Let Mommy have a look."

The finger looked red, but the skin was intact. Becca gently pressed on the finger. "Does this hurt?"

"Uh-huh," Emma said, tears streaming down her rosy cheeks.

When Becca was sure no damage had been done, she kissed Emma's finger. "Your finger is going to be fine. How about I rub it for a minute?" Becca offered.

Emma continued to sniffle, as if the chair hurt her feelings.

Becca's phone beeped with a text. She glanced down to see that her dad had sent her a message telling her he was stopping at the hospital on his way home, so he would be later than usual.

While Becca was looking at her phone, Emma reached into the side pocket of the tote bag. The little monkey pulled out her binkie and popped the pacifier into her mouth.

She sucked for all she was worth, soothing herself. Emma stopped crying and only a random hiccup slipped out of her occupied mouth.

Becca had been weaning Emma off the pacifier so she would be ready for the preschool program in the fall. It hadn't been easy. Some children were more attached to their security item than others. Besides, Becca knew Emma wouldn't be sucking her binkie forever.

Right? Right.

Megan came over to make sure Emma was okay and handed her a baggie of extra marshmallows, which immediately cheered her up.

Plucking the binkie from her mouth, she said, "Tank you," through sniffles. Then popped the thing right back in.

Megan chuckled.

Feeling a bit chagrined, Becca said, "I know. I know. She's getting too old for a pacifier. I shouldn't let her have the darn thing."

"Oh, don't worry about it. I was only chuckling because Kell and I both loved our pacifiers, too. Mom has said she had the hardest time taking them away from us. She was afraid we'd still be sucking on one when we went to school," Megan joked.

Becca listened to her friend. What an odd coincidence. "Well, at least I know Emma is in good company."

"She certainly is."

Chapter 12

Kell rang her doorbell at exactly half past seven on Wednesday night.

The man was prompt. She'd give him that.

Becca opened the door. "Brr. It's freezing out there. Come in, come in."

He handed her one of the two hot beverages he carried.

She accepted the cup. "Oh, thank you." She sniffed and lifted the lid to take a peek. "Mmm, you brought my favorite. How'd you know?"

"Megan knows what you like," he answered.

"Oh, this is so nice of you. You're the perfect *boyfriend* to think about bringing me something hot to drink on such a frosty night."

He cocked his head and took a step back. She had to hold back a laugh. Was it suspicion, surprise or fear on his face? A little of each, perhaps?

"What's the matter, Kell, sweetie? Haven't you heard? The gossip is all over town. After the auction and then us having drinks on Monday night, it seems the town is buzzing with rumors that it's only a matter of time before our wedding." She did laugh now.

"Wedding?" he sputtered, lowering his cup. "What are you talking about?"

"Oh, you really haven't heard?"

"Nope. Must have missed the memo. Fill me in."

"Give me your coat first."

He handed her his to-go cup. With his hands free, he removed his coat and passed it to her, exchanging the coat for the cup. Becca folded the coat over the banister.

She turned towards him. "Follow me. There is only one place to sit. I've got furniture on order, but for now there is just a card table and chairs I set up in the tiny dining area outside the kitchen."

Kell followed, and when they were both seated, she said, "Okay, so my staff came back from lunch today with the gossip. Then, after work, I stopped by the senior center to drop off some puzzles and books. My great aunt Esther was there, and she could talk about nothing else." Becca placed her hands on her hips. "Apparently your mother is happily spreading the news all around Lucky."

He rubbed a hand across his forehead. "Damn. I'm sorry. I thought after I talked to her, she'd back off. But I don't think she understands the term 'back off.' I'll talk to her again."

"Kell, talk to your mom or not. I can deal with a little small-town gossip. I was just teasing you. You should have seen your face."

"You have an odd sense of humor. You know that, right?"

She shrugged with a grin. "I've heard that before. Sorry."

"No, you're not."

She clapped her hands, and her smile widened. "No, I'm not. Not really. I had a feeling being told you were engaged to a woman would get a reaction from you."

"You're hilarious."

She blew on her cup and took a tentative sip. "Okay, now would you like a quick tour?"

"Any more surprises?" he asked.

"Nope. I promise."

"Then lead the way."

She led him into the kitchen. "Whoa. This looks like my grandmother's kitchen. No offense," he said.

"None taken. Don't worry, I totally agree. Awful, right? Look past the wallpaper to see the big picture," Becca said.

"Which is what?"

She described her plan to paint cabinets and replace a few of the wood fronts with glass. New appliances, flooring, and painted walls.

"Sounds great. It's easy to imagine." He gestured to one of the kitchen walls. "It really is a mess, like you said."

Laughing, she said, "You can see I utterly failed stripping wallpaper 101."

"Don't worry. We'll get it down," he said. She appreciated his confidence.

She walked back into the main living area. "On this floor, there are two bedrooms and a full bathroom besides a half bath off the kitchen." She pointed to the tiny bathroom. "Upstairs, there are two more bedrooms with a Jack and Jill bathroom. The house is a typical Cape Cod."

He had a quizzical expression. "What's a Jack and Jill bathroom?"

"Oh, it's a bathroom with access from two bedrooms. Not sure where the name came from. Something to Google later." She laughed.

Nodding, he asked, "What's the square footage?"

"A little over thirteen hundred."

"Nice. It sure beats my tiny studio. Eventually, I'm going to have to look for a bigger place. But for now, it works."

"I know what you mean. I had a studio in my senior year of college. The only time I appreciated the three hundred and fifty square feet was on cleaning day."

"My place isn't too bad, and it's a step up from what I was used to overseas."

"Oh, I bet."

He looked around the room. "This is a nice, comfortable space."

She headed back toward the kitchen. "Let's sit and finish our drinks. My evil plan is to torture you with that wallpaper, so you'll be more than ready to help me strip it on Saturday."

"Oh, I'll be ready."

After Becca's tease about being his girlfriend, an idea began brewing in his head. What if they pretended to be in a relationship? That should get his mom to back off. Right?

He liked Becca. When she allowed herself to relax, she was fun, although her sense of humor was a little sadistic.

He considered pitching the idea to her. But there was one obvious problem. Could he ask her to be his fake girlfriend and still want to touch her as if they were in a real relationship? Because if he was honest with himself, he definitely wanted to touch her. That was some mixed-up shit.

Still, she needed help. He needed a girlfriend. Win-win. And if he was lucky, they could mutually agree to a friend with benefits arrangement. But that wasn't as important as getting his mother to stop her antics.

He took a deep breath.

What do you have to lose?

He set down his cup and slid back from the table. "I have an idea I want to run by you."

"Okay. Go on." She smiled, giving him a sideways glance.

"Would you consider, I mean, only for a while."

"Kell, say it. Whatever *it* is."

"Since we have already put the groundwork in place, I mean with the auction."

"Kell, hesitation doesn't look good on you."

"All right." He took a deep breath. "Would you agree to be my fake girlfriend?"

Her eyes widened. "What?"

He frowned. "I think you heard me." He didn't want to have to repeat it out loud because it sounded juvenile.

She shook her head. "It's not that I didn't hear you. It's whether I heard you correctly. What is this, a Hallmark movie?"

"I know nothing about Hallmark movies. But I know I like you and I need a fake girlfriend to get my mother off my back. Besides, everyone in town already believes something is going on with us. Right?"

"True. But I don't know."

"I'd rather it be with someone I can tolerate."

Eyes narrowing, now she frowned at him. "Tolerate?"

"You know what I mean."

"No. I'm afraid I don't." She pinched her thumb and pointer together. "I'm this close to being extremely insulted. Why don't you explain?" Becca scooted her chair back from the table and folded her arms across her chest. "Start at the beginning, please."

"All right. So, you know my mom is a relentless manipulator. She's a schemer, and she's determined to find me a wife."

"I know Megan had some issues with her over the years. But they're getting on better now."

"Right. She did. But Megan is now happily engaged to Chase. So, my mom has turned her evil tricks on me."

Becca's brows arched. "Oh, come on, Kell."

He was getting ahead of himself. "Wait. I'm not explaining this well at all, am I?"

"Nope."

"Okay, let me back-up." He massaged his forehead. Shit, he was uncomfortable. He'd never enjoyed talking about himself, or God forbid, his feelings.

"Good idea," she said.

"First, after I became sheriff, my mother spent weeks getting herself pulled over for speeding so she could get my attention. As a matter of fact, the morning we met at the clinic, I had just come from pulling her over." He inhaled deeply and powered through the rest of his explanation.

"Mom said it was the only way she could see me because I boycott our family's Sunday dinners."

"You do? Why?"

He sighed. "Because she does nothing but talk about how much she wants grandbabies and I end up going home with indigestion and a headache. So, anyway, she pulled that speeding stunt for several weeks until I finally put cuffs on her —"

Her eyes widened. "Kell! You didn't?"

"You're missing the point," he said.

She motioned with her hand for him to continue. "All right, go on."

"After I got that situation under control, she made an account on Swingr for me."

"What? Isn't that for...?"

"Yep, it's exactly what it sounds like, for swingers."

She put her hand over her mouth, but her giggle still slipped out, then she gave up and flat out laughed.

"No way. Really?"

"Oh, yeah, way." Now he grinned, too. "Go ahead, have a laugh at my expense."

Shaking her head, Becca said, "I'm sorry. I shouldn't laugh, but it is sort of outrageous."

"I know. By the way, I believe your great aunt helped with that one, too."

"Oh, that doesn't surprise me a bit. My great aunt Esther is quite a character."

"Tell me about it."

"That's an odd friendship, don't you think? There must be at least a twenty-year age difference," Becca said.

Shrugging, he said, "Maybe it's a small-town thing. Plus, they both are... I don't know how to describe them." He didn't want to lump her great aunt into the same pain-in-the-ass category as his mom.

"Busy bodies?" she suggested.

"Well, that's a nice way to put it, yes."

"Okay, let's get back to your story. Were you able to delete the account?" Becca asked.

"Yeah. I talked to my mom, and I thought she'd back off. But then she signed me up for that damn auction." He shook his head.

"Oh, Kell, I'm sorry. The whole situation is a little crazy."

"Believe me, I'm well aware. I hate to think of what she'll plan next. Anyway, I thought since we're going to be spending a lot of time together doing the renovations, it's easy to imagine we would get involved, especially after there are already rumors." He raised his brow. "What do you think?"

"Don't you think it's an awfully drastic measure to take?"

"You obviously don't know my mom," he said, wryly.

"Can I think about this?"

"Sure. Keep in mind, it's only a matter of time before she concocts her next evil plan."

"I understand. Let me sleep on it."

"Speaking of time." He looked at his watch. "It's getting late. I'm sure you need to get home to your daughter, and I have an early appointment with the town council."

"Oh, sure. Of course."

"What time do you want to get started on Saturday?"

"Is nine o'clock too early?"

"Not at all. I'll be here at nine. I'll walk you to your car if you're ready to leave," he offered.

"Thanks. Just let me turn off the lights."

For the rest of the night, Becca thought of little else but his crazy idea. She went over everything Kell said. He'd been fidgeting, which seemed so out of character for the guy. Becca almost felt sorry for him. *Almost* was the key word.

While she understood his frustration with Ruby and his desire to protect himself from further manipulation. However, it was dishonest.

She had zero tolerance for liars. She'd learned the hard way with Josh. But if Kell and she pretended to be dating, who would get hurt? If she went in with her eyes wide open, she couldn't get hurt. Right?

It wasn't as if she was looking for an actual boyfriend. She was happy with her life. Adding the complications of dating into the mix was simply not something she'd thought much about. Perhaps this would be a chance to dip a toe into the dating pool, even if the pool had no water.

The next morning, before she could talk herself out of it, she stopped at the sheriff's office.

Someone walked her down the hall to his office and offered her a cup of coffee, but she declined. She was told he'd be with her momentarily. She had her back to the door, looking at the few photos he had on the bookcase behind his desk.

"Good morning, Doc."

She jumped and turned. "Oh, you startled me."

He held up his hands in surrender. "Sorry," he said, though she didn't think he looked sorry at all.

"Good morning, Kell. I stopped by—"

He cut in. "Have you had enough time to consider my proposal?"

"Can we not call it a proposal?"

He chuckled. "Would you prefer the word proposition?"

"Oh, never mind. It doesn't matter what we call it. I have to say up front I don't like dishonesty. We'll be lying to the whole town and especially to our families."

He held up his hand. "I understand. It was worth a try. I just need to do something before my mom concocts something even more crazy."

"As if railroading you into a bachelor auction and registering you for Swingr isn't nutty enough?"

"Right."

"For how long?" she asked.

"What?" he said.

"For how long do you think we'll need to pretend?"

"Not sure. A few months?" he said. "To be honest, I haven't thought that far ahead."

"So, I would have a date for Megan and Chase's wedding?"

"Sure. We can make that work." He grinned.

She took a deep breath and blurted, "I'll do it."

His grin grew to a full smile.

"I do have two conditions."

He nodded. "Go on."

"First, I refuse to lie to Megan. She needs to know the truth. And second, I don't want Emma confused. I won't have her bond with you only to have you walk away once you don't need me to be your fake girlfriend."

"Megan will figure it out anyway, but she has to keep quiet. And I know my sister, she'll tell Chase. Tell you what, why don't we clue your dad in, too? Then the people we are closest to will know."

"Except your mom."

"Yes, that's the whole point." He shook his head and moved on. "And I can certainly abide by your second rule."

"Okay, then we have a deal," she said.

"We can shake on it. Or I can write up a contract," he offered.

Her eyes widened. "Seriously?"

"No." He lifted a brow. "Just giving you back some of that teasing you love so. much."

"Wow, it's nice to know you have a sense of humor under that gruff bluster."

He winked.

"See you Saturday morning."

"See you then."

Chapter 13

In the few days leading up to Saturday, Kell contemplated his new "friendship" with Becca. A big part of him thought he should walk away while he still could.

He stood at Becca's front door, debating the wisdom of spending so much time in her company. Being in close quarters with her would put any man's self-control to the test. But a deal was a deal. Besides, this was his idea, not hers, and he needed to make it work.

The door opened and sure enough, one look was all it took. There was no hiding his body's response to her.

Despite the wintry morning, she wore an oversized shirt with the sleeves rolled up to her elbows. The top two buttons were open, and he could see her creamy, pale collarbone. Her bare feet peeked out from beneath a ratty pair of jeans with gaping holes in the knees. There was far too much skin exposed for his peace of mind.

Her hair was in a single braid down her back, with loose strands framing her face. She sure as hell didn't look like any doctor he ever had. How the hell was a guy supposed to concentrate on stripping ... wallpaper?

"Morning." His voice came out gruff even to his ears. He shifted from foot to foot, to keep warm, and held out a cup to her. "Brought hot beverages again from our favorite place."

"Thank you, brr, it's still freezing out here. Come in," she said.

He quickly slid past, mentally cursing when he heard her quick intake of breath after his snowy coat brushed her arm accidentally. His chest tightened.

"Can you hold both cups? I'll take off my coat and boots." He left his boots on a laminate square inside the door.

"No need to strip yet," she said and laughed.

The woman was an enigma. She sure kept him guessing. She could be so serious and yet, the woman he'd been getting to know had a wicked sense of humor.

He laughed. "Good to know."

She raised the cups. "Thanks again."

"No problem. Perks of living above Espresso Yourself. It sure smells good in the morning." He shrugged. "So, it looks like you've already been painting this morning."

"How'd you know?"

"I don't need to be Sherlock Holmes to see the paint in your hair and here on your cheek." He brushed at the smudge with his thumb. "An educated guess."

Damn, how was he going to keep his hands to himself? He hadn't been there for five minutes and already he'd found an excuse to touch her. While his head chastised him, his dick was cheering him on.

"Oh right. I woke up early, so I came over and started on the half bath."

Kell followed her into the pint-sized kitchen. He liked her house. Of course, the kitchen was the exception. But that's what he was there to fix.

If it were his house, he would knock out a wall to open the space between the kitchen and living room. But it wasn't his place. He had to admit, her enthusiasm was contagious. She had him excited over the possibilities.

At ease. You're only here as free labor.

She pointed out the slider. "Another selling point, for me, was the fenced backyard. The big maple tree will give us shade in the summer, and having a fence will give me peace of mind when Emma is old enough to play out there by herself."

Becca waved her hand, gesturing to the room they were standing in. "I know this kitchen has potential, but first, this awful tribute to fruit has to come down."

"I would agree." They both chuckled.

They each took a section of the room. He took the tougher places above and below the cabinets, while she worked on one of the other walls. They worked companionably for several hours, scoring, spraying, and peeling until there was no trace of apples or bananas.

She checked the clock on the stove. "Oh, wow. I lost track of time. We've worked right through the lunch hour. You must be starving. Can I make you a sandwich? I have some turkey and Swiss cheese in the fridge. I'm afraid that's it."

"Sure, I could eat something. Thanks." He was used to missing a meal or two when out on maneuvers or on a mission. It wasn't like they took a lunch break in the middle of warfare. When the fighting broke out, he learned to go long stretches between meals.

"Good. Sit. I have beer. Would you like one?" she asked.

"I'll heat my coffee in your microwave, if that's okay?"

"Of course. Here, give me your cup. I'll do it," she said.

"Yes, ma'am." He saluted her and did as he was told.

☘

After they ate, he glanced out the slider to the small patio, which was covered with at least two inches of snow. He'd already noted the number of windows and exterior doors on the ground level. After the doors, the next most vulnerable points are a home's ground-floor windows.

His overzealous vigilance was an unwelcome souvenir from the war.

Nodding to the slider, he said, "You need to get a dowel, or a broken hockey stick, to put in the bottom track of your door."

She paused and looked at him, cocking her head. "But there's a perfectly good lock on the door."

"You still need a dowel for added security."

"It's Lucky and—"

Frustrated, he frowned because he was unaccustomed to people not listening. "Doesn't matter. You need to do it," he snapped.

Her eyes widened, and she took a step back at the harshness in his voice. He hadn't intended to scare her. Shit. Here was another reason he should forget any ideas he might have about them.

The words of his shrink during the mandated therapy sessions still resonated. *Irrational bursts of anger, quick temper, are all signs that point to PTSD.*

Shaking his head, he lowered his voice, and, in a calmer tone, he apologized, "Sorry."

She stared at him. "Are you okay?"

"Yeah. I'm fine. I'm concerned about your safety. As a young woman with a child living alone, you can't be too careful. Taking precautions even in a small town like Lucky is still sensible. You should know that after the break-in at your clinic."

She held up her hands in surrender and said, "Yes, you're right. Thanks." She took a few steps towards him. "Are you sure you're fine? You seem pretty tightly wound."

"I'm fine."

She didn't back down. Instead, she continued to look at him. As if she was assessing him.

Son of a bitch.

He didn't need her doctoring him again. The incident with the blood on the day of the break-in was bad enough.

"Look I'm fine. I'm still not sleeping well."

Becca frowned. "Still? How long has this been going on?"

"Not long. I'm fine. I'm tense because I need to solve these damn burglaries. It's important to make your home safe. I didn't mean to scare you."

"You didn't scare me." She sighed. Rolling her eyes, she continued, "Men. My dad is the same way. He always wants to solve all the problems. Won't let me help him. Gee, just what I need."

He raised an eyebrow. "What don't you think you need?"

Becca put her hands on her hips. "What I don't need is another man in my life who thinks he knows what's best and won't accept help from anyone."

She sure was cute when she got mad. Kell smiled.

"Why are you smiling? It's not funny."

Thinking there were a couple ways to defuse her mini rant, walk away or he could distract her.

It was no surprise that his dick voted for the second option. Kell tried to ignore his semi-erect dick and the tightening of his balls. Finally, his brain took over, and he reminded himself that he had to keep his distance.

They had agreed to a fake relationship. He just needed to convince his dick. And it would send out mixed signals if he pulled her to him and kissed her.

The sound of voices came from the garage.

"My dad," she stuttered.

Kell blew out a breath and ran his fingers through his hair, positioning his body behind the counter. Any evidence of his arousal was now hidden. He tried to think of something to help shrink the problem. Puppies ... kittens ...

The door flew open, and a little pink and purple bundle of energy bounced into the room.

"Mommy!"

Bingo.

"Mommy, Mommy, look what Gampa buyed me."

"Let me see, sweetie." Becca picked up Emma, moving to the card table and chairs. She sat with Emma in her lap. "What's in the bag?"

"Guess!"

Before Becca offered her first guess, Emma noticed Kell by the counter. "Who's you?"

"Emma, that's not polite."

Emma ignored her mother, and before Becca realized what Emma was up to, she slid off her mom's lap and hopped up on a stool beside Kell. It wobbled and quick as lightning, Kell reached out to steady the stool.

"Are you my mommy's friend?" Her headstrong child was determined to find out who this person was. No one could accuse her daughter of being shy. There wasn't a person in Emma's life who she hadn't charmed. Emma outstretched her arms to Kell, *inviting* him to pick her up.

Becca grinned at the look of utter terror on the big, bad sheriff's face. Taking pity on him, she swooped her daughter up, but not before she whispered in his ear, "She's harmless."

Her dad had come in from the garage by then. He set the bag of paint supplies he'd picked up for her on the counter.

"Kell, how are you? Good to see you." The men shook hands.

"Good to see you, too. Looks like you've had your hands full."

"Oh, my granddaughter keeps me on my toes. Keeps me young, right, princess?"

She nodded vigorously. "Right, Gampa."

"Emma, this is Sheriff Howard," said Becca.

"Hi. What's a sher-iff?"

"It's like a policeman," Becca answered.

Emma nodded, then, as if she'd already moved on to another equally important topic. She pulled her *surprise* out of the sack and proudly showed the adults a paintbrush. "See, he bought me my very own brush. I can help paint my room, Mommy."

Becca looked over Emma's head. "Great idea, thanks Gampa." He grinned. "I was getting food out for lunch. Are you two shoppers hungry?"

"We stopped by McDonald's before heading back to Lucky," her dad said.

"Dad, you're a doctor. Hello. Nutrition."

"I know, but occasionally, for special outings with my granddaughter, I make an exception."

His exceptions were more like the norm lately, but she didn't call him out. He was doing her a big favor by entertaining Emma so Becca could get work done in her house. If weekly Happy Meals were part of the deal, so be it.

After her dad and Emma left, Kell helped her finish up in the kitchen. They moved into the larger of the two first floor bedrooms to discuss the plan for next time.

Before Kell headed out, he asked, "Are you going to the Super Bowl party tomorrow?"

"Yes, I'm bringing Emma. Normally I wouldn't, but Megan insisted I bring her, at least for the first half."

"It should be a fun time."

"I'm going for the food and company. I don't care about the game."

He grabbed his chest as if she'd wounded him. "What? You're not a football fan?"

"I don't mind football, per se, just not a big fan of the two teams. I will pay closer attention to the commercials and the half-time show."

"Fair enough." At the front door, Kell put on his coat. He opened the door, but Becca stopped him with a hand on his arm.

"Kell, thanks for all your help today."

"No problem. See you tomorrow."

She nodded. "Bye."

Becca watched Kell get in his SUV. There had been a few times when she could have sworn Kell was interested in her. For real. Like he wanted to kiss her. At least before her dad and Emma showed up. If they hadn't, would he have kissed her?

How did she feel about that?

She could feign indifference all she wanted, but if she were honest with herself, she'd have to acknowledge her curiosity. Was he a good kisser? Oh, of course he was. That man was probably good at much more than kissing.

It didn't matter how curious she was. She needed to remember the agreement. It was a faux relationship. Nothing more.

At least, that's what she told herself. Right?

Chapter 14

The next day, Kell arrived at Chase's house in the middle of the afternoon. He wanted to get an hour of ice fishing in on the lake before the party got started. He parked out front and walked around to the back of the house and down to the edge of the lake.

Chase had set up a pup tent at the end of his dock where two chairs sat stationed with a cooler in between. He pulled out his phone and texted Chase.

Kell: *I knocked, but you must not be home. I'm at your place. Mind if I do a little ice fishing before the game?*

The response bubbles popped up immediately.

Chase: *Sure thing. The gear's all there.*

Kell: *Thanks.*

> Chase: *I still have a few things Megan asked me to get done. But I'll join you in a few, if I can.*

> Kell: *Whipped!*

> Chase: *Yes, I am and loving every minute. Fuck you, man.*

Kell laughed when he read the reply from his best friend.

He got comfortable and kicked back in the chair. Kell loved being out here in this peaceful spot. He had a lot to think about.

Was he crazy to involve Becca in his family drama? Had he asked her out of desperation after Mom's latest attempt to marry him off, or was that a safe excuse to get closer to a woman he liked?

She certainly wasn't hard on the eyes. But it was more than that. Because he did like Becca James. She was smart and witty, and she also had an edgy side that he liked.

He'd debated the wisdom of his proposal, considering Becca had a daughter. But then he'd realized the idea could work even better for him. If he could convince Mom that he had a serious girlfriend with a kid, she might get off the grandbaby kick.

Or it could be a clusterfuck.

For now, he needed to shake off his concerns. He took several slow deep breaths and slouched back, eyes closed, listening to nature.

His phone buzzed with an incoming call, disturbing his brief respite. "What's up, Gibs?"

"Sheriff, I thought you'd want to know. We just got a call from Art Bartley. He noticed movement in the Park Street Pharmacy when he was walking his dog. I'm headed there now," Deputy Gibson said.

"Damn. Lights, no siren. I want to catch these guys tonight."

"What's your ETA?" Gibs asked.

"I'm at least ten minutes out. I'm at the lake." Kell said.

"Roger that, sir."

It wouldn't surprise Kell if they were looking for the same cough and cold medicine Becca had described. Dextromethorphan.

He set the fishing equipment aside and hustled to his vehicle. Duty called. Looks like he'd be late for the party.

The drugstore was in town, unlike the last hit. So, he hoped they'd get lucky.

Becca finished dressing and stopped at Emma's bedroom door. "Ready, kiddo?"

"Yep, all ready, Mommy." Emma held the adorable canvas bag that Becca had found at a craft show. Emma's embroidered name stood out in bold, bright primary colors on the tote. The bag had quickly become one of Emma's cherished possessions.

"I gots books, and puzzles, and coloring books with my crayons and ..." She hesitated and looked in the bag. "Oh, my Old Lady cards and my rocks and my jump—"

"Tell you what, how about we leave a few things at home?" Becca suggested, noticing how the bag bulged,

"But I need my stuff."

"Did I tell you there'll be a dog and a cat you can play with at Megan's house?"

"Weally?"

"Yep."

"What's their names?"

"The dog's name is Brady. The cat's name is Emmie."

Her daughter's eyes lit up. "Like me?"

"Close. You're Emma, and the cat is Emm*ie*."

"How come?"

"I don't know. You can ask Megan when we get there. We better get going or we'll be late. Why don't you go say goodbye to Gampa?"

"Okay, Mommy."

Becca removed a few of the items from Emma's bag. A few books and the coloring book with crayons should keep Emma busy.

She stopped at the door to her dad's den where the pre-game show was airing. Becca needed to clue him in on her agreement with Kell, and she would. Just not while there were little ears in the room.

"Enjoy the game in peace."

"Thank you, sweetheart." He held his hands out to Emma. "Give me another hug and kiss."

Emma outstretched her little arms. After the hugs and kisses, he said, "Have fun, Peanut."

The drive out to Chase's beautiful lake house took less than ten minutes. For purely selfish reasons, she was happy that Megan had moved in and that they were making it their home. It would be cool to have a friend with access to a lake for swimming and sunbathing come summer.

"Here we are," she said, as she parked in the driveway.

"Yay!"

When Megan greeted them at the door, the first thing out of Emma's mouth was, "Where is the cat and dog? Why does your cat have my name?"

"Emma, how about we say hello first?" Becca said.

Looking only slightly chagrined, Emma said, "Hello."

Megan laughed. "Brady is outside with Chase. Emmie is most likely upstairs on my bed. Want to find her?"

"Uh-huh," Emma said, jumping around with excitement.

"Okay, come on then." The two headed toward the stairs, hand in hand.

"I'll put this dessert in the fridge," Becca said.

She wandered from the kitchen into the large living room to wait for their return. She marveled at the view of the lake through the expansive floor to ceiling windows. The patio beyond the windows looked bare without the usual outdoor furniture.

Chase came in through the garage with Brady scrambling to get past him to greet the new people who came to visit him.

"Hey, Becca. Glad you could come."

"Thanks for inviting us." She bent over to scratch Brady behind the ears. "Hey, how are you, pretty boy?" She was happy when he sat and gave her his paw. What a sweet dog.

Chase glanced around the large open area. "Where did Megan go?"

"Oh, she had to show Emma the cat."

"Aha. Of course. Can I get you something to drink? We've got wine and beer."

"Wine sounds wonderful," Becca said.

"Red or white?" Chase asked.

"White. Do you have a Pinot Grigio?"

"Um, does Megan live in this house?" He laughed, and she joined him. She knew her friend loved the white wine as much as she did. "I'll be right back. Sit. Relax," he said.

When Megan and Emma returned, and Chase was back with her glass of wine, the absence of Kell was obvious. Should she ask? Would that look like she was too interested? Before she could decide, Chase answered the question lurking in her mind.

"Kell got an emergency call a little while ago. He'll be back as soon as he can."

"Oh dear, I hope everything is all right," Becca said.

"I hope so, too." Megan agreed.

No time like the present. "Hey, Megan, I need to talk to you about something."

"All right, why don't you come into the kitchen with me? You can help me get things ready while we talk," Megan said.

"I'll be right in. I'll get Emma set up with her coloring book. Is it okay if she colors at the dining room table?" Becca asked.

"Of course, but she might like the little desk I had Chase put in the corner of the living room. It's one of those old-fashioned ones. It was collecting dust in the garage, and I figured Emma would be coming to visit pretty regularly, so he cleaned it up and brought it in just for her."

"Oh, Megan, how sweet of you and Chase, of course. Thank you. I know she'll love it."

Megan passed Chase in the doorway into the kitchen. "Hey, Emma is going to color at the little desk. Would you mind keeping an eye on her for a few minutes?"

"Sure thing. I'll even keep two eyes on her." Chase grinned.

"Thanks, you two. I'll be right back," Becca said.

Becca set out the crayons and coloring book. "Here you go, Emma. Look at this cool desk Megan and Chase set up for you to use."

"Weally?"

"Uh-huh." Becca nodded. "Okay, so I'll be in the kitchen with Megan if you need me."

Megan set a bag of chips on the counter. "Want to sit down?" She gestured to the barstools. "Is everything all right?"

"Sure. Everything is fine. I didn't mean to alarm you. There's something I want you to know about before you hear through the grapevine."

"Now that sounds ominous."

"It's about Kell and me."

"Oh, that gossip. I already heard. Someone came into the cafe and spilled the beans." She cocked her head. "Get it? Coffee beans." Megan laughed at her own joke.

"Funny, you can do stand-up if you tire of singing," Becca said.

Megan shrugged. "Don't worry about the town gossip. My mom probably started it."

"It's kinda related to that. But not in the way you're thinking." She sighed deeply. She spit it out as fast as she could. "I agreed to pretend to date Kell to trick your mom so she will stop setting him up with women."

"What? Are you joking?"

"Nope. Kell thinks this might be the best way to get your mom off his back. We haven't discussed details, except that I told him I didn't want Emma to be hurt or confused. As far as she is concerned, he's a friend, not a boyfriend. Although I think she's too young to discern the difference."

"Of course."

"And I told him I had to tell you. I don't want to keep secrets from you. I value our friendship too much."

"Aww, I do, too." Megan reached across the counter and squeezed Becca's hand.

Megan suddenly frowned.

"What's wrong?" Becca asked.

"That brother of mine. He's being an ass."

"Why do you say that?"

"Because he is too clueless to see he should date you for real. Weren't you insulted?"

"No, well, maybe a little taken back at first. But remember, I'm not looking for anyone either. I'm content with my life. We made a bargain. He's going to work at my house, helping to get it ready for Emma and me to move. In exchange, he gets a fake relationship to keep your mom happy."

Megan shook her head. "Sounds crazy to me."

"No, it's a win for both of us. If he is half as handy as your mom said, I will be lucky. I don't know what I would do without his help."

"Yeah, yeah, I get that. But he's still an ass."

Becca laughed. "If you say so."

"I can't keep this information from Chase. We promised no more secrets. Not after last summer."

"Don't worry. You can tell Chase. Kell may have already done so."

Megan shook her head. "No way. Chase would have told me."

"Only you two and my dad will know the truth, though."

"We'll keep your secret."

"It's only for a little while so he can get a break from your mom. Hey, at least I could have a date for your wedding. If we don't pretend-break-up beforehand." She laughed.

"Oh, stop. I'm sure you wouldn't have had any trouble finding a date."

Becca shrugged. "I don't know about that."

When Kell got back to Chase's place, the game had to be into the second quarter. By the looks of the driveway, there were several other guests at the party.

He would not be the best company for anyone. All he wanted to do was kick back and watch the rest of the game with a cold brew. Should he skip out and go home? He hadn't quite made it to the front door and was about to turn back to his SUV when he heard Chase call out.

"Hey, man, glad you made it back. Anything serious?"

Kell glanced around. Chase was in the driveway with Brady. He didn't want others to overhear. Especially Becca. He knew she was there somewhere since he'd seen her car. There was no reason to get her upset. But the two men were outside and looked to be alone.

In a low voice, he replied, "Another break-in. Looks like the same MO as the other places. I think we only missed them by a few minutes."

"Shit. Where?"

"The Park Street Pharmacy."

"That's a little close for comfort. I hate to think we have these thugs hanging out in our town."

"You and me both."

"I know you and your people are working hard to solve these cases. Sorry you have another one piled on." He clapped Kell on the back. "How 'bout a beer? You can sit next to the fire and get warmed up."

"I was debating heading home."

"Nah, you need to hang out here for a while, right Brady? You want Kell to stay?" As if the dog understood, he nudged Kell's leg.

"See, you can shake off your dark mood," Chase said.

Kell gave his friend a half-hearted smile and Brady a pat, then followed the two into the house and straight to the kitchen where Megan stood at the counter unwrapping platters of subs, and Becca dumped chips in a large football shaped bowl.

"Sorry I'm late." His gaze must have rested on Becca a little too long, because when he turned back toward Megan, he caught her grin.

He shook his head. God, Megan could be as bad as their mom.

"You're not late. We're just putting the food out now," said Megan. But Kell's focus was on Becca. She looked hot in her snug jeans. The pants hugged her in all the right places. She wore her hair swept up in a ponytail and had his fingers itching to tug on the loose strands. He was so wrapped up in his thoughts about Becca he missed his sister's question until she swatted him on the shoulder. "Hey, bro, are you listening?"

"Yeah, sure, um, what did you say?"

Megan smirked. "I asked if you would do me a favor and get the vegetable tray from the garage fridge?"

"Yep." He wondered if Becca told Megan about their arrangement yet. He needed to have a chat with his little sister, similar to the one he had with Mom. He could take care of his own love life or, in this case, fake love life.

Actually, tonight would be a perfect opportunity to get the ball rolling on the *Kell and Becca* rumors. There were enough people at the party that it justified a little PDA. Purely for show.

Speaking of PDA, he returned to find Chase kissing Megan. Kell cleared his throat. Becca was doing a good job of studying the chips in front of her.

"I'll go stoke the fire ... in the fireplace," Chase said with a chuckle.

Kell set the tray down in the center of the island and winked at Becca, but before he could do anything else, her daughter bounced into the room. She was certainly full of life.

She made a beeline for him. "Hey, I member you. You were at my new house with my mommy."

"Yep, I was. I helped her take down the wallpaper in your kitchen."

The child was studying him, and he felt a tad uncomfortable. He did not know what he was supposed to talk about with a little kid. What was she, three or four?

Megan walked over and said, "Emma, how about we get your crayons, and you can color Emmie and Brady a picture? I have some paper you can use. What do you think?"

"Yay. Let's do that." Emma clapped her hands in excitement. "Bye, Mommy."

"Bye, Peanut."

Megan took Emma's hand, and the two skipped into the living room.

That left Kell and Becca alone in the kitchen. "Did you have time to talk to Megan about our"—he lowered his voice—"arrangement?"

"Yes," she whispered back.

"What do you think about adding some fuel to flame the gossip?"

"What do you have in mind?"

"Nothing specific. I figured we'd make it up as we go," Kell said. "Maybe a little PDA?"

"All right."

"Follow my lead."

"Got it." She chuckled. Then she added in a more hushed tone. "Remember, we're keeping Emma in the dark."

"Gotcha."

There were half a dozen others at the party. He knew a few of the guys from the fire department and Megan's assistant, Brenda, had come up on Friday. She planned to be in Lucky for the week because his sister was working on a new song.

He took Becca's hand and walked her into the living room, straight over to the sofa where there was space for both of them. He pulled her down next to him, nuzzling her neck, he whispered in her ear, "Relax, Doc."

"You know, for this to be convincing you might want to call me Becca instead of Doc. Just saying," she whispered.

"Roger that."

He felt her body slowly loosen up.

At the next commercial, he stood. "Want anything from the kitchen? More wine? I'm going to grab one last beer."

"No, thanks. I'm fine for now," Becca said.

Chase came up to him as Kell was closing the fridge. "What the fuck, man?"

Kell frowned at Chase.

"Why the hell don't you just date her for real?" Chase said.

Ah. Megan told him. "Not you, too?"

"Just saying you might find you enjoy your time with her. That you like her."

"I do like her. That's why I asked her to help me out. Can you imagine pretending to be interested in someone you can't stand to be around?"

"No, I can't."

"Can I, at least, count on you to keep your mouth shut? At some point my mom will find out. But for the time being, I'm going to ride the fake-dating wave as long as I can."

Chase shrugged. "It's your funeral, Pal. I don't want to be around when Ruby discovers the truth."

"Thanks. I think."

"You know Valentine's Day is next week, right?" Chase asked.

"Guess I've had some other shit on my mind," Kell replied. He figured he put just enough snark in his reply to let his friend know he didn't appreciate his interference. "Like these fucking burglaries, for example."

"Yeah, I'm aware. Just thought I'd mention it. We could double date. Take them to a movie or a nice restaurant. We could get out of Lucky for the night. What do you think?"

Kell stared at his friend for a beat.

"Has my sister been making helpful suggestions?"

"Nah, I came up with this idea all on my own," Chase grinned. "I think it could be fun."

"I'll think about it," Kell said. "I'll let you know."

Chase nodded. "It's on Thursday."

Kell shook his head. "I said I'll think about it. Now, can we get back in there?" He waved his arm toward the living room. "I don't want to miss any more of the game."

Kell returned to the living room and sat down next to Becca again and put his arm along the back of the sofa, just grazing her shoulders.

The half-time show was lame. Or was he out of touch with current trends in music? Being halfway around the world could do that. He was nursing his beer when little Emma popped over. It was getting late, and she wasn't nearly as exuberant as she'd been earlier.

Before he realized what she was doing, she crawled onto his lap. He had mere seconds to set his beer down and balance her precariously on one knee.

Emma put her hands on his cheeks, and leaned in close and whispered, "Do you know Megan's cat?"

He cleared his throat. "Sure. Cute little gray thing, right?"

"Did you know the cat's name is Emmie, kind of like my name, but a little not the same?"

"Yep, I know that. She's Emmie. You're Emma."

She smiled and nodded vigorously, like she was happy he understood. Then she yawned.

"Your face is scratchy. How come?"

Becca had been sitting silently beside him, watching the interaction. Now she said, "Okay, looks like it's time we head home. Tomorrow is a workday for Mommy, and I need to get you to bed." She stood as if she was going to pick Emma up off his lap.

"In a couple whiles," Emma answered. "I gots to finish my story."

Becca exchanged a glance with Kell, and he shrugged.

"Okay, finish your story." Her mouth quirked upward, and she sat back down.

The child snuggled closer and took his chin in her tiny hand and turned his head, so he was looking directly at her. Guess she wanted him to pay attention. Smart little cookie. Like her mom. The thought made him smile.

"Do you know why Emmie is named Emmie?"

"No, but I bet you do." He grinned. He had to admit, this was one super cute kid. Precocious, but cute.

She nodded her head. "Uh-huh, it's cuz her eyes are weally green like emer-olds. I don't 'zactly know what emer-olds are, but that's what Megan told me."

Kell chuckled as he shifted her over slightly so he could reach the phone in his pocket. He scrolled to Google and typed *emeralds* into the search box. He clicked on an image and handed his phone to Emma. "This is what emeralds look like."

"Oh, pretty. Mommy, look at the pretty emer-olds."

Becca leaned closer so she could see the photo. "Oh, wow, yes, Em, beautiful. That's your birthstone?"

"What's a birthstone?" Emma asked.

Becca laughed. "How 'bout I explain on the drive home?"

"No, Mommy, can't we stay, puh-lease?"

"Nope, sorry, Peanut, time to go. Let's make sure you have everything you brought. Why don't you go tell Megan and Chase thank you for inviting us?"

"Okay." Emma crawled off his lap, but turned back to Kell and said, "Tanks for showing me the emer-olds."

"Sure thing," Kell said. Wow, he'd need to be careful. He could easily see himself getting wrapped totally around Emma's pinky. There was just something about her. To say she charmed him was an understatement.

Megan and Chase came into the room from the kitchen, and Emma thanked them. "Tank you for inviting me to your party. I think I need to tank Brady and Emmie, too."

Megan knelt in front of Emma. "Sounds like a great idea. Let's go find them."

"Okay," Emma said.

"We'll be right back, Becca. We have a cat to find," Megan said.

Becca turned to Kell. "Thanks, it was sweet of you. I know you haven't been around kids much."

Embarrassed at being caught doing something *sweet,* he shrugged and said, "Nah. She's a cute kid. She makes me laugh."

"She is, and she makes me laugh, too."

"So, with the little person out of the room and the big people still here, is it okay if I kiss you good night? That should stir up some rumors."

"All right."

He moved in and took her chin in hand. When his mouth was nearly on hers, he whispered, "Relax." Then he slowly, gently, kissed her mouth.

He had planned for it to be a quick kiss. But as soon as his lips touched hers and she made a tiny sound. Something between a gasp and audible breath. He was a goner.

Before he realized he was going to say it, he whispered, "Would you like to double date with Chase and Megan on Valentine's Day?"

"What?"

"Valentine's Day. It's this Thursday. I thought a night out might be fun." He quickly added, "If you don't already have plans."

"Well, as far as anyone knows, you're my boyfriend, so no, I don't have Valentine's Day plans with anyone else." She laughed. "A fake date, right?"

Kell hesitated. How to answer this question? "Well, the date itself will be real." Shrugging, he continued, "I'm not exactly sure what the plan is yet, but with Chase and Megan planning it, I know we'll be entertained."

"All right, it sounds like fun. If my dad doesn't have plans and he doesn't mind babysitting, then I'd love to go."

"Great."

He pulled her in even closer and kissed her again. Lost in her sweet mouth until he heard someone clearing his throat, then cough.

Chase said, "Little person coming down the stairs in three, two, one…"

"Mommy, I gots to give Emmie a kiss goodbye."

Becca quickly stood and tucked her loose strands of hair behind her ears.

"Oh, good. I'm happy you have a new friend."

She gathered up Emma's stuff and put her in her coat. Then put on her own coat.

She hugged Megan and Chase and thanked them.

Kell stepped forward. "I'll call you with the details about Thursday."

He didn't miss Chase's knowing smile and slight nod to Megan.

These two were almost as bad as his mom. Almost being the key word.

Have a good week, D—, Becca."

"You too, Kell."

When Becca was gone, Kell turned to his best friend and sister and said, "Not one word from either of you. Understand?"

Chapter 15

Becca took a little extra time getting dressed, fixing her hair and make-up for the date. Kell rewarded her extra effort when he picked her up and his gaze traveled down her body. He smiled and said, "You look really nice."

She felt a blush creep up her neck at his compliment. "Thanks."

Kell said, with such a serious expression, "You know, you might be a tad overdressed for McDonalds," almost making her fall for his joke until he grinned.

"Ha, ha. Very funny," Becca said.

"You ready?"

"I am." She looked over her shoulder toward the living room. "Bye, Emma. Bye, Dad. Enjoy your date tonight."

She heard their chorus of goodbyes as she closed the front door. If she didn't adore her father so much already, the extra care he took with Emma would seal the deal.

The Valentine's Day dinner was at a place called Giacomo's Italian Bistro, about a half-hour drive from Lucky. The four of them met in back of Espresso Yourself and left Chase's truck. Kell drove his roomy SUV. Becca and Megan sat in back and chatted as the men discussed sports.

The food was delicious, and the conversation flowed easily without those awkward silences that can come on a first date. Megan and Becca were drinking cappuccinos and sharing a dessert. A unique twist of the classic tiramisu dessert with coffee sponge, layered with mascarpone cheese and espresso cream, topped with premium cocoa powder. It was unbelievably good. Everything was going smoothly until Megan mentioned Becca and Kell's fake relationship.

"So, is this a real or a fake date, Kell?"

Megan might have had a little too much wine earlier with her meal. She wasn't drunk, but she'd had enough to loosen her lips, because she didn't seem to realize the awkwardness of her question. Or did she?

Kell set his drink on the table and stared across at his sister. How would he respond? When he turned toward Megan, Becca studied his rugged profile. He had shaved his beard, but his clean-shaven face was now showing the telltale signs of a five o'clock shadow.

It wasn't as if she hadn't noticed his good looks before, but tonight she believed she could see beneath his public face. He had been comfortable with his best friend and sister... until this moment.

His jaw clenched as he answered Megan. "Well, sister dear, since we're here, some distance from Lucky with the only two people who know about our fake relationship, I guess you can say, yes, it's an actual date."

Becca looked between the brother and sister, then to Chase and he looked surprised that Megan would ask that question.

Wait. He just admitted they were on an actual date.

When Megan opened her mouth to reply to her brother, Chase interrupted, "Let's dance, babe. I've been dying to get my arms around you all night." He stood, pulled her chair back from the table, and walked her over to the small dance floor.

Becca reviewed the evening so far. When they arrived at the restaurant, Kell pulled her chair out for her, like any considerate date would.

He'd picked her up like an actual date. He'd even given her a single rose with a little pink card attached that read, *Be My Valentine*. Now that she thought about it, that last one felt totally out of character for Kell.

Kell interrupted her contemplation when he asked, "Would you like to dance?"

"Sure. But I have to warn you, I'm not much of a dancer."

He reached across the table and grasped her hand in his large, roughened one. The warmth at his touch sent feel-good tingles through her body. They joined the others on the dance floor. He wrapped an arm around her waist and pulled her closer.

He actually could dance. This man was full of surprises. "Where did you learn to move like this?" she asked.

"Oh, I think you're giving me too much credit. There isn't much talent to swaying to the music and twirling you around a few times." He laughed.

"Well, I'm impressed."

"In college, there were a few campus dances. It was one way to meet women."

"Ahh, I see. Well, I was too busy with my nose in my books to go to the dances."

He gently pulled her into him. She was so close to his whiskered cheek she ached to feel it against hers. As if he sensed her scrutiny, he looked down and met her gaze. She ducked her head into his shoulder to hide the heated, telltale blush she felt on her cheeks.

Confusion followed her embarrassment. Sure, she'd had flutters of attraction when they first met, but honestly, it seemed so much simpler when they were sparring. Even when he asked her to be his accomplice in his charade to fool his mother, things were light between them. She'd been able to suppress her attraction, well, almost.

It was a moment before she realized he'd stopped moving, but still held her in his arms. She pulled away quickly. "Thanks for the dance."

He nodded, but didn't say a thing. What was he thinking?

Later, when he walked her to her door, he looked so uncomfortable she took pity on him. "I think the flower and Valentine was very sweet, by the way." She bit her lower lip. "I'm sorry Megan put you on the spot earlier."

"Yeah, no big deal. I love my little sister but she has always been a handful."

Becca cocked her head. She wasn't sure she'd describe her friend as a *handful*. Though she could imagine Megan was a *spirited* child.

"Well, thank you. I had fun tonight."

"You're welcome," he said with a chagrined tone. He thought for a minute, then continued. "To tell you the truth, we've been doing such a good job faking it. Sometimes I totally forget it's not real. I know we agreed to fake dating and a few PDAs, but sometimes, it feels like it could be more."

"I know what you mean."

He brushed a light kiss on her cheek.

"Good night, Becca."

"Night, Kell."

On Saturday, she pulled up in the driveway behind Kell's SUV. He sat on the front steps with two to-go cups from Espresso Your-self, one in each hand.

"Hey, got your favorite here," he said as she approached.

She took the cup and smelled. "Mmm. Thanks. This is perfect. Have you been sitting here for long? I imagine those steps are cold and damp."

"Got here a minute before you pulled up. Not long enough to freeze my ass." He chuckled.

"I'm glad. I don't want any ass-freezing on my watch."

"No worries. So, what's on the list this morning?" Kell asked as he took her keys and unlocked her front door. "Are you still thinking of painting the bigger bedroom?"

"Yep. I bought the paint on Thursday over my lunch break." She talked as she walked through the house, flipping on lights as she went. "The paint is on the kitchen counter. Tell me what you think."

Kell strode into the kitchen. "The color will be easier to see once we put it on the walls," he said.

"Yes, that's true. But then what if we hate it?"

When she saw the skepticism on his face, she laughed. Oh, never mind. Actually, I bought a sampling of two colors to compare."

"Noted," he said. "Guess you will have to decide which you like best."

"Exactly. Can you help me lay the tarp down in the room?" she asked.

"Sure thing."

After they prepped the room, they each took a different color and wall. When they had covered about half of each wall, they both stepped back into the center of the room, staring at their work.

"So, what are your thoughts?" he asked.

"I like both. Wow, this is harder than I expected. What do you think?"

"Doesn't matter what I think. It's your room. Honestly, there's not much difference." He gestured between the two walls.

"Oh, yes, there is. That shade is called Demure. And this one is Innocence," she said.

He grinned.

"What? What are you grinning about?"

"This is going to be your bedroom, right?"

She stared at him for a few seconds before realization dawned on her. She felt the heat color her neck and face. "Oh, never mind."

She was stepping back from him when a loud, firecracker-sounding blast exploded.

Kell shouted, "Get down." Lightning fast, he lunged for her, taking both of them to the floor with a thud. She wasn't surprised that her body hadn't been jarred from the fall because he used his body to protect her. Somehow, he covered her, and still kept her from hitting the floor hard.

She squealed managing to cough out. "What the hell? What's wrong —"

"Stay down," he barked. He was shaking, and his breaths came short and fast.

"Kell, relax. Can you hear me?" It was as if he was in another place and time. "Kell, you need to roll off me. I'm fine. It was my neighbor's old car. It must need a new muffler. Kell!" Becca gave an awkward shake from beneath him.

He gasped, expelling quick bursts of air. "Fuck," he finally said as he rolled off her and stood. The tremor in that single word was clear. He put his hand out to help her off the floor. "Did I hurt you?"

"No, Kell, I'm fine. You just startled me."

His breathing was still off as he strode out of the room.

In the silence that followed, Becca debated going after him. Should she confront him head on or let it go? She'd seen signs of PTSD while working in the ER in Cleveland. It wouldn't surprise her if Kell suffered with these kinds of issues. After doing four tours, she couldn't even imagine the horrors he'd witnessed.

Her friendship with Kell was still new. But thinking about it now, she realized she'd seen other signs. His unusual reaction to the blood on her hands and blouse. He'd turned green and had to step away, which was odd for a man in his field. Then he was uncharacteristically short-tempered about the missing dowel in her slider. He wasn't sleeping well. And now his intense reaction to the car backfiring.

But he was a proud man. Would he welcome her help or resent it? Taking a deep breath, she went in search of him.

She found him in the kitchen, bent over the sink, splashing water on his face. His back was to her. Becca walked to his side and placed a gentle hand on his arm.

"How long have you been dealing with post-traumatic stress disorder?"

Kell straightened. Grabbing a paper towel, he mopped his face with it. Disgusted with himself for showing his weakness in front of Becca, of all people, he turned away from her and sat at the card table.

"Talk to me, Kell," she said. "Please. I believe having someone you can trust to talk to might help. Who better than your fiancé?"

Kell jerked his head up in time to see her teasing expression.

"Ha. I figured that would get your attention. Seriously, though, I'm here to listen. I have some experience dealing with PTSD from when I worked in the ER."

When he remained silent, she took the seat across the table and reached for his hand. "Please, let me in. I'd like to help," Becca said.

Kell met her gaze and sighed. "This shit began after my buddy was shot and killed during night maneuvers. Sniper. His name was Michael Fawcett, but we called him Leaks. We had orders to clear out buildings to make sure there weren't hostiles hiding out.

"Leaks had this damn coin he loved to toss. He wanted to flip to see who took point that night." Kell shook his head. "I told him it was my responsibility."

"Point?" she asked.

"Being the point person is the most exposed position in military formation and can be the most dangerous. I was the officer in charge, so the job fell to me."

"Only a bullet hit me in the thigh, and I went down." Kell rubbed his thigh unconsciously. "With me down, the sniper's second bullet hit Leaks in the head. Not sure how they knew where we'd be. That fucking sniper took down several of my men like we were sitting ducks. Leaks was the only fatality, but there were five other casualties, including me."

"So, you blame yourself?"

"Of course, I do. The safety of those men fell on me. Who else?"

She cocked her head. "Perhaps the people over you. Someone above you gave the order. You must know it wasn't your fault that your buddy got shot after you went down."

His skepticism must have shown on his face.

"No, Kell. Getting wounded wasn't your fault. And the subsequent next shot that hit your friend wasn't your fault, either."

"Yeah, I can get by most days without an issue, then something like that damn car backfiring sets me back."

"What else are you dealing with? Nightmares? Panic attacks?" she asked.

He stared at her for a moment before saying, "If anyone finds out..."

"You need to trust me. I will not discuss you with anyone. But I'd like to recommend that you talk to a professional who is more qualified."

When he was going to interrupt, with a hell no, she held up her hand, raised her voice and plowed on. "Someone who specializes in this kind of bad shit you're still dealing with."

He lifted a brow. The pretty doctor wasn't afraid to use language or raise her voice.

"My friend from medical school, Sam Winston, just moved to Lucky to join the hospital staff. He specializes in counseling individuals who have experienced trauma or violence. The money we made from the auction will help him establish some group therapy."

"I don't know. I had my fill of shrinks after the incident."

"Megan attributes a lot of her healing after the stalker attack to his group counseling. He drove in from Cleveland last summer for a group therapy session for victims of crimes."

Kell stood and walked over to the counter, leaning back with his legs braced a foot apart. "Can I think about it?"

"Absolutely. In fact, since he's new in town, I've been wanting to get a group together at Joe's. I'd like to introduce Sam to some folks. It'll be a nice opportunity for you to meet him in a totally social space. Get a feeling of what you think of him. If you would be a comfortable fit. No pressure.

Becca pushed up from her seat. "Now, how 'bout we get back to painting?" she asked.

"Lead the way. Oh, and we really need to discuss your paint choices for your bedroom. *Demure* and *Innocence*, seriously?"

❧

The next day, a chilly but sunny Sunday, Megan surprised Becca with an invitation to skate on the lake. In Emma's case, walking around in her little pink boots while holding tight to Becca's hand. She wasn't quite ready for a pair of skates.

Kell topped off their fun afternoon by showing up with the fixings for s'mores.

"Mommy, look, we can make snores."

"Yes, Peanut. But they're s'mores, not snores. Want me to show you how to build one? You can only roast a marshmallow with the help of a grown-up. Understand?"

"Uh-huh." Emma danced around on her tiptoes. Then she scanned their small group, and as if she sized them up, marched over to Kell and took his hand.

"Will you help me cook my s'more?" She emphasized the m sound.

He chuckled. "Sure. Okay with you, mom?" He glanced at Becca and winked.

Why did he have to be so damn charming? Wait. *Charming*? What happened to her first impression of him? Perhaps getting to know him, and it was seeing his vulnerable side that had swayed her opinion.

Plus, she had agreed to be his pretend girlfriend, so her subconscious was persuading her that he was charming.

Yes, that had to be it.

Then he'd asked her out for Valentine's Day. Talk about mixed-up feelings. He sure kept her on her toes.

"Sure, that's perfectly okay with me."

Kell sat down on one of the benches Chase had built to surround the fire pit. "Sit here next to me." Kell motioned for Emma to sit. "There's room for your mom, too."

Becca felt her face flush. Hopefully, with the cold weather, no one could tell the difference between cold cheeks and her hormone-induced flush.

Why did he affect her so? It had been a long time since she'd felt the flutters from a guy. She brushed aside her starry-eyed thoughts and set about making her s'more. Kell was surprisingly good with Emma. Last weekend at the Super Bowl party and now with the s'mores, she was impressed with his ability to engage her little girl.

Before long, Emma needed to wash the sticky marshmallows from her fingers and her s'more-smeared cheeks. "I think you've had enough. Let's go inside and get cleaned up."

"Do I hafta?" Emma whined. Hearing the tone in her daughter's voice confirmed the little girl had enough sweets and was getting tired.

Megan stood. "I'm heading inside. I'll take her. Hey, Emma, want to go inside and see Emmie?"

"Can I, Mommy?"

"Yes, but you need to ask Megan to help you wash up first. You don't want to get a marshmallow in Emmie's fur."

"Okay, Mommy." Her daughter skipped to Megan but stopped and returned to Kell's side. "Tanks for the s'mores." She threw her arms around his neck and kissed his cheek. And then turned and took Megan's hand.

Becca smiled at the surprise on his face. "Oh, no, now you have marshmallow and chocolate in your beard. Here, let me—" She wiped his cheek with her finger and realized she needed a wet paper towel, but before she could grab one, he took her finger and sucked off the gooey mess.

A tiny gasp escaped, and she was certain her face reflected the red blush she felt creeping up her neck. Thank goodness Chase had followed Megan and Emma into the house.

She was at a loss for what to say. The awkward silence didn't last long. He surprised her by saying, "You have a terrific kid."

"Thank you. Is there a but coming?"

He abruptly looked up from gazing at the fire. "There's no but. She's a fun little person. You've obviously done a great job raising her."

"Thanks. I love being her mom."

Kell shuffled his feet in the snow. "I can tell." He kicked at the snow in front of him. "So, is her father in the picture? I guess I should have thought of that before asking you to be my..." He whispered, "girlfriend."

Smiling, she said, "No, the birth father isn't around at all. I adopted Emma when she was a newborn. From what I understand, he was never part of the equation."

"Adopted? Hmm, I never would have guessed."

She cocked her head, studying him for a moment. "Why would you? It's not like she has it tattooed on her arm. I couldn't love her more if she was my biological daughter."

She didn't realize she'd raised her voice a notch until he raised his hands in defense.

"Hey, sorry. I meant nothing by the comment."

Her cheeks burned from embarrassment. "No. I'm sorry because I get carried away. I'm probably overly sensitive about her adoption. There are so many misconceptions."

She shook her head. "Do you know, I've had someone actually say to me, 'Oh, I'm sorry you couldn't have a real child. Do you believe the audacity? As if Emma isn't a real child. Or my child. Plus, that person knew nothing about my life and if I could or couldn't have a baby."

"It's been my experience over the last sixteen years that people can be assholes."

She studied him. "That's pretty cynical, don't you think?"

"Maybe but seeing the shit I saw in the Middle East was tough." He blew on his fingers, then tucked his hands under his arms for warmth. "The description fits."

"I guess so. I can't imagine what you, and all the others, for that matter, experienced," she said.

"About Emma, I only meant that you're a natural mom," Kell said.

"Thanks."

His phone beeped, and he pressed the button to listen. "It'll take me ten minutes. I'm out at the lake. Got it." He shoved his phone in his pocket and stood up. "Duty calls. Nice seeing you today. And Emma. Tell her I said goodbye."

"Nice seeing you, too. Be careful."

He nodded.

Chase stepped outside and Kell turned to him and said, "Hey Buddy, thanks for the day, but duty calls. Tell my sis bye."

"Will do. See you later," Chase said.

Kell jogged up the lawn, heading to his SUV.

Turning to Becca, Chase asked, "Where is he going in such a hurry?"

"He got a call. I hope it isn't another break-in."

It was a pleasant afternoon while it lasted.

It wasn't another break-in, but an accident out on Old 52. A pickup, driving too fast for the road conditions, tried to pass a slow-moving car in a section of the road with a double solid yellow line. He ended up in the ditch. The driver of the car was spooked by the truck's accelerated passing and threw the brakes on, which caused the vehicle to slide, nearly missing the same ditch.

Luckily, neither driver was seriously injured. The driver of the pickup would have some bruising from the seat belt and the air bag. He would also face a fairly hefty fine.

Kell was relieved on the one hand that this particular Sunday had gone without another burglary. But he'd bet they'd be facing another before long. If only he and his men could pinpoint the next target.

Chapter 16

That Friday night, true to her word, Becca organized a group to meet at Joe's for drinks. They ended up with quite a crowd. Fortunately, she checked with Joe earlier in the day and he reserved a table in the back for their group. There were nine. She purposely made the gathering an odd number, so no one felt they were being paired off.

Besides Kell and her, the group included her cousin Lori, Chase, and Megan. Brenda, Megan's assistant, was in town, so she joined them. Bruce Kincaid, a single dad who was a local realtor and her medical school friend Sam, and rounding out the group, was Paul, Kell's deputy.

The Detroit Red Wings were playing the Columbus Blue Jackets on the bar TVs, which immediately caused a friendly debate over which was the better hockey team. When Becca noticed Sam and Kell having a conversation at the bar, she sighed, happy to see Kell getting to know Sam.

Megan came over and took Kell's empty seat. She leaned in and whispered, "What do you think of Bruce and Brenda?"

Becca's gaze darted to the opposite end of the table, where the two appeared to be having a friendly chat. "Am I supposed to have thoughts about them?" She laughed.

"Yes. I mean, look at them. They haven't spoken to anyone else all night."

Becca studied Brenda and Bruce. "You know, that might be because they ended up next to each other," she said wryly. "Has your mom's matchmaking rubbed off on you?"

Megan shot her friend a mock glare. "Nope, absolutely not. How can you say such a thing?" She clutched her heart.

Becca arched her brow.

"Oh, all right." Megan shrugged. "I get your point. But I want Brenda to find love and a happy relationship."

"I'm sure you do. But she'll be much happier if she figures it out for herself."

"Aww, you're no fun. But you're right." Megan sighed. "I'm going on the record saying they look good together."

"Noted."

A few minutes later, Kell wandered back to his seat. He leaned in as his sister had done, but this time, Becca's body tingled from his closeness. When she felt his breath, hot on her ear, goosebumps broke out on her arms.

"Thank you for introducing me to Sam. He might be the right person for me to talk to. I'm going to check my calendar and call him on Monday to set up a preliminary appointment."

She squeezed his hand. "Oh, Kell. I'm so glad. I hope he can help you."

He nodded. "So, do I. Time will tell." He looked at her empty glass. "Would you like another glass of wine?"

"Thank you. One more, then that's my limit. Especially if we're going to get any work done tomorrow."

Returning a few minutes later, he put the fresh glass of wine in front of her and said, "About tomorrow, would you be able to manage the painting alone?"

She frowned. She should have realized there was a limit to his attention span when it came to women. Fake or not. And he was a busy guy. "Sure. We've seen each other a lot this week."

He cocked his head, giving her a quizzical look. "No, that's not it at all. I've enjoyed our dates. Actually, I have a surprise for Emma."

That could have knocked her off her feet if she hadn't been sitting. A surprise for Emma? "It better not be a dog, Kell."

A loud guffaw escaped. "I would never buy your kid a dog without your permission."

She narrowed her gaze. "Or a cat."

"No, it's not a pet of any kind. Chase is going to help me build her a swing set. With the warm spell, we thought it was a good time to do it. If it's okay with you, of course."

Becca was at a loss for words. What could she say? How incredibly sweet of Kell and Chase to do this for Emma. She sputtered before she got the words out. "Wow. That is unexpected. And very nice of you guys. Thank you. I know she'll love it."

He nodded. "I think so. I hope she does. We wanted to get started since your moving day is coming up in a few weeks."

"Oh, gee, I need to get working." She laughed.

It warmed her heart to think of the big tough Marine building a swing set for her little girl. Emma would be delighted.

Later, Kell pulled up to her father's house. He'd picked her up so they could arrive together, for the fake dating pretense. He'd put his arm around her at the bar, and at one point he leaned into whisper in her ear. Before he pulled back, he placed a light kiss on her cheek. A little PDA to keep the grapevine busy. Silly butterflies danced in her belly, which she recognized as ridiculous.

As he walked her to the door. She wondered if Kell would kiss her again.

The kiss at the Super Bowl party had been nice. Better than nice. The man seemed to do everything extremely well.

But on the Valentine's date he only gave her another brief brush of his lips on her cheek at the end of the night.

Now, on the front step, Kell reached for her hand and held it as he moved in closer.

"I need to be honest with you about something."

"Okay," Becca replied.

"I've wanted to kiss you, for real, for a while now. Maybe you figured that out the other night," he said.

"Hmm, I don't know that I did, "she said. "It's a little difficult to jump back and forth from fake to real to fake again. And we agreed to the fake thing."

"Yeah, I know," Kell said. "But here's the thing...." He tugged her slightly closer. She felt his warm breath on her chilly face.

"What's the thing?" She laughed.

"The thing is, I know if we get started, it will be hard to stop."

A small breathless whisper escaped her lips. "I see your point."

"So, here's what we're going to do."

She smiled, enjoying this almost playful side of Kell. He had to be so serious most of the time.

"I'm going to give you a perfunctory kiss goodnight now and send you inside before your dad wonders what we're up to out here in the cold. Tomorrow afternoon, after Chase and I finish in the backyard, I'll pop in to see if you need a hand with anything. After we finish whatever, you need my help with, we'll have some time alone at your place and we can revisit this topic."

Becca swallowed. "Aww. All right. Good plan."

He kissed her, the way he said he would. It was a pleasant, but quick, kiss on her lips. He took two steps back, winked and said, "Night, Becca."

"Good night," she said.

Kell felt like shit the next morning. Leery of another nightmare, he sat up in the recliner, watching the spoon and fork on the kitchen clock slowly tick. It was too much time to think.

Of course, his mind went to Becca and their fake relationship. It must be working. Mom had backed off. No more stunts. Although now he was dealing with her incessant questions and comments. How old is Becca? Is she interested in having more children? Time is ticking. Don't want to dawdle on that issue.

He finally told Mom to stop asking questions. If she needed to know something, he'd tell her; otherwise, they'd appreciate some privacy as they were getting to know each other better. She *humphed* at his request, but so far, was respecting his wishes.

He met Chase at Becca's house. His buddy's truck was parked in the driveway, and he was already hauling the swing set materials out of the truck bed.

Chase watched Kell walk up the drive. "You look like you lost your best friend. But I know that can't be it since I'm right here. I didn't think you drank that much last night." He cocked his head and waited for Kell to reply.

"No, I only had two beers. It was a terrible night. I didn't sleep well." Again.

Normally, he'd respond to his friend's concerned expression by changing the subject. The first step to getting past some of this shit was to talk about it. At least, that's what Becca thought. And ultimately, that's what he would do at his sessions with Sam.

If you couldn't talk to your oldest and best friend, who could you talk to? As if the floodgates were unlocked, he said, "I don't sleep. I've been having nightmares or night terrors, depending on the night. Some are worse than others."

Chase set the stuff he was holding back down on the tailgate. He put his shoulder to the truck and crossed his arms. "For how long?"

Kell shrugged and said, "It started after Leaks was killed."

Chase's eyes widened, and he whistled. "Shit, Kell. Why haven't you said anything before now?"

Shaking his head, Kell said, "Thought I could manage it. Don't wanna be a fucking pansy. Don't want to wind up in the Lucky gossip mill. Or screw up my job. Pick one."

Chase nodded and put his hand on Kell's shoulder. "I'm glad you finally told me. What can I do?"

"Nothing. I'm going to see Sam Winston. Becca referred me to him."

"That's great. I hope he can help you. I know Megan liked him." Then he asked, "So, you and Becca ..."

"Oh, fuck, can't we give it a rest for a day?"

Chase stared at Kell.

Finally, Kell said, "What about Becca and me?"

"For one thing, your face lights up when you look at her. I noticed the afternoon we skated and had s'mores. Then again, the other night at Giacomos. And last night, too."

"I don't think so," Kell said.

"Yes, you were looking at Becca as if she hung the moon and stars. I haven't seen that look on your face since sixth grade and you had a crush on Susie Robinson, and she traded her Spunky the Cocker Spaniel Beanie Baby for your Peace Bear."

"Whatever, man. We're pretending to date for my mom's benefit. That's all." He wasn't ready to admit, even to his best friend, that he might have genuine feelings for Becca.

"Hmm, well, good luck with that," Chase said.

"What the hell is that supposed to mean?" Kell glared at his friend.

"It means there is nothing fake happening between you and Becca James. But if that's how you want to play it." He shrugged.

Kell shook his head. "You don't know what you're talking about."

"If you say so. Let's get this stuff to the backyard. The clock is ticking. I've got a date with my hot fiancée."

Kell cringed. "She's still my sister."

Chase chuckled as he walked around the side of the garage to the back of the house.

Chapter 17

Putting the swing set together ended up taking the guys longer than they thought it would, so there wasn't any time left for Kell to help Becca. Instead, he suggested he come back over the next day. If she planned to be there, he would join her.

Becca hated to admit it, but she took a little extra time getting ready the next morning. It wasn't like she could wear a nice outfit to paint so she focused on her hair and makeup.

Would Kell notice?

She was looking forward to seeing where this mutual attraction took them. Their relationship was a bit confusing. Although they pretended to date for the benefit of his mom, they were clearly attracted to each other. She realized there was more for them to explore.

When he arrived at ten o'clock, he brought her latte. She was excited to see him on her doorstep, holding the to-go cups. It had become a mini ritual of sorts.

But on this morning, he handed her both cups, then said, "I'll be right back."

She tilted her head, "Okay."

He jogged back to his vehicle and pulled out what looked like a long stick.

When he was inside, she asked, "What's that?"

"It's a dowel for your kitchen slider. I assume you haven't taken care of that yet."

She folded her arms across her chest. "Oh, you do? What makes you so sure?"

He lifted a brow. "Am I wrong?"

She hated to admit he was right. Normally, his presumption would perturb her. Instead, if she admitted the truth to herself, she found it touching that he remembered and picked up the dowel despite his busy week.

"It was on my to-do list, but I hadn't gotten to it yet," she said. "So, thank you for picking one up for me."

"You're welcome." He moved into the kitchen, squatted by the door, and placed the piece of wood in the track of the slider. "You'll need to move it when you're using the door. But be sure to put it back in place afterwards."

"Got it. How much do I owe you?"

He shook his head. "Don't worry about it. I can afford the two bucks."

"Well, thanks again."

"Something's different."

"Oh, they delivered the living room furniture yesterday afternoon while you and Chase were out back. I guess I didn't think to mention it." She gestured back toward the room they'd just walked through.

Oddly, he didn't even glance at the furniture, but kept his gaze trained on her. Her face heated with embarrassment at his scrutiny. He cocked his head. "No, that's not it."

Maybe he had noticed.

"My hair is different; I decided the sloppy ponytail could take the day off." He didn't need to know she was wearing a little more makeup than usual.

"Looks good. Before we get started...."

"Yes."

He moved to her side, took her hand, and walked them over to the new sofa. He pulled her down beside him and leaned in. As his lips barely touched hers, she felt his phone vibrate in the front pocket of his jeans.

"Shit," he said.

"I'll second that."

He pulled his phone out. "Howard," he barked.

She couldn't hear the person on the other end. But judging from the frown that instantly appeared on his face, he wasn't happy.

"Hold tight. Give me fifteen."

He disconnected the call and turned his attention back to her. "I'm sorry. I have to go. There's a problem at the station."

"Oh, no. I won't ask."

He gave her an appreciative smile. "Sometimes being the boss sucks."

"I can relate."

He stood, then quickly sat back down beside her again.

"Listen, I've been thinking. Would you like to get away for a day?"

"What?" she asked.

"I thought it might be nice to get out of town and spend some time together. Without all the interruptions." He rubbed his index finger across the bridge of his nose. "We can do whatever you like," he added.

"Really? What if I want to shop?"

He gave her a pained look but replied, "If shopping is what you want to do, then we can shop."

"I was teasing you. Most men—"

"I thought you knew. I'm not like most men." He grinned. "Tell you what. You think about it. I'll be in touch after I'm done at the station. We can work out the details."

"Sounds good to me."

He pulled her in for a disappointedly quick kiss, then grabbed his coat and was gone.

It was late by the time he finished up at the station. It was too late to show up at Becca's house. They both had to work tomorrow. It would seem like a blatant attempt at a hook-up more than anything else, and that wouldn't be cool. So, he texted her.

Kell: *Hey, wondering if you finished every-thing you wanted to get done.*

Becca: *I wish.*

Kell: *What's left?*

Becca: *Enough to keep us both busy for sev-eral more weekends.*

Kell: *Fine by me.*

Kell: *Do you think we can play hooky next Saturday? Did you give anymore thought to the idea of getting away for a day?*

Becca: *I did. Have you ever been to the Rock and Roll Hall of Fame?*

Kell: *Years ago. I'm sure it has changed.*

Becca: *Might be fun…?*

Kell: *I'm game.*

Becca: *I'll double check with my dad to see if he still plans to watch Emma for the day. But I doubt that will be an issue.*

Kell: *Okay, then. Let's plan to get an early start. Is 9:00 all right?*

Becca: *Perfect. Let's hope that the late winter storm doesn't come through as predicted.*

Kell: *Yes, let's hope!*

It was only Tuesday evening and Kell hadn't planned to see Becca until Saturday for their adventure to Cleveland. When she called to invite him for Taco Tuesday and a movie, he accepted. Why not?

He figured it beat his cooking or another takeout meal. He'd been right, too. Becca's tacos had been delicious.

It was also another chance to spark more rumors to the Lucky grapevine. Besides, if he was honest with himself, he wanted to see Becca again. Touch her. And the thought of having to wait until Saturday made him irritable.

After the meal, they moved into the living room.

"Do you like Nemo or Dory?" Emma asked with such an earnest expression, Kell didn't know how to respond. Who the hell were Nemo and Dory? He looked at Becca for help.

"Em, sweetie, I don't think Sheriff Howard has ever seen Finding Nemo. He'll have to decide which character he likes best after he sees the movie."

The kid sighed like this was a total bummer, and Kell laughed.

Emma interrupted his amusement with a question. "Why haven't you watched it?"

Watched what? Ah, got it. The movie.

"Until a few months ago, I wasn't here."

"Where were you?"

In hell.

"I was in a faraway country." He picked up the DVD from the coffee table and read the title. "Sadly, I wasn't able to watch fun movies like Finding Nemo."

Becca interjected, "Emma, are you sure you want to watch it again? Didn't we watch it a few weeks ago? Or was it last week? You know, he might enjoy Toy Story or The Lion King."

The little munchkin twisted her face. "Hmm, what about Elsa's movie?"

Becca glanced at Kell, and he shrugged. He had no clue who Elsa was.

"Okay, Frozen it is," Becca said.

"Yay!" Emma clapped her hands.

"Let me make the popcorn and get your juice box. I'll be right back." She headed toward the kitchen, then turned back. "Kell, want a juice box, too?" She waited a beat until he looked at her and then gave him a smirk. "I mean, another beer?"

"A beer, sure, thanks. Need help?"

"I've got this. But would you mind stoking the fire?"

"Sure thing." He was relieved to have something to do while Becca was out of the room. He'd never been around kids, and while Emma was smart little person, he wasn't confident of his ability to keep her attention.

He was relieved when Harper came into the room.

"Hi, Gampa."

"Hi, Pumpkin." He kissed her on top of her head. "Hello Kell. How are you doing this evening?"

"Good. Better than good after Becca's tacos. How are you, sir?"

"Couldn't be better. Ah, yes, I'm sorry I missed Taco Tuesday. And you can cut the sir. You're not in the military any longer. Harper is fine."

"Got it."

"What's mil-tary?" Emma asked.

"It's ..." He was at a loss. How to explain the military to a three-and-a-half-year-old? Luckily, Harper answered for him.

"You know the G.I. Joe dolls that they have at your daycare?"

"Uh-huh."

"The military is a bunch of GI Joes. Men and women who protect us."

Kell didn't know if the U.S. Department of Defense would approve that description, but the answer seemed to satisfy the child.

"Are you gonna watch Elsa, too?"

"No, sweetie, Gampa has some work he needs to finish in his office. You enjoy your popcorn and movie."

"Oh, okay, you can watch it next time. I know you like Olaf."

"Yes, I do."

"Good night, Kell. Bye, Pumpkin."

"Bye, Gampa."

With that matter settled, the child moved on. She took Kell's hand and walked him back to the sofa. "You sit here." She patted a cushion.

"Gotcha," Kell said.

"I'll sit in the middle and mommy will sit next to me." She continued to show by patting each cushion.

Becca returned with a full tray: a larger bowl filled with popcorn, three smaller bowls, a juice box, and two beers.

"Here we go." She set it on the coffee table. "I hope you like your popcorn with butter, because we do."

"The more the butter." He winked.

"Aren't you the clever one tonight?" Becca laughed. She moved to put the DVD in the player and sat beside Emma with the remote in hand.

By the time Elsa was belting out "Let it Go," Becca noticed Emma had snuggled closer to Kell. He was relaxed too, because he had his arm draped leisurely across the back of the sofa, opening himself up for her to snuggle. She knew he wasn't used to being around children, so she found his behavior endearing.

Equally endearing and interesting was Emma's behavior toward him. Each time Emma and Kell were together, her child seemed to gravitate toward him. Should she be concerned that Emma was getting too attached? Becca had made it clear to Kell that if they were embarking on this fake relationship to appease his mom, Emma was not to be affected, and yet here she was inviting him into their life. But as far as Emma knew, they were simply friends.

She watched Kell and Emma eating their popcorn and a giggle escaped, which she quickly smothered with her hand. Both tilted their heads slightly to the right as they tossed the popcorn into their mouths. She'd never noticed it before with either of them separately, but, side by side, it was blatantly obvious. They were in perfect unison.

Despite the heat from the fire, she shivered. What was she missing? There was something. She just couldn't think what it might be. She shook the strange thoughts away and focused her attention back on the movie.

Emma conked out even before Elsa and Anna were reunited at the end. Kell offered to carry her to bed, and Becca tucked her in, skipping her daughter's nightly routine, which usually included toothbrushing, prayers, and a story.

When Becca and Kell were back in the family room, Kell asked, "Would you like to take a walk? Downtown is pretty, with the new twinkle lights." The mayor had ordered the year-round decoration to make the downtown streets sparkle at night.

"Oh, I don't think so. But thank you. Between the popcorn and beer and the heat of the fire, I'm wiped out."

"Well, thanks for dinner. The tacos were great."

"You're welcome. Thanks for watching the movie. I'm sure it wasn't your first choice for a movie genre." She smiled.

"It was fine. I liked Sven, the reindeer. Though Olaf was a close second. I better get going. We both have to work tomorrow."

She walked him to the door. "See you on Saturday."

He leaned in and kissed her cheek. "Looking forward to it."

She watched him walk to his SUV. After he had pulled away and was halfway down the street. She sagged against the door. She realized she was smiling. She was in deep.

The problem was, what was she going to do about it?

Chapter 18

The cheerful mood Becca had been enjoying all week evaporated on Friday morning when she read the name on the patient file in her hand. It couldn't be right.

She doubted there could be two Jodi Riggs in the vicinity. What were the chances? She hadn't seen Jodi in over three years. They agreed no contact would be best.

She cautioned herself not to jump to conclusions. Perhaps the woman was only there because of stomach cramps, as stated in the note on the chart, and had nothing to do with Emma.

She evened out her breathing and kept her face neutral and professional as she stepped into the examining room. She realized she was on target as soon as she saw Jodi. The young woman, dressed in her street clothes, sat in the chair against the wall, and the paper gown still lay folded on the examining table.

Becca closed the door and sat on the stool across the room. Sighing, she set the file on the desk and folded her arms across her chest. "Hello, Jodi."

"Hi, Dr. James."

Becca's eyes narrowed as she said, "What can I do for you? I take it you aren't here because of stomach cramps or for an exam?"

"Nah. I was afraid you wouldn't see me if I didn't make up a medical excuse."

The lie irritated Becca, but she held her tongue. She squeezed the fleshy part of her arms just above her elbows with her clenched hands.

Jodi was thin. A little too thin for her height. But from where Becca sat, her eyes looked clear. Becca assumed her little girl must have inherited strong genes from whoever her father was. The child didn't look like her birth mother. Becca saw no resemblance at all.

The young woman avoided eye contact and fidgeted with her purse. "How's my baby girl?"

Becca bristled. "My daughter is wonderful. She's a healthy, happy child."

"Sorry. Chill out. I didn't mean nothing."

"What do you want?" Because her gut told her Jodi was there for something.

"Nothing. I was passing through Lucky and thought I'd say hi. It's been a while. I wondered how she was doing, that's all."

Oh, yeah? Not sure why, but Becca wasn't buying what Jodi was selling.

"Why didn't you call? Why all the subterfuge? I would've been happy to speak with you on the phone. You didn't have to waste my time and take away an appointment from one of my legitimate patients."

The young woman shrugged. "Like I said. I figured you wouldn't talk to me." She hesitated a moment. "Me and my boyfriend are moving away, out of state. I guess I'm curious. I just want to see her."

"See her?" Panic surged through Becca, and she shifted forward on the stool. Like meet her. Talk to her? No way. She was becoming more anxious with every word that came out of the young woman's mouth.

Jodi held up her hands. "Relax. Don't get all freaked out. No big deal. I thought I could see her from a distance, you know, so I know she's doing okay. I bet she's pretty?"

"Yes, she is. Inside and out." She couldn't help but smile, thinking of Emma. Hesitant to share too much, but bursting with pride, she added, "She is smart and funny and strong and sweet."

Jodi said, "She must have gotten her strength from her daddy." She shook her head. "She didn't get it from my side, and she sure didn't get her reddish hair from my side, either."

"I thought you didn't know the father."

Jodi shrugged. "I was drunk, so my memory isn't clear. He was in the military and older than me. But hell, I was only nineteen." Becca listened, interested in learning as much as she could for the day Emma asked about her dad.

Jodi shrugged. "I don't think he had shaved in a day or two and, oh, his beard had some red in it. He sure wasn't hard on the eyes. He had muscles. Know what I mean?" Jodi paused for a second, then continued, "Oh, yeah, he had a bandage on his leg." Jodi pointed to her upper thigh. "Gunshot wound; I think he said." Before Becca could assimilate all that information, Jodi added, "Isn't there a way I could see her without her seeing me?"

Did Jodi somehow know that Emma was right next door at the daycare center? There was the observation window they'd installed between the daycare facility and the clinic. Becca used it many times a day to take a quick peek to check on Emma, and if she had a break between patients, she'd pop over for a visit. How would Jodi know that?

She wasn't sure if she believed Jodi. But she nodded. "Sure. We can do that. Come with me."

Jodi stood up and followed, but Becca noticed she was limping. The limp was slight, but she noticed. "What's wrong?" Becca pointed to Jodi's leg. "You're limping."

"Aw, nothing. I scraped up my leg."

Becca frowned. If it hurt enough that the girl was limping, there could be an infection, or need medical attention. "Did you see a doctor?"

Jodi shook her head.

"Okay, why don't you go over and sit on the table. Roll up your pant leg so I can take a look."

"It's nothing."

"I'm the doctor and I want to see for myself."

"I don't have any money to pay you." When Becca continued to stare her down, she sighed dramatically, and limped over to the table and sat on it. She rolled her pant leg up to her knee.

Becca looked at the inflamed cut. Red and puffy. Infected, as she had feared. "Did you put anything on it?"

Jodi shook her head again.

"Okay, we'll clean it up and I'll give you a prescription for an antibiotic." When Becca saw the worried look on Jodi's face, she asked, "What's wrong?"

"I don't have money for a prescription. Don't have insurance neither."

Becca studied her for a moment. "I can cover that. But you'll need to take the medicine, or this will get worse."

"All right. I will."

Once Becca had cleaned, applied an antibiotic cream and bandaged Jodi's leg, she gave her the antibiotic pills and explained the dosage. They walked the length of the hall until they reached the large window. "Go ahead, have a look."

Jodi stepped closer to the window. There were three girls and three boys in the room.

Becca knew the minute Jodi recognized Emma by her sudden intake of breath.

"Is that her? In the purple top?"

"Yes."

Jodi nibbled her bottom lip and twisted her hands. "She sure is a pretty little girl," Jodi said wistfully.

Emma saw them and ran to the window, jumping up and down, waving, with a big smile on her face. "Hi Mommy" she shouted through the glass.

Becca waved back, smiling at her daughter. She didn't miss as Jodi's hand came up to wave, too.

She cleared her throat and said, "We need to move away from the window before Emma decides she would rather be on this side instead of in the daycare room."

"Oh yeah, sure." Jodi turned and headed back the way they came.

Becca took another second to blow Emma a kiss, then caught up with Jodi and escorted her to the waiting room.

"Sorry, I lied to get in today. Thanks for letting me see her. And for taking care of my leg." The young woman sounded so sad it almost elicited sympathy from Becca.

"Good luck to you," Becca said.

"Thanks," Jodi said.

Becca didn't wait to watch her walk to her car. There were patients to see. There were three individuals in the waiting room. Becca smiled at the patients and walked back down the hall to her office.

Closing the door, she collapsed behind her desk. She put her head back and closed her eyes. She remembered the day she'd offered to adopt Jodi's baby.

Jodi's grandmother had come into the clinic because of her arthritis. It was during one of her appointments that she mentioned her granddaughter was pregnant. It was over the course of the elderly woman's treatment that Becca learned the baby was going to be put up for adoption.

It had been a long process. Becca had used the time to prepare her life for motherhood. She read every related book at the Lucky Township Library and quickly was on a first-name basis with her delivery man. She ordered books she couldn't get from the library. Books on adoption and parenting. *Baby's First Year* and *Newborn 101* were two of her favorites.

Thank God for Amazon, because she bought a ton of baby items. It was just easier than trying to shop with her busy schedule.

After Emma was born, they agreed there would be no further contact between them. And, until now, there had been none.

She inhaled, exhaled, and stood up. It was time to get back to work.

After bath time, and all the other bedtime rituals, Emma was snug in her bed, asleep. Becca found her dad in his study, reading. She tapped on the doorframe. When he looked up, she asked, "Have a minute?"

"Always for you. Take as many minutes as you need, sweetheart. Come sit down." He pointed to the well-worn leather sofa across from where he sat in his recliner. Once she sat on the sofa, he slid a bookmark into place before closing the book and asked, "What's on your mind?"

She twisted her hands in her lap and swallowed. "I had a visitor today."

"Are we talking a non-patient kind of visitor?"

"Yes."

"At the clinic?" he asked.

"Yes. It was Jodi Riggs."

Dad's eyes widened. "What did she want?"

"That's just it. She said she wanted to check up on Emma. Make sure she's good. Apparently, Jodi is moving away with her boyfriend."

"And?"

"She didn't tell the truth. She lied about having stomach cramps so she could get an appointment."

"So, you think she had a hidden agenda?"

"Yes, no, I don't know." Becca shook her head. "I was jumpy all afternoon. It wasn't until after I had Emma home that I finally calmed down. I know it's silly. But I got a strange vibe from Jodi."

"I've always told you to trust your gut." He scratched his head. Putting the book on the table beside him, he then leaned forward, elbows on his knees. "It has been over three years. With no contact at all. Was that all she wanted?"

"She wouldn't be the first birth mother to change her mind and wreak havoc on the lives of the adopted family. Do you remember that case in Michigan, years ago? It made headlines."

"I think so. But if I recall, it wasn't the birth mother, it was the birth father. He hadn't been told about the child, and they had violated his paternal rights. I can't remember all the details, but I believe there were lots of unusual circumstances in that case."

Whether or not it was unusual, the fact remains that they forcefully separated that young girl from the only parents she knew, taking her away from the only home she had ever known. It was cruel." Becca wasn't aware she was raising her voice or the fact that she was now pacing the small space with her hands clenched at her side. "Blood isn't the only thing that makes someone a parent. Anyone can make a baby —"

"Honey, calm down. You're preaching to the choir, here. Let's not jump to conclusions yet."

She took a deep breath. "You're right, Dad. But just in case, I'm going to call my college friend, Sara Davis. Do you remember my roommate and sorority sister? She's an attorney who specializes in family law in Cincinnati. She might sort through this situation and give me some advice."

He took her hands and squeezed. "I remember her. Petite, sweet, with a beautiful smile, and smart, right?"

"Yep. That's her. Wow, you have a great memory, Dad."

"Not really. She was one of your closest friends, so I paid more attention than I would have otherwise. I'm glad you two have stayed in touch."

"I believe Sara will consider the overall situation for me."

"That's a good proactive move, sweetheart." He kissed her forehead. "Is there anything else you want to talk about?"

She shook her head.

"Then I'm going to say goodnight. Mornings come earlier and earlier the older I get." He chuckled as he walked out.

"Really, Dad? You're not that old. Thanks for listening."

"Anytime."

"Night, Dad."

He called over his shoulder, "See you in the morning."

That night, Becca tossed and turned, ruminating about every detail of Jodi Rigg's visit to the clinic. Something Jodi said was needling in the back of Becca's brain.

What was it?

At half-past three, she fell into a fitful sleep.

I remember he was in the military. He was easy on the eyes. She didn't get her reddish hair from my side.

Becca suddenly woke. *That's it.* That was what had been bothering her. How did Jodi know Emma had red hair? At birth, Emma barely had any hair, but the little she had was light brown. The red showed up when she was almost a year old.

That meant Jodi had already known what Emma looked like. Had she been spying on them? Why did she act like she'd never seen Emma before?

Becca would definitely call Sara. It wouldn't hurt to talk to Kell, too. After all, he was the town's sheriff. Or would he think she was overreacting? It didn't matter. For Emma's well-being, she didn't care what anyone thought.

With so little sleep, Becca was dragging the next morning, but after two cups of coffee, she began to feel human again.

She passed her dad in the hall. "Good morning, Becca … whoa, rough night, sweetheart?"

"Gee, thanks, dad. Yeah, I had a bad night. Nothing like a bit of insomnia to put dark circles under a girl's eyes."

He squeezed her shoulder. "I'm sorry. Talk to Kell about your visit with Jodi Riggs. It might relieve some of your worry. You will have the time in the car on your way to Cleveland."

"I plan to. I just don't want to jump to conclusions. But I have a bad feeling about her. Actually, I'm wondering now if I should cancel the trip to Cleveland. I'm not sure I'm comfortable letting Emma out of my sight. No telling what Jodi is up to."

"Oh, honey, don't change your plans. I will keep her safe."

"I know you will."

He squeezed her hand. "You'll figure it all out. Hang in there. I'm always here if you need me."

Nodding, she said, "Thanks, Dad. So, what do you have planned for today?"

"I don't know. I thought a trip to the library for Saturday morning Story-time. Then onto McDonalds for a Happy Lunch."

"Happy Meal," Becca corrected.

"A Happy Lunch is a Happy Meal," he said with a grin.

Laughing, Becca said, "Ugh. I give up. You're incorrigible. I'm getting my shower."

"Have fun today and be safe on your fake date," he said with a wink.

Chapter 19

Jodi didn't know how she'd explain her bandaged leg or the antibiotics to Jimmy. He'd been on edge ever since they botched the last job. They hadn't even made it into the store before they heard the sirens. They had to abandon the plan and run.

They had scored nothing big since Super Bowl Sunday. She did not know what he was planning, but she'd discovered it was better not to question Jimmy. So far, being with Jimmy and Ben was better than being on her own.

She was grateful that it was cold in the place they were staying. It gave her an excuse to leave her pants on when they were getting ready for bed.

Of course, Jimmy noticed. "What's up? Why are you wearing your pants to bed?"

"I'm freezing."

"Who isn't? But I'll keep you warm."

"That's okay, my leg still hurts."

Jimmy narrowed his eyes at her. "So? Your leg will hurt whether or not you take your pants off."

Jodi bit her lip. She didn't want to hesitate long enough to make Jimmy mad.

"Come here. I'll help," he said.

"No, that's okay. I need to use the bathroom first. I'll be back in a second."

He shrugged and turned his attention back to the TV.

Once in the bathroom, Jodi quickly peeled off her jeans. Then carefully unwrapped the bandage and looked around to find some place she could hide it so she could put it back on in the morning. She reached in her pocket and drew out the pill bottle with the antibiotics. If Jimmy found the medication, he would take it and sell it to the highest bidder.

She finally settled on the wastebasket under the trash bag liner. She figured neither brother would find the bandage or the medicine, since neither of them ever took care of the trash.

When she walked out of the bathroom, Jimmy and Ben were arguing. She heard Ben ask, "What's this about?"

Jodi wondered what she had walked in on, but kept her mouth shut. Jimmy had been acting more volatile towards both his brother and her.

"Here's our next job," Jimmy announced. No discussion. No vote. It was his way. "I got to thinking about that picture of the kid you're so interested in." He looked directly at Jodi.

She straightened. "What are you talking about?"

"I did a little snooping of my own. You didn't tell us that the kid belonged to the doctor at that clinic. There could be a profit here if we play our cards right."

"Now, what are you concocting in that head of yours?" Ben asked.

"It should be an easy job. Kidnapping always looks easy in the movies, right?"

"Yeah, I guess. But they almost always get caught in the movies, too. And I won't hurt a kid," Ben said.

"Calm down. I don't want to hurt her, Jimmy said. "There'd be no money in if she was dead."

Jodi put her hand over her mouth to block the sound of her shocked gasp. Kill or hurt Emma? She couldn't think of it.

She'd never win a mother of the year award. But giving her baby away had been the right thing to do. It was more about not having the means to support herself, let alone a baby back then. After all, she wasn't heartless. She knew Emma had a wonderful life with the doctor.

Jodi spoke up. "What are you saying?"

"I'm saying I'm pretty sure the doctor would pay a nice tidy sum to get her kid back. Simple job. I cased the place again. That side entrance door doesn't shut quickly. We stand to the side and wait until someone exits and we're in. We grab the kid. Around noon, when they're all taking breaks for lunch. We will be in and out of there before anyone notices."

Ben stood, slammed the chair he'd been sitting in up to the table. He shook his head at his brother. "I'm done. Enough of your bullshit. I'm going home."

"Yeah? How you gonna get there? I have the keys to the car."

"I'll hitchhike if I have to. I've gone along with you for too long, but no more."

Ben stalked over to the backpack in which he kept his clothes and few belongings. He swung it over his shoulder and walked out.

Jodi was alone with Jimmy. She needed to get out of this place, too. She could ask her grandmother if she could come live there for a while. No, for now, she needed to stay put so she could watch Jimmy.

When she'd found out she was pregnant, she'd crashed at a friend's place in Toledo. She had tried to save money from her job at the Dollar Store so she could go to the local community college for some business classes.

After giving birth, she experienced depression and questioned her decision to give her baby away more than once. She partied too much, which made saving money difficult. That was when she met Jimmy and Ben.

Jimmy always had a get-rich-quick idea. He could be a charmer. Now she questioned her decisions over the last three years.

She shook her head. "I'm going to bed." She didn't wait for a response before she walked away. She barely noticed the pain from the cut on her leg because she now felt sick. Her stomach churned from anxiety and fear.

Jimmy thought he was so smart. She didn't know if he realized there was a second door from the clinic into the daycare. And there was no way she would tell him. There was no way she would allow Jimmy to steal Emma.

Could she expose Jimmy without getting herself in trouble?

Chapter 20

By the time Kell picked her up on Saturday morning, Becca felt like she belonged in the land of the living again. Nothing a little, well, maybe a lot, of concealer and some caffeine couldn't fix.

Perhaps after she discussed Jodi with him, she could relax and enjoy their day.

"Good morning," Kell said after she opened her front door. "Ready to hit the road? I picked up your latte on my way out."

"Oh, thank you. That is perfect. You're spoiling me. Just a sec. I just need to give someone a hug and kiss before we head off."

He nodded. "Of course."

She raised her voice, "Emma, I'm leaving. Come give me a kiss goodbye."

Her daughter came skipping into the hall.

"Mommy, where are you going?"

"Kell and I are going to Cleveland."

"What's Cleveland? Can I go, too?" Emma looked between Becca and Kell.

Becca knelt down so she was at Emma's height. "Cleveland is a city. No, sweetie, not this time. This is for grown-ups. But tell you what, if you are a good girl for Gampa, I'll bring you a surprise."

"I like surprises," Emma said as she clapped her hands. "How will you know if I'm good?"

Becca laughed. "Gampa will let me know. Now, do I get a hug and a kiss?"

Emma gave Becca a big hug and kiss, then turned to Kell. "I need to give you a hug and a kiss, too."

Kell's eyes widened, but he covered his surprise and bent down so Emma could give him the hug and a kiss, too.

"Okay, we have to get going. Love you more than mac and cheese."

Emma giggled. "Bye, bye."

Once settled in his SUV, Becca said, "Thanks for humoring the hugs and kisses portion of the day."

He glanced over at her, shrugging. He dodged her statement. "She's a cute kid. I bet she keeps you on your toes."

Becca smiled. "She sure does. But I wouldn't trade a minute."

"Anything special you want to listen to?" Kell asked as he fiddled with the radio.

She looked over at him. "Actually, Kell, there's something I'd like to talk to you about."

"Uh oh. Should I be worried?"

"No." She sighed. "Sorry, I didn't intend for it to sound that way."

He shrugged. "All right. I'm all yours."

"It's sort of a complicated story."

Kell leaned back. "We've got about an hour ahead of us. Seems like a perfect time to talk."

Relieved, Becca inhaled deeply. As if by Kell listening to her concerns, it would be easier for her to tackle the situation. He had a calming presence. She exhaled and jumped into her story. "Yesterday, I had a surprise visit from Emma's birth mother."

He took his eyes off the road for a second so he could look directly at her. "At the clinic?"

"Yes, she feigned a health issue to get an appointment. When I walked into the examining room, I was completely surprised to see her there."

"I bet. Go on."

Becca relayed the unusual visit from Jodi. "Honestly, I don't know the girl well enough to trust her or not. My gut tells me to be cautious."

"I've always listened to my gut. Kept me alive more than a few times."

"My situation doesn't compare to the dire circumstances you must have been in over the years, but I am worried."

"What worries you?" Kell asked.

"I don't know exactly." She hesitated, sighed, then continued, "That's not true. My biggest fear is that she wants to take Emma back. There, I said it out loud."

She twisted her hands in her lap.

Kell reached across the center console and squeezed her hands. His touch gave her the courage to go on.

"I called a college friend who is an attorney in Cincinnati. Family law. I hope she'll be able to give me some legal advice. Just in case."

"Smart. What did she tell you?"

"I didn't reach her yet. Just her voicemail. I left a message."

He nodded. "Have you seen—"

"Her name is Jodi Riggs."

"Have you seen Jodi anywhere else in Lucky?"

"No." She shook her head. "Just her impromptu visit to the clinic."

"What did she want yesterday?"

"She wanted to see Emma."

He gave her a sharp look. "What did you do?"

Becca chewed on her bottom lip. "At first, I balked at even the thought. But then Jodi asked if there was any way she could see Emma without actually meeting her."

"That seems like an odd thing to ask."

She nodded. "I know. I thought the same thing. It was almost as if she knew there was the viewing window. But how could she know about it, right?"

Kell said nothing.

"Something else occurred to me later. Jodi commented about Emma's hair color even before I took her to the viewing window."

He straightened in his seat, and she noticed his hands tightened on the steering wheel. "She's been watching Emma."

"That's what I'm afraid might be true. Oh, I don't know what to think." She wrung her hands.

"Is she in town alone?"

"She has a boyfriend. She said they were planning on moving away."

"The birth father? I thought you told me he wasn't in the picture?"

"I did. I don't think the boyfriend is the father. My understanding is she had sex with a stranger in a bar. I'm not sure she even knows who the guy was."

"And you probably don't have a photo?" he asked. "Of Jodi, not the birth father." He winked.

His bit of odd humor made her smile. "Sorry, no. Neither."

He smiled then. It was a silly distraction. But she appreciated it. "Did she put an address down on the clinic paperwork?"

"Oh, I don't know. I didn't think of that. I'll check when we get back home."

He nodded. "And I'll talk to my deputies to see if they have noticed any strangers in town. But unless there is a crime committed, we really can't do anything," Kell said.

"All right. Thanks. I don't want to get the woman in trouble, but my first priority is protecting Emma. Just knowing that you know about the situation has helped to calm my nerves. I hope I'm not making a mountain out of a molehill." When Kell gave her a quizzical look, she rolled her eyes.

"Why is it when I'm stressed about something I resort to using my dad's old-fashioned words and sayings? It's not like I've used that expression ever before. But today it popped right out." She shook her head in both embarrassment and frustration. "You knew what I meant, right?"

"I did. And in this situation, I think we're better safe than sorry." He grinned, and she grinned back. He reached across the console and gave her hand a quick squeeze.

They spent the rest of the drive talking about songs and bands, which made sense given where they were going. They discussed contemporary music, but admittedly Kell was at a disadvantage, having been basically out of touch, more or less, for over a decade. He recognized the name of more country music artists than any other, thanks in part to his sister's contacts in Nashville.

Before they arrived at the Hall of Fame, they passed a cute bookshop.

"Hey, do we have time to make a quick stop?" Becca asked.

"Sure. Our entry time isn't until 11:15."

"If you don't mind, I'd like to pick up a book for Emma. Her surprise." Becca grinned.

She found, as usual, it very difficult to decide on just one book to buy. Becca loved books and wanted Emma to love them, too. She chose two; *I Love You as Big as Ohio* and *Sport: Ship Dog of the Great Lakes.*

The first was an age-appropriate read-aloud board book with charming rhyming text and featured favorite local landmarks such as the Rock & Roll Hall of Fame, which would be perfect.

The second would be a book for when Emma was a little older and could sit still for a longer story. But it was too tempting not to get the beautifully illustrated book which told the true story of a Newfoundland-retriever mix who lived the life of a ship dog.

Kell was waiting next to the check-out counter when Becca walked up to pay for the two books.

"What did you buy?" she asked when she stepped away from the counter and noticed he held a bag. Realizing it was none of her business. She quickly added, "Sorry, I didn't mean to pry."

He shook his head. "You didn't pry." He opened the bag and pulled out a stuffed gray kitty with big green eyes, very similar to Emmie. "I saw this and thought Emma might like it." He didn't look directly at Becca when he spoke.

Becca noticed his demeanor. Was he embarrassed?

She was at a loss for words. His sweet gesture touched her. But she didn't want to embarrass him further by making a big deal of it. Instead, she joked, "So this was your way around my no-pets rule?" When he cocked his head in confusion, she reminded him, "I told you no dog or cat."

He laughed. "Yes, you did. But this is a good alternative to a real animal, don't you think?"

"Yes, I do. Thank you, she'll love it."

"All right. Let's get going or we'll miss our entry time."

The staggered entry times made the Hall of Fame manageable, despite the crowd. They headed to Level 3, to the Signature Gallery first.

"I didn't realize how little I knew," Becca said.

"I know what you mean," Kell said. "Many of the newer artists are foreign to me."

When they passed The Garage on Level 2, Becca said, "Here's your chance. Want to try out an instrument? See if music flows in your veins like it does in Megan's?"

A loud guffaw from Kell was all the response she needed. But he still said, "That would be a hell no. Megan got all the musical ability in our family."

Becca laughed. "I'll be honest. I'm relieved you feel that way. I'd be afraid you would want me to jump in, and I can't play anything, and as my father likes to say, I can't carry a tune in a bucket."

Kell smiled. Reaching for her hand, he said, "Another one of your dad's old expressions?"

"Yep."

They'd stumbled into a friendly debate over who made a greater impact on rock and roll. Becca was pro-Elvis and Kell was pro-Beatles. Finally conceding that they each had valid points, they let the topic drop.

By the time they finished visiting the exhibits and made a stop in the museum store, it was almost five o'clock.

Their hope for decent weather didn't hold off Mother Nature's blast of lake effect ice and snow. A light snowfall on the drive turned wicked while they were inside. Through the expansive windows, they could see the heavy snow accumulating on the pavement outside.

"Looks like the weather turned worse while we were in here," Becca said, realizing how futile her comment was since Kell had two eyes and could see for himself that the wind was blowing much harder.

"Wait here. I'll pull the SUV up," Kell said at the exit doors.

"No, I don't mind the walk. It wasn't too far," Becca replied. They'd parked in a parking garage close by so at least they wouldn't need to scrape off the ice and snow. "As long as we don't turn into ice statues."

"I'm not making any promises." Kell chuckled. He turned to her and wrapped her scarf closer around her neck. "Ready?"

"Or not," she said and smiled when he took her hand before exiting.

The dark clouds made it feel like it was much later in the day. Once in his vehicle, Kell tuned in his two-way radio gadget, and they learned several of the roads were closed because of ice.

"Road conditions are worse than I thought." He turned toward her. "Between the power outages and the black ice, this could be a much longer ride home."

"I was thinking the same thing."

"If you'd rather, we could stay over at a hotel. We can start for home early tomorrow morning."

"That might be the safest decision. Let me call my dad to let him know we won't be home tonight."

He nodded, reached for a CD, and popped it in. "I Want to Hold Your Hand" came over the speakers.

She laughed. "You aren't going to let it drop, are you? I thought we agreed to disagree?"

"What? I'm just playing one of my CDs. If it happens to be the most iconic band, what can I say?"

"Hmph," she said as she folded her arms across her chest.

The visibility was terrible, but thankfully, there wasn't a lot of traffic downtown. If you were smart, you stayed home during the winter storm.

"Is there a hotel you prefer?" he asked.

"Not at all. I suppose someplace close. Or if you get reward points at one … I'm fine with whatever."

Kell pulled up to a hotel and parked under the porte cochere. He turned in his seat, so he faced her.

"I don't want to presume anything, and I certainly don't want you to feel pressured or uncomfortable. Should I get two rooms? Or one?" His voice deepened on the word one. "We can get a room with two beds," he quickly amended.

"Oh." Becca was so out of practice. Talk about awkward. "I'm not opposed to one room."

Was one room code for sex?

She wasn't sure how she felt about that. On the one hand, they had gotten much closer over the last several weeks. But would it be crossing a line since their relationship was still supposed to be for show only? If they slept together, what would that do to their actual relationship?

As they approached the front desk, Becca wondered if she should feel conspicuous as Kell checked them in. One night. No luggage.

But surely, they couldn't be the only people who got stranded by the winter storm. Besides, they were two consenting adults and could stay in one room if they felt like it.

Kell addressed the young man at the registration desk. "We'd like either two rooms or a room with two beds, please."

"Let me look," the man said. He typed on the computer keyboard. "Looks like between the weather and the two weddings, the only room we have available is a king."

Kell looked at Becca. He arched a brow and hoped she understood his nonverbal attempt to find out if the room situation was okay.

She nodded.

Their room was on the fourteenth floor, and the silence in the elevator on the way up had been torture. All conversation between them had evaporated, and they stood in awkward silence. It seemed absurd considering they had enjoyed a fun, relaxing day together.

Conspicuous? No. Nervous? Hell, yes. Especially when the door to their room closed with a loud clunk.

They stood mere feet from the king bed, and every thought in her head vanished.

As if he sensed her unease, he said, "Tell you what. Why don't we go back downstairs to the restaurant and get drinks and an early dinner? Talk about our day. Unwind, how does that sound?"

"It sounds perfect." She pointed to the bathroom. "I'm going to wash up and be right out." She knew she'd have to face being in the room with him later, but she had to admit to herself she was relieved for the brief reprieve.

As they approached the elevators to go down to the restaurant, she said, "Why don't we enjoy our dinner and let the night unfold naturally?" She tilted her head and smiled.

"Agreed," he replied.

Was that relief she heard in his voice? She chuckled to herself to think that her big, tough sheriff might be a little nervous, too.

As the elevator zipped past the ninth floor, Kell said, "Listen, I don't want you to read anything into the single room. There are no expectations on my part."

So did that mean he *wasn't* interested in having sex with her?

"I didn't," she said.

"Oh good. Like you said, let's enjoy our dinner."

"Sounds good." She smiled, determined to put the sex thoughts aside so they could have a relaxed meal.

Chapter 21

The restaurant wasn't busy, and the host seated them immediately in a cozy booth near a beautiful stone fireplace with a roaring fire. On the other side was a wall of windows to a beautiful inner courtyard.

Becca stared out the window. What a pretty sight. The ice had encased everything, and the snow glittered under the lights. It was a dreamy, magical scene.

She realized Kell had been saying something. "I'm sorry. The sight of the ice and snow is mesmerizingly pretty."

He followed her gaze. "Yes, amazing that something so beautiful can cause such damage."

She frowned. "Yes, true. But we aren't going to think of that. Are we?"

He grinned. "No, ma'am."

"Good. let's simply enjoy the beauty."

"Got it. Have you been able to use your phone?"

"I sent a text to my dad, but I'm not sure it went through."

"If you don't get a reply, I'll use the radio in my SUV to send a message to the station and ask one of the deputies to get in touch with him."

"Thank you."

"Would you like a glass of wine?"

"I would. Thanks."

"Your usual?"

She cocked her head. "You know my usual?"

"Well, you were drinking it at the Super Bowl party, and you've ordered it the few times we've been out. It isn't a big stretch to think it could be your usual."

She laughed. "I guess I'm predicable. Yes, that would be perfect."

"Nah, we like what we like."

Kell ordered their drinks.

The dinner that followed was good. Nothing fancy. He ordered a Cleveland favorite, a Polish Boy. The kielbasa sausage, topped with coleslaw, french fries, and barbecue sauce, which he said was tasty. She went with a lighter option, ordering a Caesar salad.

"Now, what about dessert?" Kell asked.

"I'd be willing to share something if you're interested."

The triple chocolate cheesecake they chose was delicious. She was so content, all warm and happy, with a full stomach. The snow and ice outdoors, forgotten for the moment. Becca felt much more relaxed on the elevator ride up than she had on the ride down. It might have been the two and a half glasses of Pinot Grigio, but she didn't care.

"Thank you for dinner," she said.

He nodded. "You're welcome. It's been years since I've had a Polish Boy."

She laughed. "That's one delicacy I've never had."

"Aw, you missed your chance."

"That's okay, my salad was tasty."

When they got to the room, she said, "If you don't mind, I think I'll take a quick shower. I'm glad I bought the Hall of Fame T-shirt. It'll make a great sleep shirt.

"No, course not, go right ahead."

She came out of the bathroom twenty minutes later and Kell had his coat on, waiting for her.

"Are you leaving?"

"I'm going to try the radio in my SUV. Want to check your phone to see if your text went through or if you have a message from your dad?"

"Oh, sure. I should have done it before I got in the shower. Sorry."

She went to her purse on the desk and pulled out her phone. "Yes, I got a message from my dad. He thinks the roads could be worse once we leave Cleveland, and not to worry, he'll take care of Emma tonight."

"Okay, great. I'll be back up in a few."

He needed to check in with his people at the station. But he felt antsy in the room. Earlier, he had given no thought to how he would deal with his night terrors. Part of him wondered if this was the right thing to do. One room?

It wasn't like they had a choice, unless they wanted to try another hotel.

He didn't want to scare Becca. As much as he wanted to get close to her, he didn't feel comfortable exposing her to his night terrors.

There was just one chair in the room and it looked uncomfortable, nothing like his recliner. Maybe he could get away with sitting up all night. Once she fell asleep, of course.

His deputies were managing the weather with no problems. It relieved him of worrying that he wasn't there to assist.

Back in the room, Becca was already curled on the bed. There was a movie on the TV screen. He wasn't sure she was actually watching it.

She lifted her head off the pillow. "Hey, are things okay in Lucky?" she asked. Her sleepy voice stirred his interest and his rapid heartbeat had nothing to do with the hike to and from his SUV.

He hung the damp coat over the desk chair and cleared the lump in his throat. "Everything is fine at home. I have faith that Gibs and the others can manage anything that happens tonight."

He sat on the end of the bed.

"Do you feel okay? You look flushed." She sat up and scrutinized his face. She didn't seem to notice that her T-shirt had crept up her thighs when she shifted on the bed.

"Did the food upset your stomach?"

"No, it's not that," he said.

"So, are you going to clue me in?" she asked, in her doctor voice.

He cleared his throat again. "My nightmares can be bad, and I don't want to frighten you in the night if I have one."

She put her hand over her heart. "Oh, Kell, please don't worry about it. First, I'm a doctor, but second, I'll understand if you have one. Maybe tonight will be the exception."

Kell looked at the TV screen. A guy was holding an old boombox over his head. "What's the deal with that guy?" Maybe he could distract himself with this movie.

"It's an old movie called *Say Anything*, and the guy is trying to win the girl. He's playing some song that must be significant. I don't remember all the details."

He shrugged. "Sounds sort of desperate."

"It's not desperate. It's romantic. Besides, there wasn't much on and I really like the actor."

"If you say so. I'm going to take a shower."

"There are robes in the bathroom if you don't want to put your clothes back on."

Did the woman not realize what she was doing to his self-control? Not only was he battling to keep his shit together, so he didn't scare her with one of his frequent nightmares, but he was also trying not to think about how sexy she looked on the bed with her long legs on display.

He tugged at the restrictive zipper of his jeans. She must have noticed his discomfort.

"Oh, God." She put her hand to her cheek. "That came out wrong. I didn't mean to suggest anything." She pushed herself up, and the T-shirt inched up a tad more. Now it was her turn to blush. A pretty pink spread up her neck.

"I'll be back in a few minutes." He went into the bathroom and closed the door. He took a quick, efficient, albeit cold shower, skipping the robe in favor of just his boxer briefs.

He returned to the main room to find Becca had fallen asleep. She was curled up, perfect for spooning. Her hand sandwiched between her cheek and the pillow.

Stop thinking about spooning, or how sexy she looked, or any other dangerous thoughts.

She looked like an angel. Then he chuckled when he heard the soft, endearing snores. The two glasses of wine must have done the trick.

He glanced at the uncomfortable chair in the corner, then back at the inviting bed, and opted for comfort over caution.

He took the opposite side of the bed, sitting against the headboard and pillows. He lowered the volume on the TV, but channel surfed until he found one of the news networks.

The clock on the bedside table only read eight-thirty. Shit, he had a long night ahead. He wished he had something to read to keep him company through the night, but because this was an impromptu stay, he only had the room service menu and a magazine about Cleveland to read.

Normally, he could zone in on something or zone out, depending on the situation. But he was finding it difficult to ignore the sweet sounds coming from Becca's side of the bed. He punched the pillows behind him and settled in for the long night ahead.

Becca startled awake. It took her a few seconds to acclimate to her surroundings. Hotel. Cleveland. Kell.

But it seemed like the bed was moving or more like the guy on the bed next to her was moving, more like thrashing and muttering.

She sat up and tried to wake him. "Kell, you're having a nightmare." She shook him as much as she dared because he was agitated. She realized trying to shake him awake could be dangerous but also futile. Instead, she spoke in a soothing voice.

"Kell, it's Becca. We're in Cleveland. There was a big winter storm. We stayed over in a hotel."

His muttering was nearly incoherent. She caught only a few words. "No. Sniper fire. Get down. Leaks."

She continued to speak in a soothing tone. Suddenly, he bolted up, breathing heavily. "Oh, fuck. Did I hurt you?"

"No, Kell, you didn't hurt me. Are you okay?" Without thinking, she put her fingers on his neck to check his pulse. After, she said, "Take a couple deep breaths. Can I get you a drink of water?"

He shook his head, then hopped off the bed and disappeared into the bathroom.

She followed him in time to see him splash water on his face. He grabbed a hand towel and turned toward her. "Sorry about that," he said with a chagrined expression.

She crossed the small space. "Don't be sorry. Or embarrassed. You can't help it." She reached up and brushed her hand across his whiskered cheek. Holding it there long enough for him to cover her hand with his.

"I sit up most nights in my faithful old recliner to avoid this happening." He shrugged.

She noticed the tacit intimacy of their hands and quickly snatched hers back.

Using her professional doctor's voice, she said, "You probably already know this, but the risk of having sleep terrors and nightmares increases with stress, sleep deprivation and fatigue. I bet not getting a good night's sleep because you're sitting up in a chair isn't helping your overall health."

He didn't reply.

"I'm sorry. The doctor in me can't help dispensing advice."

"Understandable."

She took his response as a green light to continue. "And stress can't be good. I'm sure your job as sheriff isn't helping. But I really think seeing Sam regularly will help, and the nightmares will become less frequent."

"You may be right. Thanks. You know you're quite commanding when you're in your doctor mode."

"Commanding, huh? Is that a nice way of saying I'm bossy?"

"Your word, not mine." All signs of vulnerability seemed to be gone. Slowly, he leaned toward her, and moved his head even closer to hers, whispering, "So, does the doctor think a distraction would help me shake off the nightmare?"

His attractive, self-confident sexual magnetism was firmly back in place as he moved even closer until he was mere inches from her lips. A long dormant feeling, a tingling in the pit of her stomach, woke and a delicious shudder heated her body.

Despite her body's reactions to Kell, she needed to be careful. This fake relationship had gotten complicated. She couldn't decipher what was real and what was for show.

As if he read her mind, he said, "I've wanted to get closer to you for a while. But I've been struggling with this, given our situation.

She sighed. "Me too."

He seemed to think about her response for a few seconds, then gently touched her cheek and said, "Tell me no. Tell me you aren't interested in more. Tell me you don't feel the same and I will step back and sit my ass in that chair in the corner of the room for the rest of the night."

She whispered, "I can't." Her desire for him overrode everything else at that moment. She told her usual practical self to shut it but couldn't resist asking, "So, the chemistry between us hasn't been fake?"

"Not on my end."

Simultaneously, they both realized they were standing in the bathroom wearing very few clothes. He, in only his boxer briefs, which did little to hide his attraction to her, and she, in only the T-shirt and panties. His gaze raked down her slowly.

She couldn't resist him any longer. She lifted her face to meet his and wrapped her arms around his neck and placed a perfectly languid kiss on his mouth.

He must have taken her actions as a green light and deepened the kiss.

Finally, he pulled away. "Let's move this out of the bathroom."

He didn't wait for her to respond. He lifted her up in his arms and carried her to the edge of the bed. She giggled. "Oh, how Bridgerton of you."

"I have no idea what that means, but I hope it is a good thing," he said.

"Oh, yes, very good."

"Well, good." Then he tossed her onto the bed and joined her.

Becca didn't waste time. She pulled him close and touched his chest and smiled at his intake of breath. Exploring his upper body, admiring his broad shoulders, muscled arms, and wide, hair-roughened chest, she traced the tattoo on his arm, momentarily intrigued by the intricate Celtic design.

He placed his hands on her waist and drew the T-shirt up and over her head. The look of appreciation in his eyes and his gentle touch as he circled each breast with his finger vanquished any lingering doubts or fears about their relationship, faux or real.

Feeling bolder, she ached to explore more of his body with her lips and mouth. She kissed his right shoulder blade, then slowly moved down his chest, leaving a trail of kisses.

His springy chest hairs tickled her nose as she progressed to the path of darker hair that disappeared beneath his boxer briefs.

She paused her exploration when he tensed beneath her touch. Suddenly, Kell flipped her onto her back.

"My turn," he said. His voice was thick with arousal.

Kell watched as the light played across Becca's pale breasts. He replaced his hands and fingers with his mouth, kissing one breast, then the other, sucking and licking her nipples until he felt her squirm beneath him. From her breasts to her collarbone, then to her cheeks, a beautiful pink color crept over her.

"Feel good?"

"God, yes."

She moaned and pulled his head up from her breasts to her mouth for a kiss. She swirled her tongue with his and threaded her fingers through his hair. He slid his mouth along her jawline, then gently traced his tongue along the curve below her ear. The throbbing of her heartbeat encouraged him.

He took his time making his way down her body with a definite goal in mind. He stopped when he got to her pretty pink underpants, caressing the skin along the rim. She whimpered and squirmed. He slowly scooted them down her legs, like he was unwrapping a present.

He put his mouth on her, sucking and licking, swirling his tongue until she was straining upward toward his mouth.

"I need you now. Please," she whispered.

She released a small whimper when he scooted away to grab his wallet on the nightstand. But he suited up quickly and moved back to her.

She gasped when his bare chest blanketed hers, and she arched to meet his body.

"Is this good, or would you like to be on top?"

"This is perfect. Next time we'll switch places."

He chuckled. "I like the way you think."

Then he lined up and pressed into her. She was wet and snug. She felt fucking fantastic.

She responded by raising her hips as if she wanted to get even closer, and they found their rhythm.

He propped himself up with his arms on either side of her head, enjoying the pleasure on her face.

Kell knew he wouldn't last long, so he wanted to make it good for Becca. He let his arms relax simultaneously as he dipped his head and kissed her lips. She exhaled and made a sound, something between a squeak and a moan, when his chest touched her breasts again. She wrapped her arms around his back and held him tight against her.

She came first, crying out with her release. He followed seconds later.

He rolled off her, and they lay silent, side-by-side for a minute, catching their breath.

Finally she said, "Wow."

"Yeah, wow," he said.

"I'll be right back." He disposed of the condom in the bathroom. When he returned to the bed, he lay beside her, wrapping his arms around her, and she snuggled into him, nuzzling her face against his throat. Holding her close felt so good.

They lay like that for a while until she finally broke the silence by asking, "Is that scar on your thigh from when your friend died?"

He tensed at the mention of Leaks. That was the last thing he wanted to think about. But he answered, "Yeah, it is."

She kissed her forefinger and placed it on the scar. Her sweet action touched something inside Kell.

He hadn't felt this relaxed in years and he wasn't just thinking of the sex, though that certainly helped. He'd gradually been feeling... what? Good about life? He hadn't felt that way since before Leak's death. Before that, he'd been a cocky and headstrong young man. Before the horrors of war had stained him.

Even after he returned home, he was still on edge, his PTSD still a constant in his life. But he was facing his demons. He had to credit Becca for this change in his attitude. Whether he wanted it, he was falling for Becca.

Kell was on patrol, bouncing along the streets in the Humvee.

He watched as a burqa-clad woman walked through the Marketplace. Her arms were full, laden with her purchases, and she was holding a child's hand.

Out of nowhere, a rusted-out Corolla zoomed past the woman, stopping on the side of the road not ten feet in front of her and blocked the bus stop.

The hairs on the back of his neck prickled, warning him of impending danger. His sixth sense had kept him alive so far, so he wasn't about to ignore it.

Seconds later, a bus pulled up behind the car, and an Afghan man jumped out of the car and sprinted in the opposite direction down the street.

Kell was still too far away when the car exploded. The bus and the people on it, other surrounding vehicles and buildings, took the brunt of the blast. The smoke and fire engulfed the area. He could hear the heart-wrenching cries of pain and anguish.

He ran toward the flames and wreckage.

He saw the woman and her child lying motionless in the street. He ran to them.

He felt uneasy. Something was off. Something was different.

When he knelt to check for a pulse, it wasn't the Afghan woman lying there, instead it was Becca. It was Becca's blue eyes that stared blankly up at him, and the child beside her was Emma.

Kell jolted awake. A cold sweat drenched his body. "Holy fuck."

Chapter 22

Kell couldn't go back to sleep, not after the shock of seeing that Becca and Emma had replaced the Afghan woman and her child in his nightmare. He'd allowed himself to get too close to them. The nightmare reiterated his fears. He wouldn't be able to protect them.

He got the connection with Becca, but not with Emma.

What the hell was that about?

Kell couldn't get on the road soon enough. He used the excuse that he needed to get back to Lucky to check on things after the snow and ice storm. They were out of the hotel by nine-thirty.

He dreaded the inevitable awkwardness that he knew would come on the long drive home. If Becca sensed his mood, she hid it well. Their conversation was stilted. Luckily for him, before he knew it, her head rested against her window. Wisps of her hair moved in rhythm to those soft, irresistible snores.

He ached to reach across and touch Becca, to tuck the loose strands behind her ear like he'd seen her do a dozen times. Instead, he clenched the steering wheel and tried to concentrate on something else. He switched to a daily news podcast he liked to listen to when he had the time.

He might as well have turned it off, because his mind continued to circle back to the significance of his nightmare.

❦

Becca couldn't put her finger on it, but something was off. On the drive home, he didn't seem to want to talk. After a couple tries without him engaging, Becca fell asleep.

Becca is with Jodi, in one of the examining rooms in her clinic. Jodi is making a list of things she remembers about the man she had sex with... the man who is Emma's dad.

Military. A head taller. Cool tattoo. Bandage on his thigh. Hot.

"She didn't get her red hair from my side of the family."

Megan's Mini-me,

Suddenly her dream switches and she's now in a bar. She blinks in confusion. The music is blasting above the rumble of conversations happening all around her. Jodi appears. She is dancing with a man. His back is to Becca. Jodi whispers something in his ear, and the two walk toward the back of the bar. The man stops, turns, and looks directly at Becca.

She gasps. It's Kell.

Kell woke her when he pulled into her dad's driveway. "Time to wake up."

She blinked and shook her head. She took a second to ground herself back into reality. "Oh, I'm sorry I fell asleep. One minute I was listening to Lady Gaga and the next I was out. I'm a terrible co-pilot."

"Nah. It was fine. Are you okay?"

She nodded. "Sure. I just had a bizarre dream." She would think about it later.

They'd shared a fun day together, culminating with awesome sex.

Had the sex been a mistake? Had they crossed a line? Was he one of those guys who ran after the intimacy of sex? Too many questions were jumping around in her head. Well, they had been kinda vague about interpreting how they each felt.

It wasn't as if they'd been dating a long time and she little to compare to, but the few previous times he brought her home, he'd walked her to the door. Had that been for show, because this morning he opened her car door, and gave her a quick kiss on the cheek. "It was a fun weekend."

"Yes, it was," she said.

"Well, I better get to the station and see if I have any disasters to clean up."

"Sure, of course. Thank you."

She turned to go inside, but just as she reached the stoop she heard, "Beatles, Babe."

Normally, his flippant tease would've amused her, but she couldn't shake the feeling that something was off between them.

But her preoccupation with Kell disappeared as soon as she opened the door and heard, "Mommy, Mommy, you're home."

Becca didn't deserve to be a victim of his living nightmare. He shouldn't have gotten involved with her to begin with, even for a fake relationship. Sure, it had been successful getting Mom off his back. But at what cost?

His feelings for Becca had been growing. But having sex might have been a mistake, giving her the impression that there could be more between them. It wasn't fair to her. His nightmare was proof that he'd allowed himself to get too close.

You can't protect them.

He drove straight to Chase's place, hoping Chase had the day off. His sister answered the door.

"Hey, big brother, when did you get back into town?"

Kell raised a brow. "How'd you know we didn't get back last night?"

"Oh, you poor man, you have no idea how fast gossip flies in our small town, even in a snowstorm." She laughed. "Maybe Chase talked to one of the men on shift last night, who talked to Paul, who you contacted. Or maybe I spoke to Harper at the Gas & Go last night and he told me you were staying overnight."

Kell nodded. "Got it. I just dropped Becca off a few minutes ago. Is Chase around?"

"Yep, he's out back, shoveling a path for Brady. Go through the kitchen and out the garage door."

"Thanks." He headed that way when Megan stopped him.

"Kell, is everything all right?" He could see the concern etched on his sister's face.

"Yeah, I just need to talk to Chase about something."

"Okay, I'm going up to get dressed. I'll be back down in a few. Did you eat breakfast?"

"Just coffee, but I'm fine."

"All right, let me know if you need anything."

"Sure thing." Kell headed toward the kitchen.

Chase looked up when he saw Kell come outside. "Hey, man."

"Hey, do you have a few minutes?"

Chase gave Kell a sharp look. "Sure. Everything okay?" Before Kell could answer, Chase led the way back into the house. "Give me a sec to wipe off Brady's paws. Go sit." He pointed to the living room. Brady trotted off before Chase caught him by his collar. "Whoa, boy. Not you. You stay. Kell sit."

"You're hilarious." Kell shook his head as he walked into the living room.

Chase joined a few minutes later. "Okay, so what's going on?"

Kell rubbed his hands on his knees. Now that he was here, he wasn't a hundred percent sure what he wanted from Chase.

"Nothing. I should go." He stood.

"Kell, clearly something is bothering you. Talk to me, man."

"I fucked up." When Chase remained silent. Kell felt compelled to continue. "You know Becca and I went to Cleveland. We couldn't get back last night, so we stayed at a hotel downtown."

"Yeah, I know," Chase said.

Kell frowned. "We had sex."

"And that's a bad thing?"

Sighing, Kell said, "Yes... No... I don't know." He stood up, then abruptly sat back down.

"Exactly what are you trying to say?"

Kell put his head in his hands. "I've fucked everything up. This whole fake relationship deal has backfired on me. While we were pretending to date, I got too close to both Becca and Emma. I care about them. I did exactly what I told my mom I didn't want to do."

"Well, you like her, right? What's wrong with spending time with someone you like?" Chase asked.

"Because I can't protect them."

"From what? Kell, this isn't Afghanistan."

How could he explain the nightmare without Chase thinking Kell had lost it? Maybe he had lost it. "I saw Becca and Emma lying on the ground. They were dead."

Chase straightened. "What the hell? What are you talking about?"

"In a nightmare. I've had the same fucking one, over and over. I had it again last night. In it, I relive something that happened over there. A car bomb exploded, and it killed many people in the immediate area. A young Afghan woman and her child were the first victims I found. They were lying on the ground, their dead eyes stared up at me. But last night, I saw Becca and Emma lying there."

"That's messed up, man," Chase said.

"No shit," Kell snapped. But immediately felt bad. Chase was only trying to understand. "Sorry."

Brady must have sensed something because he moved in between Kell's legs and laid his head on Kell's thigh. "Good boy," Kell said as he ruffled Brady's fur.

When he looked up, Megan had returned. She gave her brother a scrutinizing look. "What's wrong? Did something happen? Is Becca all right?"

Chase shrugged, then said, "You know she'll figure it out... eventually. You should hear what your sister thinks. You know, get a woman's perspective."

"Yes, you need to listen to your sister," Megan said. "Actually, you look like you need a hug or a drink, or both."

He cocked his head. "Since it's too early for that drink, even for me, I'll take the hug."

She obliged. "Now can I help? Talk."

Kell repeated what he'd just told Chase.

Megan listened. Finally, she asked, "Why do you think you feel this way about Becca and Emma? Why not Mom or me? Or Chase?"

Kell didn't have an answer.

"You're my big brother and I have always admired and looked up to you. I'm so proud of you."

"Why do I think there is a *but* coming?" Kell said.

"But sometimes you can be a real dumbass."

"Gee thanks," Kell said, "Very helpful."

"Life is short. You know that probably better than any of us. Sadly, you've seen far more than your share of death and the evil in the world. But there is also so much good, too. You just have to open yourself up to it. Let yourself love and be loved."

Kell didn't say anything, so Megan continued, "I think you aren't giving Becca enough credit. The woman I've gotten to know over the last year is understanding and compassionate. You need to talk to her. Explain to her what your fears are, but I also think you need to consider the implications of having a genuine relationship with Becca. Emma is part of the package."

"Thanks, You're probably right."

"I know I'm right." She grinned.

He nodded. "Okay, I'll think about everything you said."

The three of them stood. Megan gave her brother a hug. "I love you, big brother. She took Chase's hand to bring him into the hug. "We just want you to be happy."

When Kell was getting into his SUV, he caught sight of the brightly colored bag from the bookstore, half hidden under the seat. He picked it up and took the stuffed kitty out. Kell stared at the toy for a long second before putting it back in the bag.

He really had a lot to think about.

Kell spotted the blue MINI Cooper parked in his spot next to the back door of Espresso Yourself.

My day just gets better and better.

After so many years in the military, recon was second nature to him, so he peeked into the cafe to locate his mom. He didn't see her. So that left only one place.

Yep, better and better.

The door to his studio was unlocked. Funny, he didn't remember giving her a key. Sure enough, she sat at his small kitchen table, drumming her fingers. As soon as she saw him come in, she frowned.

Before he could remove his coat, she jumped up. "How could you?"

"Mom, I just got back from Cleveland. I have no idea what you're upset about."

"I'll tell you what I'm upset about. How could you?"

Still unclear. Kell scrubbed his hand over his face and threw his coat over the back of one of the kitchen chairs.

"Mom, I love you, but I've got a headache and I'm beat. Is there any way you can cut to the chase?"

"You've been faking your relationship with Becca."

Since it was a statement and not a question, Kell figured she'd gotten her information from a reliable source. Why deny it? "How'd you find out?"

"So, it's true?"

"Look Mom, after all your attempts to meddle in my personal life, I thought the only way to get you to back off was to create a scenario that you'd be happy about."

"You make me sound awful."

"No, you aren't awful, but you took your determination to have me married with kids too far."

"But faking a girlfriend? Really, Kell?"

"It was survival."

His mother was quiet for a moment, then she began to cry. He hated tears, especially from his mom.

"So, you came up with this plan to have a fake girlfriend instead of being honest with me?"

"Mom, I tried being honest. Many times, in fact. You just didn't listen."

She thought about it, and finally she said, "I'm sorry, Kell. I should have listened to what you wanted. I can't believe you had to get a fake girlfriend."

He wrapped his arms around her and drew her into a hug. "Mom, I know you mean well. But you have to let me find my own way."

She nodded. "All right, I'll do my very best to stay out of your affairs."

"Thank you."

After his mom left, it occurred to him that this might not be the time to tell her what a clusterfuck he'd made of his relationship with Becca.

Chapter 23

Becca hadn't heard from Kell all week. Since she had believed things were going well, she was all mixed up, and honestly, feeling hurt. Having sex had been a mistake.

Obviously, Kell hadn't been ready. It was probably best to end things now before Emma got even more attached to him.

However, if she were being honest with herself, the distance he was keeping had given her the time she needed to consider the dream she had on the drive home. All the seemingly inconsequential things added up to a big possibility. Could Kell be the mysterious man from the bar? Is he Emma's father? For the time being she would keep her suspicions to herself.

After all, it was only a dream.

Talk about complications.

On the morning of the blood drive, Becca arrived at the fire station at eight-thirty. They set the blood drive schedule from nine to four. She helped Chase and the other volunteers set up the small conference room. The Red Cross representative was already on hand supervising.

Being a doctor, Becca knew how important blood drives were, and she always tried to volunteer if her schedule allowed it. The conference room was already full, but it was great to see the community getting involved. It didn't surprise her that people stepped up in a small town like Lucky.

At noon, Kell stopped by to give his blood. Becca figured she might as well get the awkwardness out of the way, so she set aside her hurt and approached him.

"Hi, Kell. There's a spot open at the end of the row." She pointed.

He nodded. "Thanks." He took a step toward the spot she had pointed to, then stopped. He turned to face her.

No, that wasn't awkward at all.

"Hey, do you have a minute?"

She checked her watch. "That's probably all I have." She would not make this easy on him. But she wanted to know what the hell was going on.

"Let's go to Chase's office."

"All right." She followed him.

When they were both in the office, he said, "Listen, I need to tell you something ..."

"I'm listening," she said. But she kept her arms folded tightly over her chest.

"I owe you an apology. I'd like to explain why I went MIA on you this week."

"All right," she said.

"I had a nightmare after we had sex on Saturday night."

"Another one?"

"Yes, and it ... well, it shook me up. Much worse than any I've had in the past."

She opened her mouth to tell him she was sorry, but that wasn't a good enough reason to blow her off for days. He held up his hand to stop her.

"It's a recurring nightmare which recounts a real incident from when I was on patrol. It's always the same. I have to watch the scene unfold like it is happening again and again.

"At a bus stop, a car bomb detonates, resulting in the death of an Afghan woman and her child. I try to reach her to warn her, but before I can the car explodes. My nightmare is so vivid. Her dead eyes stare up at me. Her child lies lifeless beside her." He shudders.

Well, shit. How was she supposed to hold a grudge after that story? "That's awful, Kell, I'm so sorry." She reached out for his hand. "I wish you had told me you had another nightmare. I understand you need some space."

He shook his head. "No, you don't understand. This time, it wasn't a stranger in the nightmare. It was you and Emma. You were both dead. I couldn't get to you in time. I couldn't save you."

She gasped and put her hand over her mouth. "Oh, Kell. I'm sorry. What a horrific experience."

He scraped his hand over his face.

"So, I pulled back. It's obvious that I've allowed myself to get too close to you and Emma. I care. And I can't afford to care."

Becca considered what he said. "So, do you think by staying away it will help you not to care about us?"

"Well, that's the thing. It didn't help. I miss you. I'd gotten used to seeing you regularly. Spending time with both you and Emma."

She blinked a few times and nodded. "You miss us, but you can't let yourself get involved? Is that right?"

"Yes." He reached for her hand. "No. Shit, I don't know. I haven't been in a real relationship since before my tours."

Someone knocked on the door. "Excuse me. Doctor James, you're needed in the other room." Becca pulled her hand away. "We'll have to talk later." She left him standing there.

If he is this freaked out now, how will he be if he believes he's a dad?

A few minutes later, he came back to the conference room and took his seat for the blood draw.

By three-thirty, she was ready for the blood drive to end. Sara Davis had called, and she hadn't been able to take the call. She wanted to hear what her friend had to say. Four o'clock couldn't come soon enough.

She was wrapping things up and looking over the paperwork from the day when she saw Kell's name. His blood type immediately jumped out at her. AB- That was one of the rarest types. It caught her attention because Emma had the same rare type.

As a doctor, she knew the reasons for knowing your child's blood type. In case of potential emergencies, it could speed up a search for a suitable donor for a blood transfusion. Using the wrong type could be fatal. Certain blood types were also at higher risk for particular illnesses.

She was still thinking about Kell and Emma having the same blood type as she was walking back to the clinic because she still needed to look over the charts for the next day's patients before heading home.

That Kell and Emma shared the same rare blood type had to be a coincidence. Right? Or not?

Emma looks so much like Megan did at the same age. Another coincidence, right?

It was silly, but the pacifier story popped into her mind.

Becca considered the times she had seen Kell with Emma. For a guy who said he wasn't comfortable around kids, he'd been a natural with her. Emma seemed quite taken by him.

She thought about last week when the two of them ate popcorn next to one another on the sofa. They looked like two peas in a pod.

Oh God, there was no way Kell could be Emma's birth father. Was there? No way! He wasn't even in the country then. It's all just a big quirk of fate. But what if it is true? How will he feel? He doesn't want kids. Or would this change his mind?

Oh God.

She was passing Joe's Grill when she spotted Jodi crossing the street.

She called out to her, "Jodi." The young woman stopped and turned.

"Hi, Doctor James."

"I thought you planned to leave town?"

"Yeah, in a few days. I'm on my way to the library."

"Oh, that's a bit of a walk from here."

"I like to walk."

"How's your leg?"

"Oh, fine. The medicine you gave me has helped. It's pretty much healed, and it doesn't bother me at all."

Becca nodded. "Good. Glad it helped. Listen, Jodi, I have a question I hope you'll be able to answer."

"Okay."

Do I really want to open this door?

"I'm wondering about Emma's birth father. I don't remember everything you told me about him. And I thought since you and your boyfriend are moving away, it might be my only opportunity to learn about the man. You know, in case Emma has questions someday."

"Sure. Umm, I don't know what to tell you."

"Anything you can remember would be helpful.

"He was taller than me." She held her hand up, at least twelve inches above her head. "Like maybe this tall. I told you I figured Emma's red hair came from him. Not me."

"That's right. I remember you saying that. Any distinguishing marks?"

Jodi gave Becca a funny look. "Like what?"

"Oh, I don't know, like a birthmark or a tattoo or scars?"

Jodi squinted as she thought about the question. "Yep, I believe he had a cool tattoo, and he had a bandage on his thigh."

Becca blew out the breath she was holding. "His right thigh?"

"I'm sorry, I just don't remember. I thought it was kinda cool. He'd been shot and was on medical leave at home. I think he was pretty messed up. He was already at the bar before we got there. I told you he was a Marine, right? Wounded over in Afghanistan."

Becca stepped back. Dizziness engulfed her and the buzzing in her ears kept her from hearing the end of Jodi's sentence.

A Marine. Wounded. Afghanistan. It couldn't be possible. Could it?

"Dr. James, you don't look so good."

Becca didn't answer Jodi. Instead, she reached into the pocket of her coat and removed her phone. She opened up the photo app and scrolled to the photos she'd taken at the Rock and Roll Hall of Fame. There was a photo of Kell in front of a Beatles mural. She held the phone so Jodi could see it.

"Is this the man?" she asked with a shaky hand and a trembling voice.

Jodi squinted at the photo. She pulled the phone closer. "Well, I wasn't exactly sober that night. But it looks like what I remembered him looking like. Does that make sense? I remember thinking he was hot. and this guy is hot."

Becca gasped for air. Kell was Emma's father. Oh my God, what was she going to do?

She jumped when the phone rang in her hand. She looked down at the screen and saw her friend Sara's face.

"I have to take this call." She walked away without even saying goodbye.

"Hi Sara," she answered the call with a shaky voice.

"Hey, girlfriend, you don't sound like yourself. Everything okay?"

Becca inhaled deeply, exhaled, and said, "Yeah, I'm just walking back to the clinic and the air is cold, so I'm walking as fast as I can. Can I call you in five minutes when I'm in my office?"

"Of course."

"Okay, thanks. I'll call you right back."

"Sounds good. I'm free for another fifteen minutes, then I'm due in a meeting."

"Gotcha. Bye."

Becca didn't bother hanging up her coat. She threw it on the guest chair in the corner after closing her office door. She sat at her desk and called her friend.

"Sara, I think I know who Emma's birth father is."

"I thought he wasn't in the picture."

"He wasn't. My initial worry, the reason I reached out to you, was about the birth mother showing up unexpectedly. But now I have pretty convincing proof of who the father is. Becca didn't realize the volume of her voice was increasing as she spoke.

"Becca, you need to calm down. You're jumping ahead of yourself at this point. Take a few deep breaths. First, if it's only a very strong suspicion, we'd need to do a paternity test. Why do you think you know who it is?"

Becca inhaled and exhaled deeply. "Okay, I'll back up. I ran into the birth mother earlier, and I showed her a photo of the man I suspected was the birth father. She said it looks like the guy. Her memory is a little fuzzy because she was drunk."

"Wait, you have a photo of the guy?"

"The guy is Kell Howard. The local sheriff." *Who I just happened to sleep with last weekend.*

"Are you in a relationship with this man?"

"That's complicated."

"How so?"

"I agreed to be his fake girlfriend to get his mother off his back about getting married and starting a family."

"Okaaaay, I'm sure there's a backstory there, but for now, what did you get from this arrangement?"

"He's been doing a lot of work at my house."

"So, he's your fake boyfriend?"

"That's where it gets complicated. We're attracted to each other, and we went to Cleveland last weekend and there was an ice storm —"

"You had sex!"

Becca rubbed her forehead with her thumb and forefinger. "Yes," she whispered. *As if anyone can hear you!*

Sara's sigh was audible over the phone.

"The friend in me says, get it, girl. But as a lawyer, I need to ask, how do you think he'll take this news?"

"I don't know. He has said, repeatedly, that he doesn't want kids. In fact, he has said he doesn't want a wife, either. That's why he needed a fake girlfriend. But that was before. If he knew Emma was his child, would he change his mind? What if he decides he wants custody? Or his mother. She's a piece of work. I really wouldn't put anything past her."

Becca realized she needed to slow down and take a breath before she hyperventilated. She missed what Sara had just said. "I'm sorry. What did you say?" She refocused on the conversation with her friend.

Sara said, "Let's back up. So you're saying he has never shown an interest in being a father?"

"No. He doesn't want to bring a child into this 'crazy world' — his words, not mine."

"Well, honey, if your suspicion proves to be true, that ship has sailed."

"True."

"So, is this a bad thing? Has he done anything that would make you truly believe he's a threat?"

"No, not really."

"You need to talk to him. He has the right to know."

"You're right. But not yet. I need some time to wrap my brain around the information."

"Becca, you really should talk to him as soon as possible before he finds out from someone else."

"That's not possible. No one else knows."

Dealing with birth father rights can be tricky. It depends on each situation. Failure to inform the birth father about the baby violates his rights.

"I understand. But my first and only concern is to protect Emma."

"I get it. Listen, I hate to leave you hanging, but I need to get to my meeting. Let me know if you need my legal help. If you want me there, I can catch a flight, and you know I always have a shoulder available for you to lean on."

"Thanks, Sara. You're the best. Miss you."

"Miss you, too."

"Love you, bye," they said in unison as they'd done dozens of times over the years.

It was a long time before Becca could concentrate on her patient files.

After supper that night, Dad took his plate over to Becca, who was loading the dishwasher.

"Thanks," she said.

"Thank you for picking up my favorite pie."

She smiled. "Of course. Maybe someday I will be able to actually make you a homemade pie."

He laughed. "Maybe. So, are you going to tell me what's bothering you. You've been unusually quiet, and you're tense."

"I'm fine. What makes you think I'm tense?"

"Oh, I don't know. Maybe the fact that you're clenching that dish so tight, I'm afraid it will break in two."

She looked at the dish in her hand and blew out a breath. Her dad knew her so well.

"There is something I need to talk with you about." She set the plate down. "Let me make sure Emma is in her room," she said as she set the plate down, "Little ears..."

She returned a few minutes later. "Can we sit? Do you want a drink?"

He frowned and sat down. "Do I need a drink? Should I be concerned? Are you okay?" Her father's voice didn't have its usual calm tone.

"Yes, I'm fine. I found something out today." Her dad sat with his hands folded on the table. Waiting patiently. She took the seat across from him.

"Remember when Emma's birth mother came to the clinic?"

He nodded. "Yes. Did you get some bad news from Sara?"

"No, not quite." Now he gave her a quizzical look.

"Oh, crap." She stood up and paced the small space between the kitchen table and counter. Sighing deeply, she said, "I'll just say it. I think Kell is Emma's biological father."

She'd give Dad credit. When he spoke, it was in his calm doctor's tone.

"What? Really?"

She nodded.

"Well, that would be quite the coincidence. What makes you think so?" he said.

Becca stopped next to the table. "There have been silly little hints I've noticed over the last few months, but today at the blood drive I saw his blood type is the same as Emma's AB- which is rare."

"Honey, that's not conclusive. Without a paternity test —"

"I know. I know. But I had a dream."

Her dad arched a brow.

She held up her hand. "I know." Resuming her pacing, she counted things off on her fingers. First finger. "She's the spitting image of Megan at that age. Same hair. Same dimple. She's like a Megan Mini Me."

Second finger. "They have some of the same mannerisms. Like it was crazy watching them eating popcorn the other night. They popped it in their mouths, tilted their heads slightly to the right, and munched. It was a little freaky."

She stopped pacing and fell back into the chair. "I know those are little things. But after seeing his blood type ..." She shook her head. "Here's the clincher. I ran into Jodi on my walk back to the clinic and asked her if she could remember what Emma's father looked like. She admitted being fuzzy on details because she was drunk." She popped back up.

"Honey, you need to sit down and take a breath."

She nodded and took a few deep breaths, then jumped right back into what she was saying.

"She remembered he had a tattoo on his arm and a bandage on his upper thigh from a bullet wound. Kell has a tattoo on his arm, and he has a scar on his thigh from a war injury."

Dad frowned. "I'd prefer not to think about how my daughter knows the man has a scar on his upper thigh but go on."

"So, I showed her a photo I took last weekend in Cleveland. Jodi couldn't be certain, but she thought Kell looked similar to the guy she was with that night. The timing works out, too. Kell was home on medical leave for a bullet wound in his thigh. It was about nine months before Emma was born. He was messed up. He had lost one of his men, a close friend, and was taking it hard. It wouldn't surprise me that he spent some time in the bars."

Dad shook his head. "Wow. That's a lot to take in. So, you haven't told Kell."

"No. I don't know what to do, Dad. On the one hand, I feel compelled to tell him. But I'm afraid of what this news will do to him. He's made it very clear how he feels about having children. But I have to be honest, I am also terrified how this could disrupt Emma's life. And then there's Ruby...she's crazy about wanting grandkids.

She'd done a good job of holding back the tears, but she broke when she thought about Emma. "Dad, I can't lose her," she gasped out between sobs.

He stood and pulled her into his arms. "Sweetheart, you need to calm down. You will make yourself ill. And you don't want Emma to see you this upset."

She drew in a breath. "You're right, dad."

"So what did Sara have to say?"

"She advised that I tell Kell as soon as possible. and she's offered to help if I need her."

"Well, that's good. Maybe a good night's sleep will help," Dad said.

Good old Dad. You could solve every problem with a good night's sleep.

"Yeah, maybe."

He kissed her forehead like he used to do when she was a young girl. "I'm sorry. I don't have a straightforward answer for you."

"I just needed to talk to someone. Thanks for listening. Night."

Later, as she lie in bed, Becca mulled over everything that had happened that day.

Their awkwardness felt disappointing the day before. The distance Kell had put between them had hurt her, but today she was glad to have that distance.

Though he had tried to explain why he'd gone MIA on her. Admittedly, she'd been shocked when he revealed his nightmare and how it had evolved. That had to mean something, right?

She had no idea how she was going to broach the paternity subject with Kell. Her head was telling her she had to be honest with him, while her heart wanted to protect Emma. But her little girl deserved to know who her father was and, more importantly, to have a father in her life.

Why did it have to be one or the other? The man she'd gotten to know was honorable and caring. Clearly, he would want what was best for Emma.

She would tell him. She just needed to work up the courage to do so. In the back of her mind, there was the hope that maybe he'd want her, too.

Becca put her relaxation music on her phone, rolled onto her side, and closed her eyes. Channeling Scarlet O'Hara, she thought, "I'll think about it tomorrow."

Chapter 24

"Today's the day," Jimmy abruptly announced on Friday morning.

"What are you talking about?" Jodi asked. She'd had just about enough of his bullshit. She'd been socking away as much money as she dared without him noticing.

"If everything goes as I planned, today will be a great payday for us."

Jodi stared at him. She knew he would continue talking. His arrogance was predictable that way.

"I need you to drive. You will park around the corner from the clinic. I'll grab the kid and we will head back here. This place is far enough from town to buy us some time."

Jodi stilled. He couldn't be serious. "You can't possibly still be considering grabbing that kid?"

Jimmy frowned. "No, I'm not considering it. I'm doing it. We are doing it. Lunchtime today."

"Jimmy, kidnapping —"

He put his hand up, stepping into her space. "Shut up. Just do as I say, and everything will be fine. Once we get the money, we are getting the hell out of here."

Jodi looked at the clock on the microwave. Nine o'clock. She had to do something. "Okay, then I'm going to gas up the van, so we'll be ready. If something goes wrong, we'll need to get away from here quick."

Jimmy studied her for a second. "Fine. Get gas. But I expect you back in a half hour. We need to talk out the details."

Jodi grabbed her coat and keys and headed out. There was no way she'd let Jimmy kidnap Emma. So she headed straight to the police station.

She walked up to the first desk. "I need to report a kidnapping."

That got the attention of everyone in the room. Three cops came over to her. "Can you explain?" one of them asked.

Jodi opened her mouth to tell them when another man walked out of an office. It was the man from the photo Dr. James showed her yesterday.

Did that mean it was the mystery man from the bar? The father of her baby. Things were getting more complicated. She waited for the man to approach.

Chapter 25

Kell overheard what the young woman said to his men.

She was staring at him with an odd expression. Ignoring that, he said, "Why don't we talk in the conference room? This is Deputy Gibson, and I am Sheriff Howard."

They walked her down the short corridor to the room. "Please take a seat," he said. "Do you want some water or coffee?"

With a shake of her head, she said, "No, I'm fine."

"All right." He took out his notebook and a pen. "What do you know about a kidnapping?"

"My boyfriend—well, he *was* my boyfriend, but he's gone too far with this plan. I'm done." She glanced at the clock on the wall. "I told him I was getting gas in the van, and he told me I needed to be back in a half hour. That was ten minutes ago."

Kell was afraid she'd hyperventilate. "Take a breath. Try to calm down."

"I can't calm down. He actually thinks I'll help him with this stupid idea."

"What's your name?" Kell asked.

She hesitated long enough to make Kell uneasy.

Finally, she said, "Jodi Riggs. Jodi with an i, J-O-D-I."

Kell cocked his head, the pen in his hand froze over the notebook. He had a strange feeling he'd heard that name before but shook it off and settled back into his questioning.

"What's your boyfriend's name?" Kell asked.

"Jimmy Kendall."

"Who is he planning to kidnap?"

Jodi twisted her hands on the table, and she darted a quick look at the door. She definitely looked uncomfortable.

She looked down at the table, mumbling, "Emma James."

Kell straightened, and his eyes widened. He asked, "Dr. James' little girl?"

Jodi nodded. "Yeah, he thinks it will be an easy way to get rich quick."

"When is this supposed to take place?"

"Later today. He figured he could wait outside the side door to the clinic, and sip in unnoticed at lunchtimes."

"Where is Jimmy now?" Kell asked.

"At the place we've been hanging. It's on the outskirts of town."

"Do you have an address? Or can you show it to us on a map?"

Gibs jumped up and grabbed the local map from the bookcase. He spread it out on the table in front of her.

She looked at it and pointed. "I don't know the official address. But it's Old Hickory Road, it's the third house on the left off the county road. Brown house with black shutters. It's not his house. We are staying there for a cut...."

Kell straightened. "A cut of what?"

She swore, "Damn. I didn't mean that."

"I think you did."

She sighed. "If I give you Jimmy, will you go easy on me? I swear I wasn't a major player. It was Jimmy and his brother, Ben. But Ben got fed up and moved back to Indiana. At least, that's what he told us."

"Depends on what you give me. Major player in what?" Kell asked.

"Break-ins. At the clinic, and pharmacies and other places that might have drugs we can sell."

You've got to be kidding. Kell exchanged a quick glance with Gibs.

"Are you telling me you and your boyfriend have been the ones breaking into places and stealing the drugs?" Kell asked incredulously.

"Us and his brother Ben, yep."

He would deal with that later. Right now, he had a more pressing matter. "How does Jimmy know about Emma James?" Kell asked.

Jodi squeezed her eyes shut and rubbed her forehead. "Well, when we broke into the clinic, I spotted the picture of the little girl in Dr. James' office. I took it. He saw the picture and came up with this plan.

"I went along with the break-ins. No one got hurt. But this is too far. I won't help him. You have to stop him." Jodi covered her mouth after a sob escaped.

"We will. Deputy Gibson, you and Deputy Tupper head over to the house and invite Mr. Kendall in for questioning. That'll keep him busy for a while. In the meantime, I will take Miss Riggs' official statement."

"On it," Gibs said.

His curiosity peaked, Kell asked, "Why did you take the picture of Emma in the first place?"

Jodi shrugged. "I don't know. I thought she was cute."

Kell sensed there was more to it.

"Can I ask you something?" she asked.

He nodded.

"Do you have a tattoo on your right arm?" She showed on her own right arm where she thought she remembered the man's tattoo being.

Kell gave her a quizzical look. "Yeah, why? What's this about?"

"I guess there's one more thing you probably should know."

"What's that?" He frowned. What the hell was this woman talking about?

"Five years ago, we met in a bar. Bernie's, I think it was called. Not sure if it's still there."

Bernie's Tavern? The last time he'd been in that place was like... five years ago. He was afraid he would not like what Jodi told him. Kell barely remembered that night. He'd been drinking to forget Leak's death, which had been running on replay in his head.

Jodi continued, "The details are fuzzy. We had a quickie in the women's bathroom."

A light bulb didn't just blink on in his head, it blasted him with a vivid picture. He had sex with this young woman. He cringed. *Shit.*

Chagrined, he said, "I'm sorry. I was drinking too much that night. I don't remember much." Sex in a bar bathroom with a stranger wasn't his proudest moment. It was that kind of reckless behavior he was glad was in his past. "I owe you an apology. I was in a bad way back then."

Shrugging, she said, "It was what it was."

"I find it hard to believe you remember so much. Enough to recognize me now. I'm embarrassed to say I don't remember you," he said.

"Well, that's just it. I really didn't remember you, either. Not until Dr. James showed me your picture," Jodi said.

Kell's head whipped around. "What?"

"Dr. James. I guess she must have suspected you were the birth father of my baby."

"Baby?" Kell's head was spinning.

"Yeah, I got pregnant that night."

"So, you're saying that Dr. James' little girl, Emma, was the baby you gave birth to? And you believe I am the child's father?"

"Yep. There wasn't anyone else it could be. The father, I mean. She was born on May 18th."

Kell dropped his head into his hands. A rush of emotions overwhelmed him. He felt disbelief, fear, and frustration, but interestingly no full-blown panic attack.

The pounding of his heart in his chest, difficulty breathing, shaking ... none of which occurred.

Why hadn't Becca told him?

"When did Dr. James find out?"

"I don't know for sure. But she seemed pretty upset when I talked to her yesterday."

Maybe if you hadn't given her the cold-shoulder for the last week.

Gibson's voice came over the two-way radio that sat on the table. "Sheriff?"

Kell picked up the radio and answered, "Here. What did you find? Over."

"We found the house. The owner was home and allowed us to look in the basement. Kendall isn't here. We can come back with a warrant to search the basement. Over."

"All right. I'm more concerned with where he went. I'll head over to the clinic in case he's headed there. Over and out."

He turned to Jodi. "Under the circumstances, I think the safest place for you is right here. I'm putting you under house arrest until I can get to the bottom of the break-ins. Please come with me."

"Yeah, Jimmy won't be happy I ratted him out."

Kell stopped at the front desk and asked the remaining deputy to lock up Jodi for her own good.

Kell rushed to his vehicle and sped out of the parking lot. The distance between the police station and the clinic was short. He observed the cars in the lot and on the street before going inside.

"I need to see the younger Dr. James. Now." Snapping at her staff was unkind, but something had been boiling inside him. How long had she known? Kell didn't wait. He headed down the hallway toward Becca's office.

Becca heard the raised voice coming from the waiting room. She headed out of her office to see what was happening and spotted Kell.

"Kell, what's wrong?"

"Where's Emma?"

She cocked her head. "Why? What's wrong?" By the look on his face, Becca figured she better just tell him. "Next door at the daycare, like usual."

He turned and pointed to a door next to the window that looked into the daycare. "Is that the entry?"

"Yes." Becca scrambled after him when he moved toward the door.

"You're scaring me. Why won't you answer me? What's wrong?" she asked, struggling to keep her voice calm.

"We received a tip that someone is planning to kidnap Emma."

Becca stopped short; her hand flew to her mouth as a gasp escaped. She couldn't form any words.

"We need to get her and keep her safe until we catch the guy," he said.

Becca unlocked and opened the door.

She surveyed the room full of children. Panic mounted when she didn't immediately spot Emma. "Susan, where's Emma?" Becca asked the childcare provider.

Susan looked up when addressed. "She's using the bathroom. She'll be right out. Is everything all right?"

Kell stepped forward. "Keep all the doors locked."

"Yes, of course," Susan said.

Becca wasn't going to wait for Emma to come out on her own. Playing in the sink was too big of a temptation. She knocked on the bathroom door. "Emma, it's Mommy. Are you in there?" It was a torturous long moment before she heard her daughter's sweet little voice.

"Hi Mommy. I'm coming." Becca heard the toilet flush and the water in the sink, and the paper towel dispenser through the thin door. Emma burst through the door. "Mommy!" Her daughter ran to her. "Look, I washed my hands."

Relief flooded Becca. "Oh, Emma" She couldn't think at that moment. She pulled her daughter up, balancing her on a hip, and squeezed her tight.

"What's the matter, Mommy? You're squishing me."

"I'm sorry, sweetie. I just missed you."

"Did you come to play with me?" Emma asked.

"Yes, I did. We're taking the rest of the day off. We're going to have an afternoon movie party and you can watch whichever movie you want."

"Even *Finding Nemo*?" Emma asked.

Becca smiled at Emma. "Yes, even *Finding Nemo*," Becca said, tweaking Emma's little nose. She turned to Kell to thank him, and she noticed he had an odd expression on his face. When he saw her watching him, he cleared his throat and said, "Let's get going."

Kell insisted he follow them home, and under the circumstances, Becca didn't argue. She hastily made a peanut butter and jelly sandwich and grabbed a juice box for Emma. She spread a blanket on the living room floor, telling Emma they could have a picnic, and turned on the movie.

"Mommy is going to speak with Kell for a few minutes," she said.

"Okay."

Kell motioned for her to step into the hallway, where they could both keep an eye on Emma.

They stood there staring at each other. It was clear he had something he wanted to say, so she waited.

Finally, he spoke. She was taken aback by his question and his tone. "Is it true?"

"Is what true? I'm sorry, but am I supposed to know what you're talking about?" Becca asked.

"Is Emma my daughter?"

"She's my daughter." She fought her body's urge to crumble from all the emotions that were churning inside her in that moment.

Kell was glaring. "Fine, I'll rephrase my question. Am I Emma's biological father?"

She sighed. The moment she had been dreading had come much sooner than she had prepared for. "How did you find out?"

"You're not denying it? So, it's true?"

She took too long to respond. Kell raised his voice, "Please answer my question, Becca."

"Yes, I think so," she whispered.

"You think? What's that supposed to mean? You know or you don't."

"It's not that simple." She sighed. "And I did plan to tell you."

"When?"

"I don't know. I barely had time to adjust to the information myself. How did you find out?" she asked again, since he never answered the question.

"We had a visitor at the station earlier. Jodi Riggs. She's the one who alerted us of the kidnapping. Her boyfriend got it in his head that there'd be money to be had if he kidnaped Emma. Luckily, Jodi wasn't interested in going along with his plan."

"Well, thank God," she said. "So, she told you?"

"Well, we stumbled onto it. But yes. How long have you known?"

She shook her head. "Only since yesterday. But that's just it. We would need to do a paternity test to be conclusive. Right now, it's just very likely."

"Except Jodi remembers me," Kell said.

"Well, yes, that's true."

He remained stoically silent. Becca filled the silence with what she hoped was a decent explanation.

"I've wondered for a while. There were little things at first. The photo of you and Megan at your mom's place. Megan was Emma's age in the photo. The resemblance was uncanny. Then there was the eating thing."

Kell was massaging his forehead with his thumb and forefinger. He stopped and arched a brow. "What eating thing?"

"You and Emma have the same mannerisms when you eat. The night you came over for tacos, and we made popcorn. It was like watching the same person, only in miniature form, shoveling the popcorn into your mouths.

"I wondered about those things, but it wasn't until yesterday when I saw that you and Emma share the same rare blood type that I thought it could be an actual possibility."

Kell waited patiently for her to continue her explanation.

"I ran into Jodi when I was walking back to the clinic after the blood drive, and I showed her the picture I took of you at the Hall of Fame. She thought you could be the guy, though she was vague on details."

"If you had suspicions, you should have told me." He paced in the small space. "I had a right to know."

He could hardly act all self-righteous. "Look you've made it abundantly clear that you aren't interested in a family, specifically kids. It was the reason you asked me to play the fake girlfriend for you."

He turned abruptly and faced her. "That was before I knew I already had a child," he said through gritted teeth.

She sighed, clenching her hands. "My priority is Emma. I wanted to protect her."

Kell shuddered and slammed his hands in his pockets. "From me?" He sounded hurt.

"From everyone," she said.

He shook his head.

"What?" she asked.

"You're the one who talked about the importance of honesty."

"Kell, I just saw the blood types yesterday."

"You could have mentioned your suspicions. Numerous times."

She was silent. He was right, but had she been too afraid? Becca dipped her head. "So, what now?"

He stared at her. "Right now, I have to get back to the station. I have a criminal to find. Lock the doors and don't answer them for anyone. Call your dad and see if he can come home." Then he turned and left her standing there.

Becca wanted to scream. Or cry. She needed to do something. The whole situation was crazy and out of control. Her first concern was her daughter. She did as Kell instructed. She checked to make sure all the doors were locked and called Dad, who said he'd cancel the rest of his appointments.

Becca grabbed another blanket and joined Emma on the floor, pulling her daughter onto her lap.

Chapter 26

Deputy Gibson radioed Kell to let him know they had apprehended Jimmy Kendall. He'd been lurking around the clinic. With Jodi's statement, it looked like Jimmy would be looking at more charges than just the attempt to kidnap Emma James.

With the burglary cases being solved, it seemed like Lucky might get back to a peaceful town.

Kell had too much time to think about Becca and Emma. He needed to talk to someone. No way would he discuss the situation with his sister and Chase. Not yet anyway. And his mother was an even bigger no. He made an appointment to see Sam Winston on Monday morning.

Sam listened as Kell voiced his feelings about finding out he had fathered a child. After Kell had explained what had transpired over the last week, Sam asked, "How are you feeling about this revelation?"

"The truth?"

Sam nodded. "Always."

Kell cringed as he admitted, "I'm terrified. I don't want to fuck it up."

"What specifically?"

"Being a father. Too many things can go wrong. That's why I never planned to be in this position."

"But despite your wishes, a child, in fact, your child is already in the world. So, could you walk away from this knowledge? From this responsibility?"

Kell leaned forward in the chair, arms on his legs, and put his head in his hands. "No. I can't say that. I've gotten to know Emma, and she is a terrific kid. Smart, funny, sweet, and silly. I care about her."

"I agree. The few times I've been around her, I found her to be quite adorable."

"What if I fuck it up?" Kell asked.

"You are going to mess up. That's a basic part of parenting. There are so many things that are out of a parent's control.

It's just such a shock. I'm still getting used to the idea. I want to be responsible."

"In what way?"

"Financial support, for one thing."

"Okay. We've been avoiding an important part of this equation. How does Becca fit into all of this?"

"They're a package deal, of course." Kell scratched his cheek. "I care about Becca, too. And I don't want to do anything to disrupt their family. I just wish she'd told me about her suspicions about Emma."

"Sounds like they were just that—unsubstantiated suspicions. And it wasn't like you were in a committed relationship. I can see why she would hold back," Sam said. When Kell said nothing, Sam continued, "As a matter of fact, you were in a fake relationship. That would hardly give a woman faith in a long-term bond."

Kell nodded. He knew Sam was right.

"Well, tell me this. Let's set aside Emma for a moment. Is there a connection between Becca and you? Would you have pursued more with her?"

"Absolutely. Our relationship was actually moving in that direction. But the problem is, I don't know how I will convince her because I've made it very clear from day one that I don't want a wife and kids."

"Well, that's why we're meeting," Sam said. "Let's come up with an acceptable plan that you are comfortable with, and which Becca and Emma will benefit too."

"Sounds good, thank you, Sam."

Becca did not know what she was supposed to do. It had been three days since Kell confronted her about Emma's paternity. Had he told Megan and Chase? His mother?

"A quarter for your thoughts," Dad said, when he walked into the kitchen and saw her sitting at the table.

"A quarter? Wow."

"Well, a penny hardly seems right, with inflation and all," he said with a chuckle.

"My thoughts aren't worth a quarter. I was just trying to decide how I'm supposed to proceed. Until we get the results from a paternity test, I feel like I'm in limbo.

"Well, I hope I helped with that situation. Kell came to me and asked me to run a paternity test. We did it on Saturday and the results should be in any day now.

"What? Why didn't you mention it?"

"Because the whole thing has tied you up in knots." I hope once the results come in, you will have a clearer picture of what you ... and Kell are dealing with."

"Why didn't Kell ask me?" Becca said.

"I think it was easier for him to come to me since things were a little heated the last time you two spoke."

"True."

She stood up and gave her dad a hug. "Thank you."

He kissed her cheek. "I only want you and Emma to be happy."

She nodded. "I know."

"Becca, what do you want?"

"I don't think it matters what I want," she said.

Her dad's intense stare made her uncomfortable, bringing back memories of having to justify a poor grade in middle school.

"I would like to go back to how things were progressing before either of us found out about Emma. We had moved beyond the fake dating. I believe we would be good together, given the chance."

"Then you need to tell him that," Dad said.

"No, the ball is in his court. He walked away."

Her dad frowned and shook his head. She hated to disappoint her dad. But she had her pride. The problem was, Kell also had a surplus of pride. One of them would need to make the first move.

She would text him to ask if Megan knew what had transpired. It would be nice to talk to her friend. Then a thought occurred to her. What if Megan holds it against Becca, too? Like she conspired to keep them from knowing Emma's paternity. She sighed. She had to have faith that Megan would still be her friend.

"Thanks, Dad. I'm going to go lie down for a little while before dinner. Thanks for picking something up on your way home."

"See you in a few," he said. He caught her arm and pulled her to him for a quick hug.

In her room, Becca took out her phone. *So much for the ball being in his court.* She texted.

> Becca: *Hi Kell, have you talked to Megan yet?*

She was relieved when she saw the responding bubbles pop up.

> Kell: *Not yet. I wanted to talk to you first.*

> Becca: *You do?*

> Kell: *Yes. Emma's needs come first. I don't want my family overwhelming her or us. As well-meaning as they are.*

Becca read over his message several times. She wasn't sure what to think about it. Was he saying this because he planned to get partial custody? Or was he respecting Becca and her relationship with Emma? His next text surprised her.

> Kell: *Can we meet?*

She inhaled deeply and blew it out.

> Becca: *Sure. When?*

> Kell: *I know it's getting late. But can you meet me at Joe's? At 8:30?*

Becca found her hands were shaking as she typed. Was she ready for the outcome? She was a lot of things, but she never considered herself a coward.

> Becca: *Yes, all right.*

At eight-thirty that evening, Becca watched Kell pull into Joe's parking lot. She stepped out of her car and met him at the door.

"Hi," she said.

"Hi," he said.

She hoped the conversation would get better. They sat down and ordered their drinks.

"Who is going first?" Becca asked.

Kell inclined his head. "Ladies first."

All righty then.

Becca drew in a deep breath and blew it out.

"I don't know where to begin. I guess there were a few coincidental signs. But nothing solid. Honesty is important to me. If I had ever been certain, I would have come to you." She shrugged. "But if I'm being a hundred percent honest, there was a part of me that was scared. Perhaps I allowed my fears to supersede my common sense. "

"Fears?" he asked.

"Yes, fears. I know you said you never wanted a kid. But I didn't know that you wouldn't change your mind. You have rights as the biological father. I didn't know if you would try to get custody of Emma."

He held up his hand to stop her, but she kept talking.

"Or what about your mom? I wasn't thinking rationally. I was just worried about what the outcome could be.

"Then we got to know each other better. I got used to Emma being around you. You're so good with her. I went from being afraid that you could be her father to almost wishing it were true. Talk about a one-eighty."

"Can I say something now?" Kell asked.

She nodded. Then quickly said, "No, wait, one more thing you should know. On the drive home from Cleveland when I fell asleep in the car. I had a dream. In it, all the pieces fell into place. I guess my subconscious really thought you could be her dad. In the dream, I saw a man dancing with Jodi in a bar. When he turned around, it was you." She breathed deeply. "Seems like both of us had revealing dreams that weekend."

Kell sat quietly. He let Becca get her breathing back to normal. Maybe she didn't realize she was talking so fast. He was afraid she could hyperventilate.

Finally, he cleared his throat and said, "Finding out that I am Emma's father was a shock. I won't lie. A bunch of emotions ran through me. Disbelief, fear, and frustration, but what surprised me was I didn't feel the signs of a full-on panic attack.

"There was no pounding heart, no difficulty breathing, or shaking ... none of which occurred. That has to mean something."

"Maybe you're making progress with Sam," Becca offered.

Kell nodded. "I think so. I used to believe I didn't deserve a family. That I couldn't protect them. Sam is helping me to see I have to let go of those debilitating thoughts. I finally see some light at the end of a lengthy, dark tunnel that I have been in since Leaks died."

He reached across the table, taking her hands, he squeezed them.

"I think we can work through this. What do you think?"

What did she think?

Chapter 27

Before they said goodnight at Joe's, Kell asked Becca if she wanted to go with him to tell Megan and Chase. She agreed, and the next night they met at the lake house.

As they walked to the front door, Becca said, "Since it's your family, why don't you take the lead? I can jump in if you want me to."

"All right," he said.

At the door, Megan gave them both a strange look. "Come on in. I'm not sure what this mysterious visit is about but I hope it's good news." Before Kell could speak Megan continued, "First, do either of you want something to drink? Bec, want a glass of wine?"

Becca sighed. "Sure, thanks. That sounds wonderful, actually."

Kell said, "No, thanks, I'm fine."

"I'll get the wine so we can get to whatever it is you two need to talk about." His sister left and returned faster than he thought possible with two glasses of wine. One, she handed to Becca, the other she held onto and took a seat on the sofa.

"Where's Chase?" Kell asked.

"Right here," Chase shouted from the kitchen. "I just got back from Brady's walk. I'll be right there."

The few minutes that ticked by while they waited for Chase felt torturous to Kell. He imagined Becca felt the same way.

Finally, Chase came in and sat next to Megan.

"Okay, spill it, big brother."

He took a deep breath and jumped right in. "Last Friday, we learned someone was planning to kidnap Emma."

Megan gasped and clasped Chase's leg. Chase covered her hand with his and squeezed. Kell saw his sister open her mouth to ask questions, and he held up his hand to stop her.

But Becca added, "Emma is safe."

"Thank God," Megan said.

"Let me get through this," Kell said. Becca nodded, and he continued, "On Friday morning, a woman named Jodi Riggs came into the station. She reported that her boyfriend, Jimmy Kendall, planned to kidnap Emma. She also told us he was behind the run of break-ins we've had around here. Deputy Gibson arrested Kendall late Friday afternoon.

"Really?"Chase asked.Riggs

Kell nodded then continued. "In the course of my conversation with Ms. Riggs, I found out that she believed that I'm Emma's biological dad," Kell said.

Megan's jaw dropped. Chase's eyes widened. Becca sighed. Then everyone began talking at once, which made it difficult to hear any one person.

"Everyone, please stop talking," Kell said with enough authority in his tone that he got the response he wanted.

"I'm sure I don't need to tell you that it came as a shock to me, too," Kell said. "Harper helped me get a paternity test done." He looked directly at Becca as he reached into his pocket and pulled out a sheet of paper. "I got the results today." He handed it to Becca. She read the results.

"It's conclusive. You're Emma's father," Becca whispered.

Kell nodded.

"I'm an aunt," Megan announced. She jumped up and hugged Kell first, then turned to Becca and hugged her friend. Looking back at her brother, she said, "I won't even ask how you had a kid while being deployed for so long."

"Listen, we'd appreciate it if we can keep this quiet for the time being," Kell said.

"So, you probably don't want mom to know yet," Megan said.

"Correct. We'll tell her. We just need a little time."

Becca glanced at her watch and stood up. "Speaking of time, I need to get going. I promised Emma I'd be home in time to put her to bed. My dad is probably on his third read through of *Goodnight Moon*." She hugged Megan. "I'll stop by the cafe tomorrow and we can chat."

"You better," Megan said. "We have a lot to chat about."

Becca squeezed Megan's hand and nodded.

"Night, everyone."

Chase jumped up and escorted her to the door and waited for her to get into her vehicle.

Megan turned to her brother. "Okay, please tell me you will not screw this up."

"Thanks for the vote of confidence," Kell said.

Megan raised her brows and crossed her arms over her chest. He hated when she did that. It reminded him of their mother. She just needed to start tapping her foot.

"Well, I hope I haven't screwed it up."

Megan shook her head. "Tell me."

He told her about his reaction on Friday. Then he mentioned his heart-to-heart talk with Becca.

"That sounds promising. And Becca certainly didn't act like a pissed off woman tonight. So, dear brother, what are you going to do about that?"

Chapter 28

A few days later, Becca was finishing up some patient notes when she heard a commotion coming from the waiting room. It was the end of the day. There were no more patients, and the remaining staff were closing up the office.

"What's going on?" she asked. The staff mingled around the glass doors that faced the parking lot. When she reached the door, she heard music. It was Elvis.

"Oh my gosh," she said and covered her mouth as a laugh escaped.

Kell stood propped against his sheriff cruiser, legs crossed, and held his phone above his head.

"Is he trying to do that bit from that old John Cusack movie?" Betty asked. "But with his phone?"

One of the other women added, "Yeah, I think so, but why Elvis's songs?"

Becca smiled. "It's an inside joke."

She knew why he chose Elvis's music. So far, the mash-up included "Don't Be Cruel" and "All Shook Up." The third song brought tears to her eyes. She held her chest when "Can't Help Falling in Love" played.

"Ladies, I'll see you tomorrow," Becca said as she walked outside, thankful she wore a sweater. She smiled at Kell as she approached him. "I love your mash-up," she said.

He lowered his phone. "I hoped you would," Kell said.

"So, are you acknowledging Elvis is superior to the Beatles?" she asked.

"That remains to be seen," he said, and chuckled.

"I really can't believe you did this. I didn't know you had the musical know-how to do a mash-up."

He nodded. "Yeah, well, it's a good thing I have a connection in the music industry. It's not exactly in my comfort zone. But I knew if I wanted to make a point, I needed a grand gesture."

"Well, this was certainly grand. And using the King was smart." She tapped her head with her index finger. So, what point are you making?" she asked.

Shoving the phone in his pocket and grabbing her hands. "I wouldn't risk my reputation as a hard ass cop to serenade a woman unless I thought it was the best way to convince her of the sincerity of my feelings."

"Your feelings?"

"I'm falling in love with you."

Becca wrapped her arms around his neck and kissed him on the lips. He kissed her back, but when they finally drew apart, he explained, "Like I mentioned the other night, I never thought I'd be able to have the whole happily ever after package. I felt like I didn't deserve it.

"Sam is helping me to wade through my crap. But, more than anything else, it was you who brought me back to the land of the living. Is it possible for us to be a family? You, me, and Emma, and a kitten someday."

She shook her head as tears welled up in her eyes.

"What's wrong?" Kell cocked his head.

She swiped at the tears on her face. "A family sounds perfect."

He nodded. "I think so."

"Since we're so familiar with the whole faking thing, why don't we start with a fake kitten and work up to a real one?" Becca said.

"That's funny," Kell chuckled, opening his car door. He brought out the bag from the bookstore they'd stopped at in Cleveland. Reaching in, he pulled out the sweet kitten plush he purchased for Emma. "With everything that's been happening, I never had a chance to give this to Emma."

"Aw, she'll love it. Want to head over to dad's house to give it to her?"

"Sure. Ride with me."

All right." Kell opened the passenger door for Becca. Once settled in the vehicle, she blew out her breath. "Phew. What a relief."

Kell gave her a questioning look.

"I was afraid I wouldn't have a date for Megan and Chase's wedding."

Kell laughed. "Put your mind at ease. I've got you covered."

She smiled. "Yes, you do."

"C'mere," Kell said as he reached across the middle console. She met him halfway. He tucked a wayward strand of her hair behind her ear. He kissed the tip of her nose and moved to her mouth. Their kiss heated quickly.

She pulled back. "You know what?"

"What?"

I think we need to stop at my house before heading to dad's place."

"Oh?"

"Yes, I need to get your opinion on the new mattress I bought for my bedroom."

He grinned. "Gotcha." He put the SUV in gear and pressed the gas.

Epilogue

Four months later

"That's everything," said Kell after he set the last box down in the living room. "It helps that I don't have much."

Becca smiled. "That's an understatement."

"What can I say? All the furniture in the studio was there when I moved in and there was no need to buy anything. Pretty much just the clothes on my back."

Becca moved to stand next to Kell. She wrapped her arms around him and put her head on his chest. "A perfect fresh start."

He tilted her head up and kissed her lips. Pulling back, he said, "A lucky break for me."

His nightmares were less frequent, and he felt he was making progress with his therapy. His PTSD was much less intrusive into his life. He knew it was still something he would have to work on and deal with for the rest of his life, but Becca's love and support gave him the confidence that he would succeed.

Moving into Becca's house made sense to the two of them. It already felt like home to him. It was more about the family who lived there than the actual house itself.

He'd like to move to the bedroom so he could show her how lucky they both were, but Emma was in the kitchen chatting with Hazel. That cat followed Emma everywhere. More like a dog than a cat.

Sure enough, Emma came skipping into the living room with Hazel trailing behind. "I want a kiss, too." She extended her arms to be picked up and Kell obliged her. There wasn't much he wouldn't do for her. She had successfully wrapped him around both of her little fingers.

"Goup hug, Goup hug," Emma said, as she wiggled with excitement. It was incredible what a one-eighty he'd made in his thinking about what he wanted, and more importantly, what he deserved. Now he couldn't imagine what life was like before Becca and Emma.

"Mommy, can I put my princess dress on?"

"You can try it on and look in the mirror and twirl a few times, but we need to hang it back up for Megan and Chase's wedding," Becca said.

"Yay." She wiggled to be set down.

All the wedding gear was hanging in the spare room they used as an office. Emma was the princess/flower girl, and the excitement bubbled out of her. Kell, who was Chase's best man, had his dress uniform pressed and ready for next week's big day. Becca's bridesmaid dress hung beside his uniform.

It would not be a huge wedding. Megan wanted to keep the details away from the press. It hadn't been easy, but with only five days and counting, they may have pulled it off.

Later, after she had hung her princess dress back up, Emma, dressed in her play clothes, asked, "Can we go play on the swings?"

Kell looked at Becca. "What do you think? Want me to push both of you?"

"Of course."

The backyard was everything Becca could have wished for, and more. Between Kell and Chase, they built a fire pit, and best of all, if Emma was asked, was the castle playhouse they added to the swing set.

The castle was complete with an ornate door, curtains on the windows, and a staircase up to a balcony where Emma could stand and wave to the peasants below.

Becca smiled. There was no place she'd rather be than with her two favorite people. This is what happiness felt like. Kell moving in was a simple decision. They were together whenever they weren't at work. He'd blended in with her little family of two as if it had always been their destiny to become a family of three.

Becca loved listening to Emma's squeals of laughter as Kell pushed her swing a little higher. That child knew no fear.

"Higher." Emma giggled.

"That's about as high as I can push you," Kell said. "You'll break my back if I have to push any higher. You don't want to do that, do you?" His easy, teasing manner gave no hint of the intensely complicated man she'd met back in January.

"Okay," Emma said.

Kell smiled at Becca. Winking when he caught her smiling back.

"Kiddo, it's time to slow down. We need to go in and get your bath and quiet down for bedtime," Becca said. With it staying light so late in mid-summer, earlier bedtimes were a challenge.

"Aww. Can't we stay for a little longer?" Emma whined.

"Tell you what, I'll give you a couple more big pushes, but when they slow to a stop, it will be time to go inside. Deal?" Kell said.

"Yay. Deal, Daddy."

Becca's breath caught. Her own swing had stopped, and she turned in time to catch the look of awe on his face. Kell and she exchanged an amazed look. Emma had never called Kell daddy before. They were taking it slow. There would be an appropriate time to explain, but neither Kell nor Becca was in a hurry.

"Here you go, Em. Hold on."

Becca stood and walked behind to Kell. She wrapped her arm around him from the back so she wouldn't interfere in his pushing. "Thank you."

He asked, "For what?"

"For being such a good man. I, no, we love you."

He let the swing slow on its own and turned to pull Becca into his arms.

Emma hopped off her swing and ran over to them, reaching her little arms to be picked up. "We love you more than mac and cheese, right Mommy?"

Becca and Kell laughed.

"Exactly right, sweetie."

"I love you both, more than mac and cheese, too," Kell said.

Acknowledgements

I want to thank my three professional writing organizations who have been supportive and offered many opportunities for me to learn the craft of writing. The three groups include my online group, Contemporary Romance Writers (CRW), and two local groups, Michigan Romance Writers (MRW), and Greater Detroit Romance Writers (GDRW).

Thank you to my editor Bryn Donovan, who I contracted through Reedsy, and my cover designer RCMatthewsArtist.

I also want to thank Elizabeth Meyette, who read an early draft and offered helpful input. I value her wisdom and writing expertise more than I can say.

Thank you to Dawn Bartley, my writing buddy, and Diana Stout, who includes me in her daily write-ins. You both have helped to keep me accountable and on-track. Also, Diana, thank you for continuing to teach me new things.

Thanks to Jenny T. and Ann R., who did a final beta read for me.

Also, I'd like to give a shout out to Dr. Ryan Gleesing for his willingness to help when I had medical questions and Retired MSG Joseph Gleesing, for answering my questions about the Marines. If there are any errors, they are solely mine.

I need to thank my daughter, Lizzy, for her willingness to help via text and Facetime, sometimes more than once a day.

Finally, thank you to my family and friends who believed in me and encouraged me to keep writing, especially to my husband, Jeff, son, Andrew, and Lizzy.

About the Author

I've always loved to read. So when I decided I wanted to write books, I knew the stories needed to be like the ones I most enjoyed reading. The books that end with a happily ever after.

A true Midwest gal, I grew up in Ohio, went to school in Indiana, and have lived in Michigan for many years. My husband and I raised two children, who are adults and out on their own. Now we share our home with a rambunctious rescue dog named Brodie.

Thanks for reading Lucky Break! I hope you enjoyed the story. Kell and Becca (and Emma) have a special place in my heart. If you would be so kind as to leave a review on Amazon.com or Goodreads, I'd appreciate it. A review can be as simple as a brief comment and it will help other readers find my books.

To receive the latest news and surprises, be sure to sign up for my newsletter on my website: www.authorannestone.com.

<h1 style="text-align:center">Book 3 is Coming Soon</h1>

You can expect to see all your Lucky friends again in Lucky Strike.

Johnny 'Rocket' Martin, a playboy big league pitcher, finds himself amid a media frenzy after authorities suspend him over allegations of steroid use. Returning to the small town of Lucky for his estranged grandad's funeral, he sees his high school sweetheart, Lori James. Now a divorced mother of a young son, she avoids Johnny. She has zero tolerance for drug use of any kind after her parents were killed by a drug addict when she was fourteen.

Johnny's plan is to lie low and avoid the media, but when his grandparent's sporting goods store goes up in flames, leaving his grandma injured, he's determined to uncover the arsonist. When Johnny and Lori revisit their past, they realize their chemistry is still intense and quickly rekindles, leading Johnny to a tough choice... is family more important than baseball?